A PLACE TO STAND

About the Author

Twenty-five years as a psychologist has given Helen McNeil's writing both insight and compassion. She writes about ordinary people dealing with the deep questions she struggles with herself. Where is home? What does family mean? Are my beliefs worth the pain? Who am I?

Helen McNeil was a migrant herself, coming from the UK in the 1950's to Kawerau in the Bay of Plenty. She has drawn on this experience for her first novel "A Place to Stand". She has studied at Auckland University and is a graduate of the Master's in Creative Writing course at Auckland University of Technology. She lives at Earthsong Eco-neighbourhood (Auckland, New Zealand) alongside chickens, organic gardens, lots of compost and constant negotiation.

In 2016 she published her second novel "A Striking Truth".

HELEN McNEIL

A PLACE TO STAND

First published 2013 by Del Sur Productions, Auckland, New Zealand.
Second edition 2016 published by Cloud Ink Press, P O Box 8988,
Symonds Street, Auckland, 1150
www.cloudink.co.nz

ISBN: 978-0-473-22152-2

Cover design: Robin Charles (robincharles.com)
Book design and typesetting: Greg Simpson

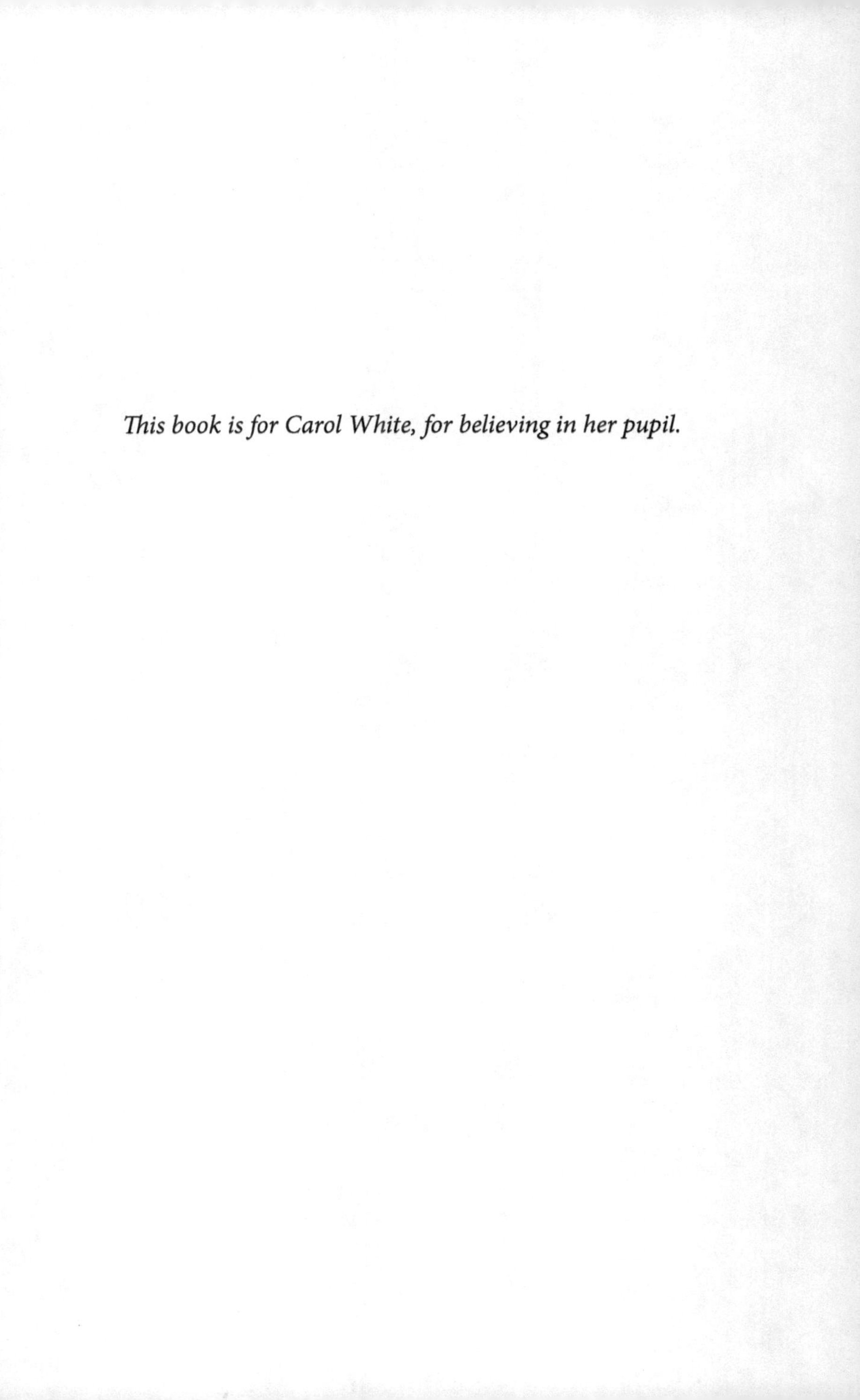

This book is for Carol White, for believing in her pupil.

Chapter One

It's nearly nine when the wind pushes her through the door into the office. The door jangles. It sounds bright, almost as cheerful as the bloody birds had been this morning, chirping their way into her hangover, dragging her out of her flat with so much promise. Spring in Auckland, rain, then sun, then wind, then all three at once. Changeable they said on the radio. The same change not happening with the pictures of houses drooping in the office window—nothing shifting, no-one buying.

She can see the boss hasn't arrived yet. His office with its large, bare desk is still dark. Leaning on the door, she closes her eyes and breathes as she counts—*in for three, hold for four, out for three.*

"You feeling all right, Sandra?" asks a voice from the reception desk.

"You know what, Melanie," Sandra replies. "Men are jerks. But, today is life, the only life you can be sure of, so live today with gusto."

"What are you on about?"

"Page thirteen, Melanie."

"You've been on that course."

"Very good it was too, you should say yes if the boss offers it."

"What makes you think he'd offer it to me? I don't make megabucks for the company."

Sandra turns to her desk. Neither does she. Her sale figures for the last month have been terrible and the boss wants to talk to her about her job. It's hardly her fault, who in their right mind would buy a house when interest rates are at twenty per-cent? She moves a pile of papers from her chair to the floor. There's lots of filing to be done. She hates it, putting old things into order. Two new listings to follow-up, she'll do those first, get something new started. Last night's wine is still making itself present as a dull headache. She reaches for a cigarette, thinks better of it and heads for the ladies toilet to check if her lipstick is still intact.

She scrubs the red from her front tooth and tries practising her smile again, the one with the bottom teeth just showing. When she scrambles in her handbag, the letter falls out, landing on the floor. Sender: Mrs B Simpson, it accuses. It's been redirected twice and still it's found her. Her headache thuds, and something stabs deep in her belly. She holds on to the cold porcelain of the sink and breathes in. Not now, she can't deal with it now. She's bending, very slowly, to pick it up when the door opens.

"Boss is here," says Melanie. "Hurry up, he's waiting for you."

"Yes, right. Just coming."

The letter glares up at her from the floor. She pushes it under the rubbish bin, for later, maybe. She stands straight, smoothing her trousers, does one more round of breathing, *in for three, hold for four, out for three* and pulls the door open.

The boss keeps his head down as she comes in She can see he's beginning to bald. As she waits for his attention, she tries to esti-mate how bald he is, forty-five years worth? He peers up at her at last, his glasses on the end of his nose and his chin collapsing into itself. Maybe fifty. His eyes flick down over her red trouser suit, a 'power colour' the course leader called it, to her stack-heeled shoes and up again. She turns her head slightly to one side and smiles, bottom teeth just showing.

"Sit down please, Sandra," he says.

She can tell from his tone. She pulls the chair close to the big desk, sits with her back very straight and leans slightly towards him. She keeps the smile, clasping her hands on her lap to stop them trembling.

"That colour looks good on you," he says.

"Thanks."

"Can't say so much for the sales figures. They're well down. Have been for the last six months."

He's staring down at the papers spread on his desk. The magic line is drooping on the page. Sandra sits straighter and lifts her chin.

"Poor sales have repercussions for staffing, Sandra."

He leans back, turning from side to side, his hands clasped in front, forefingers tapping.

"And you were the last one taken on."

He's pursing his lips and nodding.

"But I've been thinking. We should be specialising. Inner city, Sandra. It won't be long before it's very desirable real estate. We should be getting in there now. I was wondering if you might be interested in a little syndication, Sandra. It's not money we need. It's you. We want to buy up inner city houses and who better to do so than an attractive young woman like you?"

What does he want? Is he trying it on?

"I'm not sure I understand," she says.

"Well. We can't do it as a firm, you understand, it's against the rules. But a new syndicate with you as its head, in name only you understand, that we can do. We stand to make a killing. Give you a fair share of the profits, of course."

He looks very respectable, the boss. He always wears a suit, he lives in Remuera and plays golf.

"I'll think about it," she says.

"Hmm. Might keep you your job. Think about it quickly, will you? I want an answer by next Wednesday, get things in motion. Now, run along Sandra. I'm sure there are people out there needing houses."

She's proud of her exit from his office. She nods slightly, smiles her best professional smile, and makes it out the door before her face changes. Her desk is in the farthest corner, past the young men who sit closer to the boss. They look at her curiously as she goes past.

By the time she's back at her desk, she's smiling so much that the red lipstick is lavish on her teeth. Here's her big chance, if she plays it right.

"You look very pleased with yourself," says Melanie.

"When you're given a lemon, make lemonade. Page seven, Melanie."

"Cut it out, will you? And take my advice. Don't let him suck you in."

Sandra pulls in her cheeks as if she's eaten something sour and laughs. She's about to turn back to the two new listings when Melanie puts something down on her desk. It's the letter from Mrs B Simpson. Sandra slits it open, still laughing. It's only one page. On white paper.

Dear Sandra,

I hope this letter reaches you. I have sent the same letter to every Sandra McLeod I could find in the Auckland phone book. I hope you are well. I am writing to say it would be a good idea for you to come and see your mum, Betty. She is living with us now. She is getting very frail. You haven't been back for a long time, dear, and it would be very good to see you. When you come, you can stay with us. Our phone number is Kawerau 7007. Pat is well, so are the kids.

Yours sincerely,
Bea Simpson.

Her mum. Her mother, Betty. She hasn't been back for a long time. The words snare her breath, pull it from her. Her belly hurts, cramps up, knots itself with her heart and her lungs and she can't breathe. Her head is flicking pictures like a mutoscape in a penny arcade, so many that none of them settle; a spoon going back and forth to a disconnected mouth in a blank face, her back aching as she leans down in a body so big it must be someone else's. And the room dark, always dark.

"You've got a sick mum, then?"

The voice brings Sandra back, to her feet on the floor, her fingernails digging into her right hand and Melanie behind her.

"Jesus, Melanie. You don't believe in privacy do you?"

"Look, Sandra. My mum died a couple of years ago. I didn't go back to see her and I've regretted it ever since."

"I said I'd never go back, Melanie. Not to that dump. I meant it."

"Doesn't sound like you. You're not scared are you?"

"Yeah, well. Got to get on with these new listings."

"Please yourself. Thought you weren't scared of anything, Sandra."

The phone rings and pulls Melanie away. Sandra folds the letter, carefully. She mutters: *Fear doesn't exist anywhere except in the mind. Page twenty-four. Fear doesn't exist anywhere except in the mind. Fear doesn't exist anywhere. Except in the mind.*

Over and over.

By six o'clock she can safely leave the office. It always pays to be the last to leave but sometimes it's a competition between her and the young men who watch each other, daring the first one to break and go home.

She has to park on the road because there's a combie van in the driveway that has an opinion about love and war. It's been around twice this week already. In her handbag is the letter, on its one white page. This time it doesn't fall out when she digs for her key, it's nestled itself in. The door sticks, she pushes it hard and is engulfed by a sharp, heavy smell, like hedge clippings burning. There's two bodies on the couch, slumped into each other.

"Hey, it's the corporate lady," he says.

"Hey, it's the dirty hippy," Sandra replies.

"Sandra, come and share a toke, come on," her flatmate says.

Her flatmate was more fun before the combie van arrived. There was someone to get drunk with. Not anymore.

"Get stuffed," Sandra says.

"May Gaia bless you with rivers of love and mountains of peace, sister," he says.

"What are you on about?"

"Our Earth mother, Gaia, she's always there for you, man. Even in your darkest hour."

Sandra goes into the kitchen. Where she came from, the earth mother was a bitch, another reason she's never going back. Behind her the two potheads have drifted to the bedroom.

The message book next to the phone has a couple of entries for her.

4.30—Barb rang. Wants you to have dinner week Saturday. Got a new possible for you. Works in a finance company. HE'S A DISH AND SINGLE. Barb'll pick you up at 6.30.

4.30ish—That creep from last night rang. Brent??? Said thanks and can we do it again!!!! Yerch.

Barb, yes that might be OK, although the last attempt at match-making was a disaster with a fat accountant who bored everyone and she got so drunk she passed out. As for Brent? Well.

The banging from the bedroom is getting louder and faster and the grunting and gasping sounds are irritating. She turns on the television, turns up the volume to try and drown it out. It's the news and the screen shows an old woman, leaning on a stick, walking across the Harbour Bridge and behind her is a tide of people, Māori people, flowing like water between the metal struts. When she stops, they lap around her, carrying her on with them.

The announcer talks about them walking for their land, for what they say has been taken from them. The Mother of the Nation, he keeps calling the old woman. 'Not one acre more', she says. 'We've had enough'. Mother of the Nation, it seems to Sandra that they keep saying it over and over.

Mothers. This one's a stroppy old woman. Or desperate. It seems some mothers fight and some just give up.

You haven't been back for a long time. She's sixteen again. Or, at least, there's a person who used to be her that's sixteen. The day she left, she'd walked out of the hospital as fast as she could.

"I'm not coming back, ever," her sixteen year-old self had whispered.

She turns the television off. There are voices down the hallway, the back door slams and the combie van stutters its way down the drive.

"Good riddance," she says.

She moves automatically to pick up the clothes that are scattered over the floor, empties the ashtrays and piles dirty dishes in the sink. Flatmates are such a bad idea, maybe it's time to move on again to a flat by herself, with no-one else to look after. By the time she goes to bed, the lounge is neat again and she's still the only one home. She props herself up with a pillow and opens the book from the course, the one that promises to change her life, to build her new personality: Sandra McLeod, professional, successful real estate agent. Her course book open on her knee, she reads: *Exercise twelve: Building Confidence by Successful Self Talk. Don't allow your thoughts to escape into anything that is not about achieving your goal. Identify your habitual SSS: self-sabotage-sentences.*

The first one's easy. She's female but that's a fact, not something she's made up. There's something about today, the conversation with Melanie. What had she said? *Thought you weren't scared of anything.* The deal the boss is offering, sounds like a challenge but Melanie was talking about that letter, from Mrs B Simpson, the one she doesn't want to think about.

She pulls her attention back to the page in front of her. Written in bold print, the words stand out from the page: *You have more courage than you ever dreamed you possessed.*

That's right, she thinks. Like Melanie said, I'm not afraid of anything. I'm Sandra McLeod, I can get what I want out of life and I'm not afraid of anything.

The bus to Kawerau leaves at eight the next morning. She sits in the second row from the front with her bag on the seat so no-one can sit next to her. As the bus fills up and people board, they try to catch her eye, to get her to move it. She stares them down. Shame her old car isn't that reliable, the bus is definitely second best but she's not going to share a seat. Bags are put up on racks, and seats are taken. The driver checks the last passenger off on his clipboard and climbs the steps. He looks over his glasses in her direction, raising his eyebrows. Sandra has the only spare seat next to her. He settles behind the driving wheel.

Her legs tense to propel her up and one hand reaches for her offending bag. She could run, now. Maybe it wasn't such a good idea. She hovers on the edge of leaving. Thought control, that's what's needed. *I have more courage.* She's caught between running and staying, unable to do either. The bus door slams. It's too late now.

Her hand is not steady as she lights a cigarette and stares at the suburbs moving past her. It's Saturday and she can be back on Monday night. That's only three days. Melanie will cover for her and that will be enough time to prove it to herself; that she's not afraid of anything.

The suburban streets end and the green begins. There's lambs, feeding with their tails twitching, jumping with all four feet off the ground and the odd one, lost, bleating for its mother. The bus driver puts the intercom on but Sandra can't hear what he's saying over the noise on the bus. His voice becomes a drone, background to the bus engine, working hard to get up the hills. She falls asleep.

The smell wakes her up. It pierces a confused dream in which she's standing on the boss's desk wearing a g-string and stilettos and twirling a 'For Sale' sign in the air and there's a woman in a floral pinny reaching out for her and she's holding up the 'For Sale' sign, to ward off the long, smothering arms. The bus is pulling into a town and she's not sure where she is, where she's going. It's the smell of sulphur that tells her she's in Rotorua. The ground is steaming its stinking breath out. She stretches her neck and gets her compact out of her bag, blinks at the half awake green eyes that look back from the mirror. The driver's at it again and he's louder. He's not going to let them out of the bus until he's told his story. It's a gar-bled story about a god of volcanoes. Something about his parents being pushed apart when she was pregnant and his mother so dis-traught by the loss of her lover that she turned over and birthed the baby god into the earth. Buried him. She grimaces into her mirror.

The bus is almost empty for the last part of the journey. She puts her bag up on the rack. The doors are about to close when the last passenger arrives. It's an elderly woman and she takes a while to get up the steps. Of all the seats she could choose, she sits right next to Sandra. Sandra hunches her shoulder to close the old woman out.

"I'm going to see my daughter," says the old woman. "What about you?"

Sandra pulls out the silver lighter, with its initials I M and lights her cigarette.

"That's an old lighter. I used to have one like that."

Sandra doesn't answer.

"Looks like it's special."

Sandra takes in the smoke and stares out the window.

I M, Ian McLeod. Her father. The last time she'd seen him, the day she'd left, he'd said to her sixteen year-old self; 'Hello lass, I've come to take you home.' Home. The word had echoed off the hospi-tal walls, magnified as it bounced from the ceiling, escaped through the open window, and melted in the drizzling rain. Home. It had echoed in her empty belly and sunk. When he'd gone to sign her out she'd groped in the pockets of his jacket. A dirty handkerchief, a lighter, and his wallet. The envelope in the back of the wallet had photos in it. Into her coat pocket had gone the envelope with the four photos, all of the money, and his silver lighter with the initials I M on it. No-one had seen her leave.

Sandra breathes out smoke and shoves the lighter back in her bag. The bus twists around the edges of the lakes: Rotoiti always choppy, white caps frothing with the wind, Rotoehu, so still, weeds reaching through its surface, and Rotoma, surface trembling and shifting. The only road into Kawerau has trees now, where once there was scrubby grass, camping on the ash. It's the same and it's different and recognition is just a little out of reach, like a half-remembered ruin that should mean something to her.

The bus pulls into the station. This hasn't changed. The seat's still there; where she'd sat for a time, resting, watching the rain stop and the cloud lift from the mountain, watching the cloud reach arms around the girth of the mountain to touch the small mound tucked into its side, the baby mountain. Those arms that would never reach her. If he'd come looking for her, he could have found her easily enough but he hadn't. No-one had and she'd said she wasn't coming back, ever.

She's the last one off the bus. She's got a handbag and a small suitcase because she's only staying for a few days. In her handbag is an old envelope, with four photographs in it.

Chapter Two

Kawerau February 1954

A photograph of Sandra and Amy with the neighbours' dog. They're sitting on the doorstep. Amy has her arms around the small terrier, she's holding it tight. The dog's squirming, arching its back. It's trying to escape. Sandra's sitting very close to Amy, with her arm around Amy's shoulders. Her dark hair is cut short, with a fringe. Her teeth stick out. Her face is screwed up and she tries to hold both Amy and the squirming dog.

Sandra was half out the door when she remembered she hadn't told her mother where she was going. She yelled down the hallway.

"Mum, I'm going to play with the Simpson kids, all right?"

"Don't you go too far away. You stay round here where it's safe."

"Yes, Mum."

"And take Amy with you, don't just leave her to me, you hear me?"

Sandra made a face at Amy.

"Did you hear me?"

"Yes, Mum."

Sandra hissed at Amy as they went out the door.

"You'll just have to keep up."

Amy nodded, stamping her heavy boot down to keep her balance.

Sandra pulled Amy into a joyous army, a savage army, a wild

army going for freedom that hooted, whooped and ran over the field together, pretending to shoot each other, rolling over in momentary death, tripping each other, tangling legs and arms. Sandra counted seven: herself and Amy, the Parker boys from next door (Lenny and Robert), the Simpsons from the other next door (Peter, Maria and Colin). If you counted Jip it was eight. Jip was the Simpson's dog and he threaded between them, yipping and skipping almost as high as the children. Sandra danced in and out of the melee, circling back to her sister who, with her mouth set hard in determination, formed the rear guard.

"We've got wounded, we have to carry our wounded," called eleven year-old Lenny.

"You heard the Sarge," said Peter, also eleven. "We've got two wounded, and the Anzacs never left their wounded."

"Neither did the British army," yelled Sarge Lenny. "Come on troops, there's a war to be won and we must take every last man. You Simpsons, you're on ambulance detail. One of you take my little turd brother Robert, and one of you take Amy. Fall in."

The army settled slowly, one random shot felling two of the Simpson boys. They shuffled to get organised, with Jip chasing his tail, tripping them up and causing chaos. Eventually Amy and Robert, the wounded, were piggy-backed by two of the Simpson boys. Sandra bit her fingernail as her little sister was jiggled along on someone else's back. Amy's arms tightened around Colin's neck and Colin, trying to balance the heavy leather boot, staggered.

"Are you all right, Amy?" she asked.

"You, soldier, you're needed in the battle. Let the ambulance detail do their job," Sarge Lenny yelled.

"My mum said I had to look after Amy so stop yelling at me. I'm nine and you can't boss me all the time."

Sandra sat down, folding her arms. She wasn't meant to be here and if anything happened to Amy, her mother would say it was her fault.

"You have to take orders," Lenny said. "You're in the army."

"I'm not in the army. My dad said girls didn't have to be in the army."

"Well, you can't play then."

"Come on, Sandra," Peter said. "You can be the dog handler, Jip hasn't got a dog-handler and he's a dangerous weapon."

Jip was capering around Amy and Colin, threatening to destabilise them further.

"Come here, Jip, come here," she said and Jip, finding someone at a more accessible level, leapt at her. She grabbed his collar and stood up. "Good boy, good boy...."

With the rebellion quelled, the army was on the move again. The destination was Sulphur Hill and Sandra hoped her mother wouldn't find out. It looked like a battlefield and it was the best place for war games. Here, the mountain had breathing holes, tiny cracks and long fissures that emitted the earth's breath, smoke and steam coming from deep hot springs in the live earth, the bubbling earth. The fissures sat like Hell's flowers in an uneven bed of bright, brittle sulphur deposits. On that sunny day they were blindingly bright, white and yellow. At the edge of the smoke, where the earth was streaked the yellow of nicotine stains, the army stopped. Sandra carried a squirming Jip.

"Fall in, troops," Lenny yelled. "That means get in line. Some of you have to be Germans so we can kill you."

As the crooked line shuffled, Jip barked and wriggled. He seemed to be the only volunteer.

"Stop it, Jip," and Sandra tightened her grip.

"The Simpsons can be Germans," Lenny said. "They've got a German name."

"No, we haven't. We're from Christchurch," Peter said. "And anyway, that's not fair, that means you get to win."

"We can have turns," Lenny said. "You can be Germans first, then we can swap over when you're all dead and you can kill us."

So it was decided and World War Two began again but Sandra and Maria defected and played together with Jip, throwing a stick shed by the stunted manuka. The wounded, Amy and Robert, found an ant nest to poke. The ants, already accustomed to dodging the hot spots in the earth, scurried away from the sharp sticks, unwilling to join a war. There was just the English army of Lenny Parker shooting at the German army of Colin and Peter Simpson. The battle noises filtered through the smoke, "You're dead," "No, I shot you first, you're dead," "You're German, you have to be dead," and arms were thrown up and bodies fell down.

As she bent to pick up a stick, the sulphur invaded Sandra's sinuses. The gases from the earth were heavy and clung to her clothes and hair. She was enveloped in the mountain's breath: sulphur dioxide (the smell of brimstone), hydrogen sulphide (the smell of farts and untreated sewage), toxic, deadening the sense of smell and bringing creeping death. The acid of it caught her throat. She coughed.

The smoke drifted, carrying the voices, fragmenting them. Bodies emerged and submerged, colliding and collapsing, swallowed by fumes. Then the earth breathed out and the weight of her breath deadened all sound and movement. Sandra held on to Jip's collar, a small, lost island.

In the silent fog, Sandra squinted. There was a wooden fence, coming and going in the billowing white, now you see it, now you don't. It was around a cauldron of a pool almost buried by the yellow sulphur, which bubbled with some potion for earth magic. As if in the slower time of the mountain life, she reached for the stick and threw it into the smoke and steam, towards the fence.

Jip was fast after it. Legs and body in one determination, he was a stray bullet. Sandra heard a splash and a high-pitched, frantic yelping. Her legs in slow motion against the heavy gases, she ran through the fumes, through the smoke and steam, towards the small bubbling pool to see Jip pull himself out of the water, out of the portal to the belly of the mountain. She reached for him, trying to help, but Jip wriggled away. He ran, with an unearthly yelping, and disappeared.

"Jip, Jip, Jip come back!" she called. "I'm sorry, I'm sorry!"

The war stopped and the soldiers came running out of the steam.

"What's the matter? What happened?"

Lenny was the first to arrive. Sandra was crying, knuckling her eyes and gulping.

"I'm sorry. I'm so sorry. I threw a stick for Jip," she said. "It landed in the hot pool. He jumped in and he's hurt and he's run off. He's hurt, he was crying and crying."

The rest of the army had arrived so she repeated her story, wiping her nose on her arm, hiccupping.

"He will've gone home," Peter said. "If he's hurt he will've gone home. He always does that, when he's hurt."

The Simpsons all nodded.

"Yeah, he did that when he got hurt in the barbed wire," Maria said. "He'll be at home."

So the little army disbanded into a group of children going home, back across the fields, following the dirt road.

They found Jip lying on the front porch. Sandra was the first one to reach him. She ran over to pick the dog up but stopped as she got closer. She stood and stared. The children joined her in a silent circle, witnessing. The white and black hair was gone from his back legs and trunk. He was a livid red, the red of meat fresh cut. And the front of his body and his head were still Jip, with his black patch on one shoulder, one black ear and white muzzle. His mouth was open, his tongue a limp pink rag on the concrete step and his open eyes were glassy marbles. He smelled of cooking meat. He still had his collar on.

~

Kawerau March 1954

A photograph of Sandra, her sister Amy, and her mother Betty
collecting pine cones down by the stream with the Parkers, Jill and
her children Lenny and Robert, from next door. Betty's bending
down, her skirt dragging on the ground and she's holding open
a hessian sack. She's stretching her face upward to look at Sandra.
Sandra has her arms full of pine cones and she's walking towards
her mother. She's saying something. Amy's in the corner of the
photo, standing, in her crooked way, staring at a single pinecone.
Her face is hidden by her wispy hair.

It was the dandelions that pulled Amy away. She wanted a great golden
feast of them. She followed the gleam further along the creek, further
from the chatter and laughter. Here the manuka thickened. It shielded
the edge of the fast flowing creek and met over the top, forming cool
shadows where the dandelions shone brighter. She dragged her ortho-
paedic boot, pushing her lopsided way through the long rye grass with
its seeds rustling and poking at her as she passed. Under the canopy
of the manuka, on the edge of the water, the dandelions promised.

She reached for those little golden flowers like small suns in a
green sky. She swung her boot over to the edge of the bank, leaning
down to pick them but the creek had swept under the bank, taking
the sandy subsoil and now, taking Amy. She slid, grabbing at a young,
rough twigged manuka. It ripped her palm as she slid further. The
water, fast, greedy, pulled her in.

They say that once the water has seen you, seen into you, you
will never fear it again. Amy would always remember the caress of
the cold creek water, the way it filled her ears, her nose, the way it
held her, carried her. Her body would remember the cold. The cold
that shocked her warmth from her then insinuated itself into her
veins. She would remember the entrancement of manuka against
blue sky, twisted, stroked into movement to mimic the water and
the feeling of water pushing her eyelids open.

Then, moving faster than her, like question marks on the blue-patched sky, the dandelions floated. She reached for them, through the insistent water, reached for the gold and couldn't catch them. She couldn't touch the bottom of the creek bed; couldn't get beyond the water's grasp. Her boot caught a large plant of rye grass growing close to the water while the current pulled, pulled at her body and the shock of the arrest broke the dream and broke the creek's possession.

She bumped against the sandy edge, grabbed at the grass tangled in her boot and it held. She hauled herself up the sandy soil. The tiny pumice stones pricked her bare arms, bit her strong knee as she levered herself up. Her heavy leather and iron boot still in the creek, she retched out the water. Numb with the cold of it, numb with the creek's bid for her, she could hear the cicadas insisting the urgency of the sun. Her name was calling her back.

"Amy, Aaameee."

Her sister's voice calling, calling. Amy pulled her heavy boot from the creek's grasp, and tried to stand up, her legs numb, refusing to hold her weight.

"Amy, Aaamee," and Sandra came running, effortless, the paspalum whipping at her bare legs. "Amy! Oh, Amy, you're all wet, all of you. And you're all dirty too. What happened?"

One of her big sister's hands was on her shoulder and one was wiping her wet face and hair. Amy couldn't speak, couldn't tell of that otherness. She gulped in this sunshine, this dry world.

"I was worried. We need to get you dry. Come on, I'll give you a piggy back."

Sandra hauled her sister up on her back, the water-logged boot awkward. Amy clung on and they staggered back along the creek. They weren't far, the creek bend had carried Amy further by water but they could hear voices close by.

"That's enough," their mother said. "It's going to be too bloody heavy otherwise."

She was overseeing the pinecone collection and the weight of the bags. There were five sacks full, one for each adult or child capable of hauling it home.

"Where's those girls? Sandra, Sandra, oh, there you are. Gawd, look at you Amy. Get those wet things off her Sandra, she'll catch her death. I hope she hasn't wrecked her boot, your dad will be furious. What were you doing, Amy? Can't leave you for a minute."

She rummaged in her cane basket and handed Sandra an empty hessian sack.

"Here, Sandra, put her wet things in here."

Amy's clothes were peeled off, gently, and her body patted dry and water squeezed from her fine white blond hair. All by her sister. The boot was waterlogged, and the leather straps were difficult to undo. It finally came free with a sucking sound. A small tadpole of a foot, bending back on itself, beached on the grass.

"I think her boot will be all right when it dries out, Mum," Sandra said but her mother was sitting on a pine log, lighting a cigarette.

"Do you think we need to come back for more of these pinecones, Jill? You said we'd get a load of wood coming too, from the camp."

She dragged on her cigarette, crossing her legs.

"How cold is it going to get anyway? Innit supposed to be a lot warmer here?"

Amy peeked out from the close hold of her sister; her thin body shaking, her fair skin bluish tinged, her club foot twisting her body so she always looked precariously placed on the earth.

"Mum, she's freezing," Sandra said. "Amy's shivering and shivering."

Her mother passed her cardigan over to Sandra who wrapped Amy, hugging her closer. It was Sandra's neck that Amy clung to, melding her body to her sister's warmth, as if the creek was still pulling at her. Around the two of them the warm, dry world continued.

"Well," their mother said. "I know we need them for the copper and I s'pose for the fire. Funny not having a gas fire, innit?"

"Lots of things to get used to," Jill said. "It takes a while. At least you're in your own place now, you and the girls and Ian. You'd never get a place of your own back home."

As the two women sat smoking together on the fallen pine, Lenny, brown from a summer of sun, dressed in shorts and plimsolls, climbed through the pine branches.

"Mum, Robert's stuck. He's got himself in under the tree and he won't come out because of the monsters," he said.

"Here, hold my fag a minute will you, love?" Jill said. "I'll fetch him out. Honestly, that boy's scared of his own shadow. It's time we got home anyway. It's nearly four and your dad will be getting off to work soon and he'll need his dinner."

Jill handed her cigarette to Lenny who pretended to smoke it, the smoke curling up over his face.

"Don't you try, I just said hold on to it or I'll tell your dad."

They straggled back across the dry, empty paddock, leaving the loudness of cicada song, the manuka dark green on the hills behind the creek. Amy was on Sandra's back. The buttons of her mother's cardigan dug into her chest and her wet hair trailed over Sandra's face as well as her own.

It was the end of summer and the ground was sandy where the grass had burned away. Only the small, yellow flowers and long paspalum fronds survived the heat and dryness, their seeds sticking to the full hessian bags and to the children's bare legs. Inside Amy, the water insisted.

~

Kawerau March 1954

A photograph of Betty, in the backyard. She's holding a hose, squirting water at something outside the photo. Her dark hair is permed and it looks like Queen Elizabeth's hairstyle, with two kiss curls at her forehead. She's wearing a sundress. The front gapes because she's thin and the sundress is too big. Her eyes are screwed up against the sun and she's shouting at whoever is holding the camera. She's agitated about something.

Dear Kath,

Am sending you a photo of our back yard. Can you believe it? That's me in a sunfrock and its March!!! Bet you're shivering in front of the gas fire. You can see we got a big lot of land, we could have a picnic out here and pretend we're on Tooting Common. You wouldn't believe the house, it's a bungalow. It feels really strange not going up the stairs to bed and it's made of wood, all the houses here are made of wood. Got three bedrooms, so much room! The girls are good, our Sandra is going to school. Do you remember them prefabs they put on the Common during the War? Well, that's what her school looks like, prefabs in a field and she doesn't have a uniform. She seems happy enough. Our big trunk has come. It seems so long ago that we packed all those things in it. Sandra thinks she's too big for her walky-talky doll. Would you believe it, all that fuss she made about missing it. Amy's been playing with it and if it says mamma, mamma one more time, I'll throttle it. Amy's happy to see her old puppet, that one you gave her, you know, from the Bill and Ben on telly and I'm glad of me old mangle, don't know if I'd get one here, at least you can get the washing dry outside!!! We got a whole lot of Poms here so we have good sing-alongs, excepting it's in each others houses because there ain't no pub down the road. Ian's working every day, in the

*mill and building houses. There's no footpaths yet, and the
roads are only dirt. I'm getting about in me old skirts and
sandals most of the time. Me flash London clothes I packed
might not get much airing. Gawd, this sounds like I've
come to the middle of nowhere and that's what it feels like!!
Remember that pamphlet we looked at, before we came?
The one that said about New Zealand being prosperous
and needing new settlers and remember how there was just
a blank on the right hand side? Well, that's where we are.
The middle of nowhere. Missing you all. Amy's really missing
her Aunty Kath, she's gone all silent on me, won't answer
when I talk to her. I suppose she'll get over it, we all have
to make big changes. Run out of room, will post this when
I go to the next town on the bus, its name sounds like
Wockertarny, lawd knows how you spell it. Have to go there
to get me shopping once a week. It is the middle of nowhere!!!!*

Love Betty.

Sandra finished reading the letter over her mother's shoulder just before it was carefully folded. She got to lick the sides of the blue aerogramme and seal it up as her mother took a puff of the cigarette sitting in the ashtray.

"Can you get that sister of yours to hurry up, Sandra," she said. "We have to meet Jill and little Robert and we might miss the bus."

Before Sandra could move, Amy came down the hall with her boot stomping on the wooden floor. Their mother pulled at the leather straps, tightening them and Sandra winced for her sister. Amy never complained.

"Did you clean your teeth?"

Amy nodded.

"Show me. You'll do. What are you doing with that old rag doll? It's your puppet. You can't take that, you're likely to lose it. Here, give it me."

Amy looked at her mother and shook her head.

"You can't take that old thing to the hospital. What if you lose it? Here, give it me."

Amy took a step backwards, away from the hand reaching for her, tripped and fell on the floor. Her precious puppet landed on the concrete base of the oven. Her mother snatched it up.

"Got it. It's going up here and I don't want to hear any more about it."

Her mother put the puppet in a high cupboard and bundled her string bag and her purse into her cane basket.

"Now come on, we've got to get up the road for the bus."

As her mother reached down to help Amy up, she pulled herself upright.

"Please yourself. Now come on, you two."

Sandra tucked her book away next to the puppet and, rolling her eyes, shrugged at Amy.

There were no footpaths so the two women and the three children walked on the road. The dust and small stones worked into their shoes and into Amy's heavy boot. Robert and Sandra both held Amy's hands so that they could walk faster but they were still lagging behind when the adults reached the bus.

"Hurry up you slow coaches," their mother said.

"Cor, bus is a bit empty today," Jill said. "Where do you kiddies want to sit?"

The two mothers sat at the front of the bus with Sandra and Robert led Amy down to the back. The two small children sat on the edge of the seat, their legs dangling, holding on to the steel bar in front.

"My Ian wants me to look for some nice pig trotters for his tea," their mother said. "Do you think they'll have some? Me and Amy have to be at the hospital first, our appointment's at half past ten. What do you want to do, Jill? You want to come to the hospital with us before we do the shopping?"

She pulled out a cigarette and offered one to her friend.

"Might as well," Jill said. "Might be a good idea to see the hospital anyway, just in case."

Sandra followed her mother's eyes out across the bumpy field with its dirt tracks and sheep that still thought this was their home. There was nothing that looked like England. The sunlight of the southern hemisphere was brighter, more direct than the soft, greyed dampness of London. The air was missing its heavy load of exhaust fumes although, as the old bus started up, it did its best. Mostly it smelled of dust and heat and the heat had a hint of sulphur in it. There was little to hear; no hum of traffic, no clack of passing trains. There was not even the sound of wind through trees, just the old bus, rumbling and coughing. Her mother sighed as she smoothed her linen skirt with one hand and pulled a plume of smoke back through her nose and mouth.

"How-d'ya-be ladies?" the bus driver asked, turning to check his load. "Anywhere you wanna stop? I'll be going through Kopie, anyone need the hospital?"

"What did he say, Jill?" her mother asked.

"Um, yes, we want the hospital," Jill said.

"Righto, off we go then," and the driver pulled out.

They sat in the waiting room at the hospital on hard chairs with straight backs. The walls had notices about washing your hands and about notifying health authorities if you were coughing blood. Sandra and Amy shared a chair, twisting around to stare at the red hanky the woman in the poster was clutching. It looked like she had sneezed tomato sauce. Robert hung on to his mother's legs and she absent-mindedly stroked his hair.

"Mrs McLeod? Amy?" called the receptionist and her mother reached over to Amy, pulling her along after the white uniform with Sandra trailing behind.

"Ah, Mrs McLeod, sit down," said the doctor. "And you must be Amy, and this must be your big sister. Come on over here Amy, let's get you up on the bed and have a look at that foot of yours."

Sandra remembered visits to St Mary's Hospital in London.

This room was white, just like the room they always went to, and it smelled sharp, of something that cleaned everything. Her mother sat on the one hard chair, very straight, crossing her legs, cradling her shopping basket and Sandra leaned against the wall. With no help at all Amy climbed up on the bed and perched with her booted leg sticking out.

"So, let's get your boot off, hmm, it's getting a bit tight. How does it feel, Amy, is it a bit tight?"

The doctor was slipping a finger into the side of the boot. Amy winced and her mother frowned as Amy pulled her foot back from the doctor's manipulations. The boot came off, leaving marks where the straps had been tightened.

"She isn't wearing a sock underneath. It would help stop the boot from rubbing. See, she's got callouses along the edge here. Did you notice how tight it has got, Mrs McLeod? I would have expected you to contact us about that. I think we might have to do some alterations. What else are you doing today?"

She reached for her handbag to get a cigarette then stopped herself. She looked at Sandra, her face pinched, as if she didn't understand some difficult arithmetic problem and she wanted Sandra to tell her the answer.

"I got the shopping to do, doctor, me and my friend. We came in on the bus to do the shopping," she said.

"Did you bring a pushchair for Amy, Mrs McLeod? I need to send the boot down to the technical department for some alterations and it will take a little while. That is, unless you want to wait here."

"No. I didn't think about that. I really need to get the shopping today."

"Well, maybe we can let you have a wheelchair on loan. We might get you to sign for it and take it home, Mrs McLeod. Amy shouldn't be walking long distances with this heavy boot on, it will ruin her posture even more."

"Bloody hell," her mother whispered. "We walked to the bus,

was that a long way? Gawd, what about school?"

Sandra shrugged and sneaked a look at the doctor. He didn't seem to have heard.

"Let me see, she will be five in … oh two weeks ago. I assume she's started school?"

"No, she's starting after Easter, doctor."

Sandra knew her mother hadn't yet told the school about Amy, she wasn't going to do it until Robert had turned five.

"I'm going to take her to school," Sandra said. "I can look after her."

"Good. Well, we had better get her measured up for a lighter-weight boot, I think. The heavier one for night-time and the lighter one for school. She can have the next operation when she's six, by the look of her growth. The clubfoot is much smaller and is likely to stay smaller than the other foot. We'll move on to a built up shoe once she's had the next operation."

He looked down at his notes and began writing. It wasn't clear if that was the end of the appointment. Amy was still on the big white bed, like an abandoned bird sitting in a nest with her one clawed foot. She had a way of curling into herself, making herself small. Sandra wasn't sure if her mother could lift her and she wondered how they would manage to get all the shopping with Amy in a wheelchair. Would they get the wheelchair inside or would one of them have to carry Amy into the shop? Her mother was blinking and her mouth was tight. Sandra crossed her fingers, closed her eyes and made a wish for her. *Don't cry, Mum, don't cry.* The doctor's voice interrupted her.

"You can pick up a child-sized wheelchair at reception, Mrs McLeod. Take this slip with you. It's on loan until the new boot is ready, then you are to return it to reception. Is that clear? The old boot will be ready around four this afternoon and you can pick it up at the same place. Meanwhile, I don't want Amy walking on that foot without a supportive boot on and no long distances until she gets her new lightweight one."

"Yes, doctor," her mother said, nodding. "Thank you, doctor."

As her mother sat up straight and carefully arranged her skirt so that she could stand up gracefully, Sandra picked up the basket. Her mother reached for Amy and hesitated. Like an infection defiling the sterility of the room, Sandra felt pain and fear spreading. It wasn't hers, it was too big for her. It lived in the hesitation, between her mother's reaching arms and Amy, curled on the bed. She willed her mother to pick Amy up. Her mother found a bright smile from somewhere and bent to collect the small, passive Amy parcel. The pain and fear scurried under the bed.

"Come on, Amy," her mother said. "Let's get downstairs. You can be the lazy one today."

As they walked down the hallway to reception where Jill and Robert were waiting on the straight-backed chairs, Sandra held her sister's limp, bent foot. The toes were cold and the scar ridge on the instep was purple.

"Cor, he was a right one, that doctor," her mother said. "Thought he was a Harley Street surgeon he did, sounding so posh, made me feel like a right pillock."

"Yeah, but what did he say about Amy?" Jill asked.

They walked into the town centre. Robert wanted to push the wheelchair and, after steering it into a hedge and down the kerb, he managed to keep it moving straight ahead. Sandra trailed behind. This time there were footpaths and sealed roads to cross and trees in the gardens of the houses they passed. They came towards the bus stop, tucked into the side of the hill.

"Here, Betty," Jill said. "Let's do the butcher's first, it's just over there. Sandra can wait here with the wheelchair."

The concrete bus shelter had a tin roof and wooden seats. The old pōhutakawa tree slopped down from the hillside above it, its branches leaning over the footpath, providing shade. The shaded footpath was crowded with Māori who had come into town from Poroporo and Te Teko to shop and to meet. Sandra could hear them speaking but she couldn't understand the language. She moved past them, hoping to sit down with the wheelchair. She tried not to stare at the old women sitting on the wooden seats. They had head scarves on and wrinkled faces scored by the thousand winters of living in this land. They had black marks on their chins and their lips were blackened. They smoked, not cigarettes but old pipes.

"Don't you go near them, Sandra," her mother said. "They look like a lot of old witches. They'll put a spell on you."

Robert wandered over and sat on the seat next to one of them. He didn't look much bigger than the old woman he sat next to. She turned and patted him on the knee. He smiled and pointed to Amy in the wheelchair and the old woman nodded.

"Come here Robert, this minute, come here!"

Her mother's voice was shrill.

~

Kawerau, April 1954

A photograph of Ian, outside the front door. He's wearing grey trousers and shirt—his working clothes. They still look new and slightly too big for his thin frame. He's got his steel-capped work-boots on. His hair's thin, his forehead shiny from the brylcream. His big, crooked nose splays to the right of his face. He stands with his legs apart, his arms at his side, holding a cigarette cupped in one hand. He's smiling at the camera.

It was her mother's sharp voice that pulled Sandra out of the dark of sleep. She listened to a taut silence. Then the back door slammed and woke up Amy.

"Mum's in a bad mood," Amy said.

"It's because Dad went to work today. I heard them arguing."

"But he always goes to work."

Sandra sighed. Dad did always go to work. He said the building on his days off from the mill was good extra money.

This morning her mother was all sharpness and slammed cupboards, making Sandra so nervous that she dropped her bowl and it smashed. That's when her mother told them to get outside and play.

It was Sandra's idea to go and visit Dad so, without telling their mother, they walked along the sandy road past the houses that were beginning to look like homes. There was the one where Maria Simpson and her brothers lived. It had curtains up. There was Robert Parker's house. It had a new flower garden in the front. His brother was playing outside on the rough grass that passed for a lawn. Robert was watching him from the doorstep.

It didn't take long to get past the houses that held people. There weren't very many of them. They huddled together on the empty paddock. Without roads or footpaths to hold them in place, they looked like the sheep, keeping together for safety. Now they were passing half-built houses, some with roofs, some with windows but no walls. Sandra wondered if they felt lonely, the ones that were not yet lived in, that hadn't quite been finished yet. The last house was only a skeleton of a house, the framing all that was standing, just wooden bones. Behind it, the mountain, Mount Edgecumbe, was hiding under a heavy cloud. There was a man standing up on the promised house. He looked as if he was standing on the flattened mountain, his head reaching into the clouds.

"There's Dad. Up on the top."

"He's the king of the mountain, Sandra."

"He's the king of the whole world."

Around the edges of the piles of building material there were bright yellow flowers, reaching high for the grey sky. They decided to pick the gold for their kingly father. They could hear the conversation he was having with someone on a ladder below him.

"I'm not a Pom. I'm a Scot. You know, from that other country. After the war I lived in London for a while, converting flats for an old Jew boy. Where are you from?"

"Can't you tell, mate? Off a farm. Lots of good mutton in these muscles. You could do with some yourself. What did you lot get to eat? You're as scrawny as an old wether. Hope you've still got your knackers."

"Cheeky sod. We still had ration books, right up until we left. Didn't get much in the way of meat. Ever tried whale? Bloody awful."

"You Scotch beat us, you know. Must've been the whale meat, made you tougher than the Poms, we beat the pants off those Poms. You know what I'm talking about, don't you mate? The All Black tour of your country. You follow the footy, don't ya?"

Her father reached for another sheet of corrugated iron. Sandra thought about his knackers and wondered what he used them for. She liked the word; knackers, it sounded like a man's kind of knickers. She sniffed the flowers she'd picked and they smelt of egg yolks.

"Yuck, Amy. These are rotten egg flowers. I don't think Dad will like these."

"Yes he will, Sandra. He will."

"Well you take them. Come on. Let's call out to him."

They stood under the forest of framing and stared up at their father. He was standing to stretch his back, balancing on the rafters and looked down at them through the gaps.

"Dad, we picked you some flowers," said Amy.

"Och. Two little lassies and where did you spring from?"

"We made a wish and the good fairy went whoosh and we came to see you."

"Are you the good fairy, Sandra? Sounds like one of your ideas. Look, you'll get me into trouble. Go and play in the sand over there. Dinna want a hammer falling on your head."

They took turns to bury the golden treasure flowers in the sand. When it was Amy's turn to uncover her eyes and dig them up, the sand she threw in the air went into Sandra's eyes and Sandra called Amy a sod. Amy started to cry so Sandra turned her back and pretended she couldn't hear. Amy was still crying when their father came over.

"Finished. Come on you two, stop your fighting. I'll just have a beer with the boys, then I'll double you both home."

Sandra followed him to the truck where another man was flicking tops off beer bottles on the edge of the tray. She sat on the step up to the truck and watched her father tip the beer down his throat. One moment she was squinting into the sun, relaxing against the warm metal, the next she was startled rigid on the metal step. The tools, loose on the back of the truck, rattled. The beer dribbled down from her father's mouth. As suddenly as the quaking started, it stopped, leaving her shaken awake and her heart speeding.

"What's that?" her father said.

"Strewth, you don't worry about a little one like that," said his work mate. "We get them all the time."

Once the beer was drunk, their father wheeled out his bike. With Sandra on the carrier, and Amy on the crossbar, he zigzagged to avoid the pot-holes and the piles of pumice sand that slumped against the boxing put in for the future kerbing and paths. Sheep scattered as they passed, colliding with wooden stakes where houses would be. One of the sheep clambered to the top of a pile of timber and the tarpaulin ripped slightly. It stood on its mountain and stared at Sandra as they wobbled down the road.

When they got home, they disentangled themselves from the bike. Their mother was frowning at them from the kitchen window.

"Does your mother know you came to visit me?"

Sandra shook her head. Maybe it wasn't such a good idea.

"We'll all get in trouble then," their father said. "Let's give her a surprise."

He leaned in the back door, easing his feet out of the constriction of his steel-capped boots.

"Got a treat for you tonight, Betty. We'll all go down 'The Caf' for our tea. Come on, get your glad rags on. You kids, get yourselves ready."

"Ian, those girls have been terrible all day. I don't think they should get a treat. I've got some chops to cook and the potatoes ready to go."

"Come on, lass, it'll do you good. Get you out of the house."

Sandra skipped ahead, looking back at her sister riding on her father's shoulders, holding his ears and getting brylcream on her best dress. There was no way she'd be dislodged. Her mother, in her elegant blue suit with the shoulder pads and peep-toed London shoes, held her father's arm, leaning on him to negotiate the uneven roadway, down the pumice road to a brick building in the middle of a field.

On a Saturday night 'The Caf' had lines of men still in their working gear and families dressed up for a night out. They all queued together. Amy and Sandra stayed close to their parents, watching some of the other children who ran around the big dining hall, dodging between the formica-topped tables and wooden-backed chairs. Amy held on to her father's trouser leg. Two men in once-white aprons stood behind a servery of deep dishes. The ash from cigarettes clamped in jaws occasionally fell in the food.

"It's mutton stew," he said. "Smells good. Wonder if this is one of those sheep that's been watching us working all these weeks, serve it right for not getting out of our road."

He laughed. He handed out plates from the stack, one to their mother, one to Sandra and one to Amy. Amy's eyes narrowed, her lips clenched. She shook her head.

"What's the matter, snookums?" their father asked, hunkering down next to his smaller daughter. "You'll need a plate for your dinner. Do you want me to get you some?"

Amy shook her head harder.

"What's the matter?" he said. "You need to tell me. Come on, we're holding up the line."

Amy shook her head again and looked at the floor.

"She doesn't want to eat the sheep," Sandra said. "She thinks it's her friend."

"Oh, Amy," their mother said, "you stop your nonsense. You'll eat your tea and that's that. She's still not talking, you know. She won't talk to me. I don't know what's wrong with her. I wish we had Kath here to help, she'd sort her out."

Their father picked Amy up, balancing her and his own plate. Their mother glared at him, pulling the frown lines between her eyebrows into a tight line. If she had tried to reach out for her mother, Sandra was sure she couldn't stretch far enough to touch her. The instant became a moment, frozen, the two of them in the harshness of the light hanging overhead.

Then the white plates on the servery rattled and the light bulbs on their long cords swayed and Sandra stared as they came closer and the floor beneath her shook itself as if to fling them all off like so many fleas on a dog.

The building shuddered and the white plates crashed to the floor and Sandra was falling; falling into the tunnel of the tube station in London, where the train would come and suck her away; away from the deck chairs on pebbled beaches and her cousins sliding on the tea tray down the stairs and Mum and Dad laughing; away from family—those people with the same noses and the same dark hair and shared stories: away from a place where everything was known. Away to this strange land that would not stay still.

The shaking stopped. Sandra pulled herself up from the broken pottery, searching for her sister. She tried to still her own terror, the sensation of being sucked off the earth. Before the bodies on the floor could pick themselves up, before the world could become normal again, she scrambled amongst the shards of pottery and spilt mutton stew, reaching for Amy, for her little sister, and pulled them both to stand upright again.

Chapter Three

Kawerau September 1975

She pretends she's never been to this town before and sets off from the bus station determined to look at it with a stranger's eye. She hasn't come back, she's visiting for the first time. A supermarket shines with fresh paint, the foreign trees that had been planted along the footpaths have grown. A new place, it looks different, she can be a different person here. Except for the smell. As she walks on the cracked footpath that never did manage to cover the hot earth, the pungent steam coming from the drains and Sulphur Hill behind her threaten to resurrect that sixteen year-old who left.

She sets off for the Simpson house. *You have more courage than you ever dreamed you possessed. Page twenty-nine.* She keeps repeating it as she walks, to keep out the confusion of who she was, who she is now and how this place shaped her. Past wooden fences encasing new residents, gardens where there was once bare ash, the house where the pig dogs were chained. The edges of the past push through, exclaiming themselves.

At the letterbox she puts her suitcase down. Only a few days, she tells herself. The air is different here, close to the mill and it invades her and eats into her nose and mouth. She knows every-thing will taste of sulphur and sauerkraut. The mountain sits under its cloud behind the house, it leans on her with a familiar weight. It was here all these years, waiting for her. There are still swings on the traffic island. One slung up over the frame, the other hanging on one chain. She remembers them swinging, cleanly, back and forth and turns away while they're still empty. *Look at the house in front. Don't look next door.* She walks up the path with her suitcase bumping on her leg. Her feet step over the cracks.

On the front door the translucent mother duck is steaming forward over the glass water. She doesn't wait for her babies. Sandra knocks, her heart beating louder than her knock. She wonders if they can hear her heartbeat, the Simpsons, her mother, and whether, even if they could, they would think this is a foreign heartbeat, not one of ours. She thinks some time has passed since she knocked but she can't be sure. She bangs harder this time and her foreign heart beats louder. Then there's the creaking of floorboards and a shadow comes across the glass and a hand reaches up to open the door.

Fear doesn't exist anywhere except in the mind. The door opens, and Sandra breathes out again. It's not her, not yet. She recognises? Bea Simpson? At least, it seems to be her, an older version of her. Sandra counts the years, fourteen, no, it must be fifteen years since the last time Bea passed her a big man-sized handkerchief and that lump in her throat is going to need a man-sized handkerchief. Swallow. Take a shuddery breath. The lump recedes.

"Can I help you?" Bea says.

"No. I mean yes. You wrote to me."

"Sandra?"

"That's me. At least, last time I looked."

"My goodness. It's really you? Come in, dear."

Sandra smiles her professional smile, with her bottom teeth just showing, and bumps her suitcase up that one step.

"Thank you for coming, dear, I'm so glad. Just leave your suitcase, we'll get it organised later."

Sandra follows her across the lounge. There's the furniture she remembers and the picture of the Virgin Mary with the red, red heart.

"Your mum's in her room," Bea says. "She'll be so surprised."

Sandra wonders why the hallway is so long, it seems to have

stretched. It wasn't this long when she used to come to visit Maria, to come to this bedroom, where that other woman is waiting. She wishes it was Maria who was waiting but it's not. Her heartbeat has taken over her whole body, her feet want to run the other way. A little duckling from the glass front door has taken over her head. *Are you my mother?* it asks, over and over. Bea's hand reaches up for the round, black door handle.

"Here she is Betty, here's your Sandra to see you."

Sandra waits while Bea steps through the doorway. In that one long moment in the hallway, her feet almost win. She wills them one step forward. She stops in the doorway. It smells, a smell she knows. A sweet smell, English Leather, that's it. She always smelled of English Leather. In that other bedroom. Even when …

The mirror on the dressing table in the corner catches her eye. She can see her own reflection in her red trouser suit, red, the power colour. She can see another reflection, a very small figure shrunken into an armchair. There are the hands. Bent fingers are picking, picking at the blanket, pulling at it urgently and she's mesmerised by the rhythm of it. She stares while her heart slows, slows to the same rhythm. Pick, pick they go. Pick, pick. She keeps her eyes on the reflection as she steps into the room. It's not real, any of it.

"Mum," she says.

She waits. The hands keep picking at the blanket and her heart keeps beating.

"Mum, it's me. It's Sandra."

As the nodding head straightens the duckling is sure. No, this is not her mother. This is a very frail, elderly person and she's small, very small. Sandra takes another step and looks closer at the reflection. There's those green eyes, vacant; her mother's eyes were vacant. They're a faded green, as if the sun has bleached away the colour but they're still green, like her own. This person is so old, she can't be her mother. The reflection in the mirror puts up a hand to where hair comes to a point on the forehead. The widow's peak that forever denotes mourning. There's a match. Sandra turns from the reflection. The old woman who is her mother nods, her lips move but no sound comes.

"Some days she's really with us, you know, Sandra," Bea says. "We're grateful for those days."

There were so many other days when her mother was in some other place. Then. Sandra wonders if she'd be grateful if her mother was really present. Now.

"I'll leave you two, shall I? I'll be in the kitchen."

Sandra nods. She nods and the old woman in the chair nods. The door closes.

"Mum," that's all she can say.

She sits on the edge of the bed, on the pink candlewick bedspread and she picks at the fluff that frets its surface. Pick, pick. She watches her fingers picking at the fluff and she catches the reflection of those old hands picking at the blanket. Pick, pick.

She has beginnings in her head.

She has: "*Guess what I'm doing now, Mum?*"

And: "*It's been a long time, Mum.*"

And: "*Do you ... *"

She stops that one. The one that goes:"*Do you remember ...*"

That would unravel too much.

How long does she have to stay here, in this room, with this elderly woman, with her mother, before she can decently go out to the lounge and ask all those questions, all the ones that are picking at her. Before she can ask them of Bea. She jumps when there's a tap at the door. Her voice is too loud when she says,

"Come in."

"Hello Sandra."

It's a man's voice. She stares at the heavy cheek and the black hair and at the brown eyes looking solemnly back.

"Do you recognise me?" he asks.

"Robert Parker, yes of course I recognise you. How are you? It's great to see you. What have you been up to? My goodness, it's been sooooo long. You haven't changed a bit."

The words get faster and higher and the last word is pulled from her like the beginnings of a shriek. She holds that brittle smile and she holds her breath but his attention has gone to the old woman in the armchair. The faded green eyes widen, they recognise this man, this Robert who's just come in and welcome him.

He bends down and lifts those plucking hands and cradles them. A pang in her belly registers how gentle he is.

"It's good to see you here, Sandra," he says. "It's good for Betty. To have you here, I mean."

He's fussing with the blanket on the old woman's knee, tucking in the edges.

"I don't think she knows who I am."

She hadn't meant to say that.

"You haven't been home for a long time," he says. "All those years, growing up here. All that happened. You never came back home. Ever."

She's relieved he's looking elsewhere so she isn't overwhelmed by the accusation that hangs in the air.

You haven't been home for a long time.

She wants to say something else:

There was good reason. This place never let me be home.

She follows Robert back along the hallway, past the framed photos of Simpson children and grandchildren, back to the kitchen. He sits down and spreads his arms on the table, taking up space he seems entitled to.

"She's gone to sleep, Bea," he says.

Bea's hands come out of the soapy sink and she wipes them on her apron. She still wears flowery aprons that tie behind her waist.

"She'll sleep for a while now, Sandra," she says. "She gets very tired, very quickly. Now, tell me how you're getting on."

Sandra smiles with her bottom teeth just showing. Her hair falls across her face and she pushes it behind her ear and looks around. There's the familiarity of this kitchen with its green Shacklock stove and the handles on the cupboards that had always flicked back to catch her finger. Just like the kitchen in her old house, the one next door. It should feel like home. There's the strangeness of these faces impersonating people she once knew. Bea's face stays immobile, waiting.

"It's good to be here. Thanks, thanks for letting me stay and for letting me come and visit."

"So, all these years you've been away," Robert says. "What have you been doing?"

She looks around for a chair and sits down, scrabbling in her handbag for her cigarettes. Her hand closes over her business card. 'Sandra McLeod. Real Estate Agent'. She puts it on the table.

"That's me. If you want a house in Auckland, come and see me. I've only come for a couple of days you know, I've got clients that need me in Auckland."

"That's nice, dear," says Bea.

"So, after all these years, you're mum's only going to see you for a couple of days?" Robert says.

Sandra breathes in for four. She loses count and her words come out in a rush of air.

"Important meeting next week, a syndicate you understand, lots of money involved. Can't let people down, Robert."

"That's right, dear," says Bea. "Can't let people down. I've put you in the boys' old room. Hope you don't mind."

"Well," Robert says. "Since you're here, for a little while at least, maybe you'd like to come with me. For old times sake. I'm in the King of the Mountain Race this year. You know, the one that goes up Mt Edgecumbe. It's my first time. I want to find my route up the mountain and walk it."

Anything to get away from here.

"Sounds good, I'd like that."

"I don't suppose you've got any sport's shoes have you?" Robert says.

"Well, actually, I have. I'll go and get changed," she says.

Her one dress looks lonely in the empty wardrobe. She wishes she'd brought a dressing gown, negotiating the bathroom in her flimsy nighty might be tricky. She slips her shoes off and one of them falls off its platform heel. Her running shoes and track pants come out of the case, they might get more wear. Her course book is placed carefully on the bedside table. *Only a few days*, she whispers at it, *only a few days*. She's almost out the door, turns back and picks it up. *You'd better come with me* she whispers and pushes it into her waistband.

As Robert drives through the twisting roads of the town, familiarity and difference play two discordant notes at the same time. She can't pretend she's a new visitor to the town anymore. There's the house where Rewi's aunty used to live, it has a new fence. The signs along the river-bank that once shouted in bright red letters, now whisper in faded pink DANGEROUS RIVER. ADULTS WARN… The last words must have been washed away. There are private homes and letterboxes where the hospital used to be. *Don't look there.*

"We'll park up by the old dump," Robert says.

"Nice car, Robert, what kind is it?"

"Oh, it's a Holden, bit of a tank but it does me."

"You must be doing well."

"The bank pays me OK. I've nearly finished my accounting exams, then I'll be worth a bit more."

"You'll move then? Away from here I mean?"

"Move away? Why should I?"

Sandra gets out of the car with the noise of the river roaring in her ears as it throws itself over the rocks and under the bridge. Behind her the mountain, stern guardian of the river and the town, has shrugged off its clouds and pushes its shoulders up into the sky. It's looking over her and keeping its silence. Her eyes stray down its flank to the smaller mound that the hot earth tried to birth. A child mountain, tucked in, held, secure. Here, close to the old hospital, even the mountain's got a baby.

Robert locks the car and shoulders a small backpack. She follows him along the rutted pumice track, with its clay bones exposed by the rain. She has to concentrate on where she puts her feet and her words. It's slippery.

"Robert, do you have any idea which way you want to run to get up there?" she asks.

"Not sure, I'll probably go around the small hill, there's a fence line up there now. I want to find it so I don't get lost on the day."

"Is there a Queen of the Mountain?"

"Well, there's Emma Edgecumbe, the wife of the Earl of Edgecumbe. In England, of course. Suppose she's the nearest thing to a Queen of the Mountain round here. She'd been buried with a valuable ring on her finger and a few days later, a thief dug her up to steal the ring. He tried to cut it off her finger and she woke up. No-one believed she was alive, thought she was a ghost."

"Buried alive. It happens. I can imagine the revenge of a woman like that."

"Oh, I don't know. It's just a story. Are you one of those women's liberation types, Sandra?"

"Oh, yes, of course I am," she laughs. "I burn other women's bras, as well as my own. And I tell mothers they can have jobs as well as kids."

"I don't think you can have any opinion about mothers and kids, Sandra."

The mountain pushes its silence down on her. She opens her mouth, closes it. The silence breaks as Robert pulls his backpack up on his shoulder and walks away. She almost goes back down the track to the car. Almost. Down to where the car is parked, near the maternity hospital. *No opinion, you should have no opinion. Page eighteen, remember, page eighteen; the only way to get the best of an argument is to avoid it.* She takes a deep breath and follows his footprints.

The track is dug into a cutting between two hillsides. Robert is somewhere ahead, around that bend, with his backpack and his stolid face. She's enclosed, held by the bones of exposed clay hill bodies, with black ash and white pumice like flayed skin clinging in the cracks. There's a piece of broken lava right underneath her heel and she stops, unlaces her shoe, and tips it out. Sharp ash fragments crunch under her shoeless foot. She pauses, listening. The scrubby manuka with blackened bark is motionless in the still, hot air; it's also listening. She can't hear Robert, just a crunching under her one shoe and that other loud noise, her own heartbeat. She brushes the underside of her sock and pokes her foot back into her shoe. The dust from the spent ash makes her sneeze and the sound of the sneeze is absorbed, with no echo.

"Robert?" her voice is loud, flattened into the hills. "Robert, where are you?"

Silence. She tries again. Louder. The hills breathe in her voice. She listens. Up to her left, on the hillside, the manuka rustles and Robert's feet appear above her. She looks up to see his face obscured by the dark green.

"I think I found the track. Keep going around the bend and you can come up. This way's too steep."

She watches the back of his heels as he pulls himself up. The track is a small break in the bushes, with steps cut into the clay. She climbs up, holding on to the bushes, pulling her body up the wide steps, placing her feet carefully, close to the shallow-rooted manuka. The dust invades her nose, clinging to the spit in her mouth. She swallows. Robert is waiting at the top of the slope. She trudges behind him again, the slope now edging up towards the small mound tucked into the mountain. The ash shifts under her feet, pushing her back down.

"It's not that easy to see," he says. "I'm sure this is the way, this path goes directly up to the little mountain and misses the swamp."

"Sheesh, it's one step up, two steps back," she says. "This stuff fills up your shoes, too."

"Do you want to stop?"

"No, I've given up on emptying my shoes."

She shakes one leg behind her. Lava bits shift inside her shoe.

There's a series of fence batons sitting like bared teeth across the slope, ringing the rocky outcrop of the small, baby mountain.

"I think that's your fence," she says. "What's it for?"

"Maybe to keep animals out."

"What animals? I haven't seen any."

"Wild pigs. People. Mostly to keep people out."

"Out of what?"

"There are caves," Robert says. "Burial caves. Old ones for the Māoris who lived here, on the plain."

"I need to sit down," she says. "Get my breath back."

These are the same caves. The ones they came to when they were children, to be explorers. She slides herself down a fence post and leans against it. The town is spread in front of her, its streets snaking black between the red and green roofs. There are trees now that soften the rawness, the newness. Like an adolescent woken too early in the morning, the town sulks under the heavy grey cloud. She's searching for her old house, intent on following the bend of the black road, its convolution around the traffic island. Her breath is slowing and then she hears it. There's a muttering, a voice not carried in the air, but embedded, inscaped into the rocks behind her where the caves live. She can feel that life pushing at her, telling her she has no business here. There are the hands of the old man, bending over next to the chicken coop, reaching. The caves breathe the muttering and the hands shake as they lift bone. Old bones, better left buried.

"Can you hear that?' she asks.

"What?"

"The mountain. The rocks. They don't want us here."

"What are you talking about? These were burial caves for Māori people. I've never been near them. Someone else's ghosts Sandra, not yours."

"I don't know about that. I've been here with Colin. He was always where there was trouble."

She almost says 'Don't you remember?' but the words stall.

Chapter Four

Kawerau April 1956

At eight o'clock Sandra was the first child to come out into the street, by eight thirty there was a crowd. There was her sister Amy (with one built-up shoe). There were the Parkers: Robert with his brother Lenny (who kept making monster faces at Robert). There were the Simpsons: Maria (who was Sandra's best friend), her older brother Peter and their younger brother Colin (who was shouting that they weren't going to leave him behind).

The road always belonged to the children. It was a dead end, with a wide circle in which a traffic island had been marked off. This morning they gathered on the Simpson's rough lawn. Sandra and Maria sat pulling long pieces of grass through their teeth. Lenny and Peter watched Colin, who had Robert down on the ground. Robert was trying not to cry.

"Little turd," Lenny said. "Little turd brother, you gonna cry?"

"He's gonna bawl his eyes out," Colin said.

"Stop it," Amy said, pulling at Colin's shirt. "You shouldn't be so mean to Robert. He's not a turd. He's my friend."

"Cry baby, cry baby, baby gonna cry," Colin said.

He rolled off Robert and pushed Amy over.

"You aren't coming today, anyway. Girls and babies aren't allowed."

"What are they talking about?" Sandra asked.

"Oh, I don't know," Maria said. "They're going somewhere today.

It's just stupid boy stuff."

"How come we can't go, then?" Sandra said. "Just because we're girls? That's not fair."

It was Lenny's idea to explore the small mound tucked into the side of the bigger mountain and he ignored Sandra and Maria when they said they were coming. He told Amy and Robert there were wild pigs that ate little children and they ran inside, just in case. But the boys couldn't stop the two girls following them and follow them they did, up the old track from the town dump, skirting the swamp that stretched between the lake and the mountain, sliding and scrambling up the dry ash slopes where the dust made them sneeze and stuck to their open mouths as they climbed. No-one had remembered to bring any water to drink.

This almost volcano had looked so smooth and rounded from the town but up close it looked very different. When the small mound had tried to reach volcano-hood, it spurted lava out, like pimples, in adolescent eruptions that had left many doorways, passageways and caves. The boys were already there, assembled outside a thin cleft in the ragged volcanic rock and they were arguing.

"It'll have to be you, Colin," Peter said. "You're the littlest. All of us are too big. You go in and see what's in there."

"What if I get stuck?" Colin said. "What if I can't get out again?"

"You're not scared are you? You sound like little turd," Lenny said. "You are, aren't you, you're scared. Scaredy cat, scaredy cat …"

"Shut up," Peter said. "We're explorers and explorers do things properly. When people go into caves, they have a rope around them. I've got one. We'll tie it around your waist Colin, then we can pull you out if you get stuck."

Peter pulled a heavy, frayed tow-rope out of his rucksack and started to tie it around Colin's middle, over the top of his dusty shirt. Colin scratched his head and pulled away.

"Why can't one of you go? You're the ones who want to do all this 'sploring. Why does it have to be me?"

There was fear in Colin's tight, thin body as he leaned away from his tormenters. Sandra knew. The fear fixed itself on her, burrowing into her, lodging itself. It was old and huge and too big for either of them. She pulled at the rope, trying to get it out of Peter's hands.

"Stop. Don't make him," Sandra said. "He's scared. You shouldn't make him."

"You shut up, Sandra. You're not an explorer."

As Sandra and Peter tussled for the rope, Lenny took it from them.

"You're not scared, are you Colin?" Lenny said.

Colin shook his head, standing still as the rope was tied around him.

"You're the only one who'll fit through that little crack, Colin," Lenny said, "and look, we've got a torch too. We're proper explorers. You can use my dad's torch."

He rummaged in Peter's rucksack and pulled out a big torch with 'Tasman' scored into the metal.

"Except don't lose it. He doesn't know I borrowed it," Lenny said.

So it was settled. Colin, with his eyes wide and rolling, was to go into the narrow opening. He pointed the torch at the jagged, sharp rock and Sandra peered at the small gap that looked like a mouth, with teeth bared. It didn't look welcoming.

"You don't have to go," said Sandra.

"Scaredy cat, scaredy cat, scaredy, scaredy, scaredy cat," hissed Peter.

Colin wiped his nose on his shirt sleeve, swallowed hard and, holding the torch, wriggled his body between the tearing, gouging rocks.

Outside, the children waited. The sun went behind a cloud and a small wind came up, stirring the dust and making them even more thirsty. Sandra was closest to the gap where Colin had gone. She could hear him in there, in the mountain. He was making whimpering sounds, like a small animal. Fear sounds. She pushed her way in the entrance and there was a narrow passageway. It hadn't just been for lava. There was a way through the jagged rocks and places to put feet. That must be where Colin had gone but she couldn't see him, he seemed to have been swallowed. She whispered his name and the whimpering sounds stopped. She couldn't call any louder; the heavy air smothered her. It smelled of damp, and mould and something very old and as she strained to hear, she could almost hear a muttering. She pulled herself out, scraping her arm, her heartbeat echoing off the edges of her body. She joined the silence of waiting, not knowing what for.

He came out of the mouth of the cave with no heed of the scratches and cuts that he gathered. Breathing fast, his out breath carried a deep sound of distress. The light was blinding him. In one hand he was clutching the torch, and in the other, a long bone, green and mouldering. It was broken and the edges were jagged.

"What did you see ..."

"What's in there ..."

"S'plorers have to give a report ..."

The tumbling words stopped. Colin sat down suddenly. He was breathing very fast and his eyes were focused somewhere else. Lenny took the torch, Colin didn't seem to notice.

Peter pointed at the bone in Colin's left hand.

"What's that?" he asked.

There was no reply.

"Come on, let's go home. I had enough of this exploring," Lenny said. "Come on."

He started moving back off the small ridge to the ash slope.

Sandra stared at the bone in Colin's hand. She blinked, she blinked away a millennia of caves and graves, of cold earth and mouldering green, of joints letting go and skulls falling away, of sweet, sickening smells of rotting and decay. He dropped the bone, stood up, swayed and started walking after Lenny.

They slid and scrambled down the dry ash slope of the mountain. Ash got stuck in their shoes, chafing their feet. The swamp that stretched between the lake and the mountain, its dark water silted, waited for them to put one foot wrong and it would suck them in. At the edge of the little lake that sat at the mountain foot they stopped to get a drink, moving carefully in silence, keeping to the edge and the shallows where the water was clear. They didn't step further in where the water was dark, held by the reeds that infested the lakebed, a close cousin to the swamp they'd avoided. There was no sound until they disturbed the stillness, carefully scooping water to slurp. Colin stood on the sand at the edge.

"We should get you a bit cleaned up, Colin," Lenny said. "Get some of the blood off you."

Colin shook his head.

"Yeah, we'll get in trouble if you go home all bleeding," Peter said. "Dad'll give us the belt. You look like something tried to eat you."

Colin shook his head again.

"We can wash him with the hose when we get home," Lenny said. "We can just say he got stuck in blackberry bushes."

The next morning Sandra and Maria were walking to school with Robert and Amy trailing behind. They turned into Newall Street, passing Atkinson Street, which should have joined up with their street but didn't. They stopped to wait. From where they stood, Sandra could see her mother in the backyard, hanging out washing. There were no trees between the snaking roads that looped and turned back on themselves, coming to dead ends.

"Did your parents ask about yesterday?" Sandra asked.

"No," Maria said, "but the boys were whispering and Colin wouldn't go to sleep last night. I could hear them 'til real late. He's got to stay home today. He must've hurt his arm yesterday because it's really swollen. He's even crying about it. Mum's taking him to the doctor."

They turned into Galway Street. It snaked around, doubled back on itself before it allowed them a short, straight street to their school. An old green bus pulled up outside the school gate, shuddering and stopping in a diesel cloud.

"Watch out! Amy, Robert, come here and we'll cross the road together," Maria called.

They skirted the back of the bus, Sandra holding her breath to avoid the smell of diesel.

"Whose bus is this?" she asked.

The ten children coming off the bus were Māori. They stopped on the footpath, all barefoot, carrying newspaper wrapped bread for lunch, crowded together with the older ones holding a hand of the younger ones. Sandra stared at brown faces with sleep still in the corners and one upper lip with a trail of old white snot like a snail trail; at tangled hair that hadn't been combed; at the dress that seemed to be for a bigger girl, the hem nearly at the ground; at bare feet that could run on stones and three knees with scabs that crusted and cracked. These were Māori children who were not like the other children in the school who wore white socks and pleated skirts and bows in their hair. These were strangers. She looked for something that said these were children her mother would approve of and she couldn't find it.

"Come on Amy," she said. "We'll be late."

They drifted up the footpath as the bell rang.

It was just after morning inspection. Sandra's group had got an extra five points for everyone having clean fingernails and only one boy without a handkerchief. Her group was winning. They all sat down as the teacher recorded little chalk marks saying so in the corner of the blackboard.

"There'll be two new children joining our class today," said the teacher. "They've come from Onepu pa, they're swapping to our school. Sandra, they can sit next to you, at the end of your group. I know we're already cramped but you'll just have to move your group further to the front. You boys, get two more desks from the library."

Sandra made a face at Maria. She got her arithmetic books out of her desk and set to work on page twenty-three:

'John wanted to make a kite. The long strut was to be three feet, four inches. The short strut was to be two feet nine inches. They were to cross over half way up the long strut.
(a) How much material would he need to make the kite?
(b) If the material cost two shillings and threepence a yard, how much would it cost?'

She had drawn the kite and was trying to think through the next steps when the two new girls arrived. They slipped into the classroom quietly. Sandra sniffed, they smelled really strong, like the kerosene heater that got lit on cold mornings. Their hair was wet, that was the smell. One of them was crying, silently, wiping her chin as the tears dripped.

"What happened to you?" Sandra asked her.

"We got kutus, this stuff kills them."

"What are they?"

"Kutus? They live in your hair, they bite you."

"Do they hurt?"

"They do now."

Her father had told Sandra once about cootees, she supposed they were the same thing. He said that he had them when he was a Prisoner of War. Some of them were almost pets, he would pull one of them out, say hello and put it back, because there would always be cootees, because there was no soap.

"How come you get those things?" she asked.

There was silence. The girl who was crying used her fingers to wipe her nose. Sandra nodded to herself. Her group would not be getting any more inspection points.

"What's your name?" she asked.

"I'm Iripeta, this is my cousin Jessica," said the other girl, the one who wasn't crying. "What's yours?"

"I'm Sandra. This is my friend Maria. We live next door to each other. Where do you live?"

"Onepu."

"Where's that?"

"Down the road, past the mill."

"Did you just come here? Like us? We've been here for two years."

"No, we've always been here, but my nan, she came from Whakatane."

"How come you just came to this school now?"

"Don't know. Didn't want to. Too many kids at Otakere school prob'ly and our little brothers just started and our little cousin. Too many kids for the school, eh?"

The teacher came across the classroom, leaving a ragged line of unsolved arithmetic fidgeting alongside his desk.

"You, you new girls, you'd better come here and get some paper and pencils. I'll give you a list of stationery to take home. Not that I expect your parents will get it. You get on with your arithmetic, Sandra, don't let these two distract you."

So by lunchtime Sandra knew how much material John would need to make a kite and that the two girls from Onepu, called Iripeta and Jessica, both had younger brothers the same age as Robert and Amy. She knew they hadn't wanted to move schools and she knew their teacher hadn't wanted them to either.

After school, Sandra and Maria were sitting in the Simpson lounge, working on their model about medieval life in an English village. They had made a plasticine family dressed in scraps of fabric and sat them in an empty shoebox that once held English shoes. Colin had been given some aspirin and was asleep on the sofa. His arm was in a cast that went from his armpit, bending around his elbow and encasing his hand, with a loop between his thumb and fingers.

Maria put down the wool and matchstick fence she'd been work-ing on. She sat on the floor beside the sofa and beckoned Sandra over.

"Watch this," she said. "He talks in his sleep. Colin, Colin, what happened? How did you break your arm?"

Colin moaned.

"Colin, you have to make a confession, Colin."

Colin tossed his head from side to side. Sandra wanted to poke at his eyeballs, she could see them through his slightly open eyes and they were a milky white.

"Jesus's bones, they're coming, no, no," he mumbled. "Got to get out. No, not me, Jesus, don't make me stay here."

He turned his head from side to side.

"He's not dead, Colin," said Maria. "He'll come and get you, Colin. Here he comes, here comes the Holy Ghost."

She moaned and waved her hands in front of Colin's face. She was almost hit by the plaster on his arm as he jerked it up and curled into himself.

"Stop it," said Sandra. "Look, he's really scared."

Maria laughed.

"I'll fix him," she said. "It's all right, Colin, Jesus loves you. Even if you are a bad boy, a very bad boy."

Colin mumbled, his head thrashing around, his knees up near his chin.

"You must say ten Hail Mary's Colin. You've been a very bad boy. Say it with me: Hail Mary, Full of Grace …"

But Colin had gone back to sleep.

"Come on," Sandra said. "He's just stupid anyway. Let's get on with our model. We need some twigs to be trees and some dirt for the floor of the cottage. Let's put in some chook poo, that'll make it smell right too."

Out in the back yard they found Peter, behind the chook house. He was squatting down with his rucksack.

"What are you doing?" Sandra asked. He jumped at the voice.

"Yesterday, up the mountain. Colin found this bone up there. He picked it up. I think, I think it's a cow bone."

Sandra looked at the long piece of broken bone, the shaft dark where it had fractured, then at Peter's face. She tried to catch his eye but he kept his face turned up towards the mountain where the late afternoon sun was tingeing the slope with red. Peter's neck was flushed.

"Oh, yeah," she said. "I was there, remember?"

"I'm just going to put it here, behind the chook house. It might have some disease."

He threw it as far as he could along the wire fence. It landed on a pile of chicken manure. He turned and pushed past them.

"You forgot your rucksack," Sandra called.

"Come on Sandra," Maria said. "Don't mind him, let's get this finished before tea."

The two of them turned from the mountain and the mouldering bone, back to their task of portraying a medieval English village, held in the confines of a cardboard shoebox.

Sandra carefully carried the shoebox to school the next day, with Maria and Colin, whose plastered arm was held in a cloth sling.

"Why do you have to come with us?" Sandra asked.

"Mum made me," he said.

"She told me I have to stop him play-fighting and I have to stop him climbing trees as well," Maria said. "His plaster's still a bit soft."

Today was assembly day, held on the asphalt tennis court. Two hundred and forty-three children were gathering there, sitting or standing in groups. Colin had got away from his sister as soon as he could. He was surrounded by a group of admirers and he was telling the story of his broken arm. Sandra could hear his voice getting louder and louder.

"Then we got to the cave and I was the only one brave enough to go in. Everyone else was way too scared, eh? So I squeezed in this little, little passage and I got to a big cave full of bones and the bones all got up and they danced around ..."

He was waving his cast and kicking out with his thin legs.

"They was grabbing me and they was all rotten and smelly and one of the skellingtons pushed me over."

He crumpled on the asphalt.

"It was going to get me and I grabbed it and pulled off one of its arms and ran out and they all chased me 'cos they wanted the arm back but I got it …"

He ran out of story and breath at the same time and lay on the asphalt with his eyes closed.

Sandra glared at him. She could see Peter and Lenny milling about, whispering. She could feel a press of children behind her and turned around. The Māori children from Onepu had come off the old green, wheezy bus and were standing in a group. Sandra looked for Iripeta and Jessica, her class mates. She could see horror on their faces.

As Sandra walked in the kitchen door, her father was having dinner. He was due on shift at four at the mill and that meant dinner when Sandra and Amy were ready for afternoon tea.

"So I said to the new foreman," said her father, "I said to him that we'd sort it out, between us I mean. Seems to be a good fella, a Finn, but a good fella. More than I can say for those bloody Māoris."

Sandra slipped past her mother, who was busy at the sink. She reached for the bread from the cupboard.

"Pat had them though. Pat Simpson. You kids play with his kids. Catholics that lot, aren't they? Bloody left footers, place seems full of them."

Sandra cut two thick bits of bread from the loaf.

"They wouldn't talk to us, those Māoris. They just stared at us when we came in. Pat tried to get them talking, said he'd seen them at church. Didn't make any difference. They just kept poking their eyeballs at us."

He put a fork full of potato in his mouth, chewing for a moment. The next words came out muffled and Sandra stopped spreading butter to listen.

"Then they kept on about some kids who went up the mountain on the weekend. One of them's called Colin. Said he pinched some bones from their burial caves."

Sandra turned back to spreading jam.

"Said they were taboo and horrible things would happen to all those kids. You know about that, Sandra?"

She shook her head.

"Anyway, they said they wanted the bones back. Bloody peculiar I tell you."

Sandra folded each piece of bread over itself, hiding the blood red jam. Her father was busy with his dinner as she went out.

On Saturday morning the children gathered in the McLeod backyard. Timber framing took up all of the space. It was the beginnings of a set for the town pantomime, with struts across, partitioning it into empty rooms that could hold many different stories. The children sat on the edge, organising.

"You can't be the princess, Amy, you're too little."

"Yes, I can, I want to be a princess with long hair, like Rapunzel."

"I want to be the king, I could have a sword, and I could kill the dragon."

"Who said there's going to be a dragon?"

"I want to be Robin Hood and you can all be my merry men."

"No, that's boring. They all just sit up in trees and we haven't got any trees."

"I want to play cowboys and Indians. We can make bows and arrows."

"You can't do any of those. Mum told me the pantomime is Aladdin, so we have to do Aladdin."

There was an argument over who would be Aladdin. None of the boys would take it on. It seemed that going into a cave to fetch a treasure didn't appeal to them. Amy was sure she wanted to be Rapunzel and demanded that Robert put on his mother's floral pinny and be the old witch who looked after her. They settled in one section of the framing. Peter had been reading 'The Lion, the Witch and the Wardrobe' and knew he was destined to be a king so he set out from the castle with his queen (Sandra) to kill a fierce dragon (Lenny). Peter told Colin he could be Aladdin and go into a cave to get a treasure but he paled and, without saying why, he refused point blank. He became the single cowboy who was relegated to the shed but was expected to rescue Rapunzel.

As stories do, this one took an unexpected turn. Rapunzel was accidentally eaten by the dragon and an argument broke out about whether killing the dragon would result in killing Rapunzel as well. It became very heated. The errant dragon, or Lenny, called a meeting, to be held on top of the flat shed roof.

The children climbed up the wood stack, pulling their cloaks behind them, dragging swords and carrying cardboard crowns. Amy got her special shoe stuck in a gap and Sandra pulled her out. Colin tried not to put weight on his plastered arm. Lenny got everyone to sit down. From the shed roof, there was a view of the street.

Sandra looked down at four men coming up the driveway next door.

"Peter, there's a whole lot of people going to your house," she said. "A whole lot of Māoris."

The children crowded to the edge of the shed, staring. There were four men, in black suits and white shirts, holding hats. Three of them had black hair neatly combed back, brylcream glistening. There was one older man with them, his hair grey, combed carefully over a balding spot. He was leaning on a stick and led the other three men up the footpath. The delegation stopped on the front lawn.

"I've seen them at our church," said Peter. "They're Catholics like us. They must want some church stuff from Mum."

Peter and Colin's mother came to the front door, wiping her hands on her apron, shaking her head. She talked, the old man talked. Sandra strained to hear but the sound didn't travel up to the shed roof. Then, her voice shrill, Mrs Simpson called out.

"Colin, Colin, where are you? You come here this minute."

Colin was biting his lip. Sandra remembered his jerky skeleton dance and the look of horror on the faces of her friends, Jessica and Iripeta, and she gave him a shove. He climbed down the woodpile and went over to his mother. She held him by the shoulder, talking to him. He shook his head and waved his cast around, looking at his mother, not the men. When she let him go, Colin escaped back to the roof.

"What do they want?" Sandra asked. "Why did your mum want to talk to you?"

Colin's face was pale and his shoulders drooped. He nursed his broken arm.

"They wanted to talk about the bone that I got from the cave. I told them I don't know what happened to it. I think I dropped it in the cave. They said it was one of their dead people," and he shuddered.

Peter had sat down. He was staring at his feet.

"What about that cow bone, Peter, the one you threw on the chook poo pile?" Sandra asked.

He shook his head. Her cardboard crown and her queenly cloak were left at Peter's feet and she climbed down the woodpile. She went over to where Mrs Simpson was nodding while the old man talked and she stood waiting for a gap in the conversation.

"I think I know," she said. "Your bones. I think I know where they are."

Sandra led the old man behind the chook house. The chooks, thinking someone had come to feed them, crowded to the fence. She leant down to pick up the piece of bone that Peter had thrown on the pile of chook poo but the old man held her arm and said something, in a language Sandra didn't understand. He gestured, said something again and she moved back from the fence, away from the inquisitive chooks and the bone. She sat on the brown, crumbly manure. He pulled a white cloth from his trouser pocket. As he bent down to pick up the bone, he talked quietly, his voice a soft cadence with the curl of chook song punctuating it. He was almost singing to the bone, gently lifting it, cradling it. He pulled the white cloth over it, gesturing her to follow him. Bent to protect his burden, the old man led them back around the house. Sandra followed reluctantly. She was back at the entry of the cave with the weight of the dank air pulling at her and the long years of death and the rotting bones and the fear.

She ran over and hid behind Mrs Simpson, watching over her shoulder as the old man nodded to them both and turned towards the three men standing on the front lawn. He passed the white cloth with its hidden contents to one of the other men and they bowed their heads. The soft murmur started again, its rhythm falling and breaking, rising and mending. There was silence. As the men turned to leave, the old man looked at Mrs Simpson and Sandra, then he pointed with his stick to the children on the roof, banging his stick on his forearm. His voice carried up to them.

"Every time you see that mountain, you remember."

He nodded a final time and turned to leave.

Chapter Five

Kawerau February 1975

"Sandra? They're not your ghosts."

Robert's voice cuts into her. She's pulled back from the terrified Colin coming out of the cave with the bone making a hole in the sunlight; from the old man's shaking hand gently lifting it and wrapping it in cloth, to Robert's hand dribbling ash.

Here. Now.

"Maybe, but they don't want us here. The caves, the mountain, the whole place. None of it wants us here," Sandra says.

"I don't know what you mean."

"Neither do I."

She takes a handful of ash and joins Robert in sifting it, as if the answer might be there, in its dry brittleness. The dust drifts, silent.

"Sandra? She's not going to last much longer, you know."

"What? What did you say?"

"I said, she's not going to last much longer, your mum, I mean."

"Oh, really? Been seeing things, have you?"

The words are out of her mouth before she can stop them. His hand freezes, with the dust from the ash haloing around it.

"God, I'm sorry," she says. "I'm so sorry Robert, I didn't mean it."

"Time we headed back," he says, brushing his pants and pulling on his backpack.

A flash of heat from the ash she's sitting on comes up through her body. The flames reach her face. Words explode in her head. *I been seeing her—the old woman, she's back Sandra.* Before she can grasp them, Robert is down the mountain in long strides, fast down the slope into the manuka fringe.

He's gone.

She waits, listening. The caves hold their silence. She wipes the sweat from her upper lip and pulls herself up, steadying herself on the fence post. Her eye travels along the taut wire. There's no sign of a gate to get into the enclosed caves but the fence shouts loudly KEEP OUT. Her gaze is repulsed by the rocks that mutter at her and the ash slope carries her feet down and away. Away from the mountain and back to the fences stretched between Robert and herself.

She turns the corner of the deeply etched track and steps into the roar made by the river. The sound buffets her and echoes through her head and her belly. It sweeps her towards the Holden with its open door and Robert sitting behind the driving wheel. She's washed into the car and … one thing, she needs to do one thing, to be here in the car. She takes off her shoes, to get rid of the mountain ash. She can feel the hard spine of her course book digging into her ribs. *Fear only exists in the mind,* it says. The lace of her shoe has lost its plastic end and is fraying. New laces, need to get new laces. *You have more courage.* One shoe emptied, she's beginning on the other.

Then there's Robert, his knuckles white on the driving wheel, staring out of the windscreen at the river. She follows his stare. The water is urgent under the bridge. Fierce in the prison of its narrow banks, it throws itself at a huge boulder immobile in the middle of the river's track. She watches the desperate water bounce back, broken by the rock dissipating its force into the air. She knows something of that violence; of no possibility of escape but she buried that knowledge long ago.

"Robert," she says. "Robert, are you all right?"

He doesn't reply.

"Robert. Come back."

He turns towards her but his eyes are focused somewhere else. In the river, in the past, in whatever he can see in the disintegrating water. The two of them are held, like the boulder, in the roar of the river. Both are pounded by the violent water.

"Robert. Please."

His eyes slide back to the river, taking her with him. From the edge of her vision she sees his hand move down and he pulls off the handbrake. The car begins to roll, slowly, drifting across the ash. Sandra is mesmerised by the water and by the gradual movement of the car, as if whatever is going to happen to her is inevitable, dictated by some force that she cannot control.

The old lady. She's been living in my wardrobe and she's been very, very angry. I been seeing her every night.

The noise of the river is drawing the car towards it, seducing, enticing. As if of its own volition, the car is drifting slowly down the gentle ash slope, to keep an appointment made long ago. Sandra can only see the pounding water. It's as if she's no longer sitting in a car. She is the boulder, caught by the river, unable to escape.

She's been very, very angry.

The car hits something, a great lump of concrete protruding from the ash. It stops. The suddenness jerks Sandra forward in her seat and she puts her hands out, pushing herself back from the river.

They sit. It's Robert who breaks the stasis. He turns on the ignition and the engine starts. It drowns out the river and its spell. Without anything being spoken, he turns the car towards the town.

Sandra swallows. *Fear doesn't exist. Breathe in for three …* The breath is shallow, pushed out quickly by her heart that is pounding hard enough to break her ribs. She tries again. *Breathe in for four, no that's not right.* She puts a hand on the hard surface of her workbook under her sweatshirt. *I'm Sandra McLeod and I have more courage …*

The car slews around the gravel bend and they're back on the asphalt road; the river behind them, the cloud heavy and grey. As the car winds back towards the street where she once lived, when she was a different person, the grey turns to rain. The windscreen wipers flick across and back, across and back, a metronome measuring those ten years. They're leaking through, fragments of those years, but she won't go there, not back there.

"It's raining," she says.

"I did notice."

"Houses must be cheap here."

No answer.

"It would be hard to market houses here, you know."

Silence.

"Hard to find the selling point. It would have to be the price. Can't think of anything marketable about this place."

The sound of the windscreen wipers is preferable to his silence. His face is saying KEEP OUT.

Sandra is not sure whether to be thankful when they reach that street, the one with the roundabout and the swings, where her mother lives now, where she used to live. *Only a few days.* She reminds herself. *Only a few days.* Soon, soon she can go back to Auckland, back to her flat and the two new listings she hasn't started and the boss and the new deal. Back to her real life. Maybe she should ring the office.

"I need to get back," she says. "I've got a life. There are people, you know, who need me."

"Yes, of course," says Robert. "People who need you. Like Amy needed you. You never really knew who she was, did you?"

Chapter Six

Kawerau May 1956

It was murky in the bedroom that Sandra and Amy shared, the heavy curtains keeping the day out. It was cold enough for Amy's breath to make a faint cloud as she leaned over to Sandra's bed, lifting the heavy eiderdown, poking the ball curled underneath it.

"Wake up Sandra," Amy whispered. "Wake up. That old lady's here again."

"What? I'm asleep."

"That old lady's back again. Look, by the cupboard."

"Where?"

"There, in the corner."

"Have you been having bad dreams again? There's just our clothes on the chair."

"The old lady was there, Sandra, she was, over there by the cupboard."

"Well she's not anymore. Don't cry, it's all right. You just had a bad dream."

"I was under the water," Amy whispered, "and there was this old lady, all bent over and she was nodding and waving a finger. She was all wobbly, like she was made out of water and I could see the wall and her at the same time. It wasn't just a bad dream."

The murkiness in the room deepened. The thickened air pressed itself against the walls and Sandra could feel her sister, inflating, dissipating, floating over her. She pushed herself upright.

"Don't be silly, Amy," she said.

Amy blinked at her, hard, squeezing the tears out.

"Come and get in bed with me."

Amy pushed the eiderdown aside, then stopped and pulled the sheet further up to her chin.

"Come into my bed, it's warm in here."

Sandra opened up the bed cave but Amy shook her head, wriggling towards the wall.

"Well, maybe we should get up anyway."

Sandra made one leap to the clothes chair, grabbed the pile, and leapt back into her warm bed. She sorted the clothes into two piles, stowing some under her eiderdown and throwing others down on the floor between their beds. Her bed became a series of bumps and heaves and she came out to put on her skirt.

"Amy, you haven't even started yet. Here, here's your vest and your pants."

The clothes stayed on the bed, then slid back on the floor.

"What's the matter?"

Amy pulled herself harder against the wall. She looked as if she was trying to disappear through it, dissolve like her old lady.

"Oh, have you wet the bed again?"

Amy nodded.

"We'd better tell Mum."

Amy picked at the sharp point of a feather that was poking through the eiderdown cover. She shook her head.

"We have to."

Amy dragged her booted foot across the bed. The iron strut snagged on the wet winceyette sheet and there was a ripping sound as she pulled her leg hard with both hands. Her heavy boot dropped on the floor, as if it was someone else's leg, lifeless. She worried at the buckles of her boot, hauled it off and headed for the door.

"I'm not telling Mum," she said. "You can."

Sandra stood at the kitchen door, trying to find a way to tell her mother about Amy's ripped, wet sheet. Her mother had her back to the kitchen door and was staring out of the window at the mountain. There was a letter half finished on the kitchen table, with a tea stain on it. It had been there for a week. Sandra had already read it.

Dear Kath,

Monday
Thanks for the parcel, I don't know what I'll do with the clothes. The big heavy coat might be useful, we get frosts here. Funny seeing Mum's old things again. What with you moving out of the old house, I suppose there's a lot of things to sort. I opened it up and thought Gawd, its been two whole years since we left. ~~It was~~ I wish we could have come home for the funeral. We never really talked about it when we left, whether we could come home. Me and Ian just couldn't afford it. ~~Don't know~~ Mum would understand. I've put the photo you sent of her grave on the mantelpiece, the flowers on it look lovely. It makes me cry just to think of you all. You know, I never really thought about how much I'd miss you

Wednesday
Sorry, I didn't get time to finish my letter on Monday, the kiddies came home from school then what with the all the roads in the town getting tar-sealed and Ian doing double shifts. Still, mustn't get too down. ~~Sometimes~~ The kiddies loved the comics you sent with the parcel. Sandra keeps them under her bed and all the neighbourhood kiddies borrow them. Just like a little library. Amy's due back at the hospital for another ~~bl~~ checkup. She's wearing a special shoe now during the day and just the boot at night. It tears the sheets something terrible. What makes it worse is she's still wetting the bed sometimes. I don't remember her doing that before we left

Her mother was wearing the old dressing gown that she'd unpacked from the parcel of clothes. Sandra remembered her grandmother in that dressing gown, on Sunday mornings. Is that where her mother was, in that memory; waving goodbye to Grandma and then sitting on the Common, with Aunty Kath's head thrown back in the sun and arms reaching up to catch a little child. Her sister Kath, with the same dark curls as herself, laughing, and everyone laughing and the bright sun. Soon they'll pack up their picnic and go home. Home.

The sun was creeping into the cold kitchen, catching the formica sink bench and the empty, upended milk bottle. It was moving slowly over the rag rug with the scarlet bits that had been her mother's best blouse. It was thin light, not promising much. Ash from her mother's cigarette was spilling on to the aerogramme, coating it. Her mother shook herself, stubbed out her cigarette, pushed the chair back to stand up, slumped back onto its hard wooden seat, put her face down into her arms and cried.

Sandra crept back to her cold bedroom where Amy was pulling on her jumper. She didn't say anything about their mother crying. Then she heard the door to her mother's bedroom close.

"Come on Amy, they're doing our road today, we can watch on our way to school."

Around the corner came a truck full of sand, which was spread and raked by men in boiler suits. The children from the street stopped and stared. After the sand came the bitumen. The bitumen truck, revving and choking on its own thick, hot ooze, came spreading tar over the sand in a fine, black mist, smelling of burnt molasses. The men in boiler suits had cloths covering their mouths and their eyes gleamed white from black faces. They appeared and disappeared out of the steam and the smoke. Now you see them, now you don't.

"You kids, keep back from the road, this stuff's hot. Keep away!" yelled a voice from amidst the boiler-suits.

Sandra saw another boy coming out of the house across the

other side of the planned traffic island. He was eating a piece of bread and stopped close to the edge of the road. The tar splashed up on his bare legs. He wiped his leg and licked at his blackened hand with a pink tongue. One of the boiler-suits waded through the bitumen and grabbed him by the arm.

"Get back from the road, you moron," he yelled.

The boy's face contorted and his mouth dropped open as if he was trying to say something. He tried to pull himself away from the gloved hand and almost fell on the road.

"You stupid little bugger, you get that hot tar on you and you'll know all about it."

The boy got himself free and ran inside the house.

"Who's that?" Sandra asked.

"That's the new boy," Maria said. "He's just moved in. He's not the full quid."

Later that day, at the dead end of the newly tarred street, Sandra got into trouble for not looking after Amy. Still in her school clothes, Sandra sat on Maria's front door step, gossiping with her friend. Amy was sitting by the road with Robert and the boy from across the road. They'd been playing barefoot in the sand that collected in the kerbing and had started moulding the still sticky tar. There were three handprints distinct in the road surface.

Sandra's mother stalked across the lawn and stopped to put her hands on her hips and a frown on her face.

"Oops," Maria said. "You're in trouble."

"What do you think you're doing Sandra, just sitting around like Lady Muck. Why aren't you looking after your sister? Haven't I got enough to do?"

She didn't stop long enough to get any answers and carried on towards Amy, Robert and the strange new boy. Robert stood up. Sandra hadn't been paying attention to them. When she did, she tried not to giggle. Robert had tar streaks on his cheek and arms. His trousers had black patches and his hands were black. Amy still sat on the kerb, bent over herself. She scrunched the toes on her crooked foot and the little toes stuck together, curled like a baby's fist. A blob of tar pulled the edge of her mouth into a lopsided smile and stuck it there. She rubbed at it with one blackened hand and smeared tar into her eyelashes. One eye persisted in sticking closed. It looked to Sandra as if Amy was winking at her mother. She felt another giggle coming and dug her fingernails into her hand to plug it.

The bigger boy jerked himself up from the kerb. His feet and legs were blotched. His old shorts and shirt, already ripped and dirty, were black with tar.

"Blimey, look at you, what a pack of little savages. What's the matter with you, Amy, you're all covered in it and you took off your special shoe."

"Richard go home now," the bigger boy said.

He waved vaguely at Sandra, backed into the middle of the road and bolted, leaving faint footprints.

"Who's that?" her mother asked. "Who's that dirty boy?"

"He's my friend," said Amy.

"His name's Richard," Robert said, pointing. "He lives over there. He nearly fell in the tar yesterday."

"He's as big as our Sandra. What's he doing playing with you little kiddies?"

"It's because he's little inside," Amy said.

"You get home, Robert and you, Amy, you come with me. Lawd knows how we'll get this stuff off and it's on your school clothes. You, madam," she said, turning to Sandra, "had better help."

Her mother pulled Amy away from the sticky road, stripped her clothes off at the door and humped her inside. Sandra lifted Amy up on the kitchen table. She was in her underwear. One strong leg and one thin wasted leg, equally streaked with black, were both dangling. Amy clenched her hand and stretched it out again. The fingers stuck momentarily, then separated. She repeated the action again and once again. For a moment Sandra felt the delight of her sister's fingers, sticking together, separating, to stick together again. Sandra held the butter dish as her mother scrubbed the grease into Amy's straight, strong leg. The smell of grease joined the smell of tar and the smell of roast beef cooking.

"I hope you're ashamed of yourself, sitting out there in the gutter, barefoot, getting filthy dirty like this and as for you, Sandra, I don't know what you were thinking of, too busy nattering away to that friend of yours ..."

Her mother reached for Amy's bent foot. The rag stopped. Sandra's heart ached with it: the rag reaching, pulling back, reaching again. As if there was some invisible barrier between that hand with the rag and Amy's little shrunken foot. As if her mother was unable to reach and hold its vulnerability. Sandra put her hand out to take the rag, to free her mother and the butter dish almost slipped from her grasp. Fumbling for it, she let her breath out in a rush as her father came into the kitchen, his hair still wet, face scrubbed. Freshly awake, he would be home tonight for dinner, cycling off back to work for the midnight shift.

"We'll have you for dinner, little buttery one," he said. "You smell as good as the joint. You want me to do that, Betty, you get on with the dinner."

He poked at the tar hardening on Amy's bent foot, trying to separate the little toes and his fingers stuck.

"You look like a little tar baby, snookums, you're all sticky," he said.

The next day was Saturday and Sandra and Amy had been awake since six o'clock, listening to the radio in the lounge. The ashes from the first winter fire were cold in the fireplace. They were sitting on the floor, on cushions from the sofa, wrapped in eiderdowns Sandra had dragged in from their beds. They were two little cocoons, wrapped against the early morning cold.

The story on the radio was about the mermaid princess who lost her home in the water, her fish tail and her voice, all for a prince who loved someone else. In the end the mermaid floated back to sea as the foam, with her sisters.

"I'm a mermaid," Amy said.

"No, you're not. You haven't got a fishtail. Don't be stupid, Amy."

"Oh, but I am a mermaid. I just don't live in the water anymore. I'm like the Sad Little Mermaid with her sore feet."

Amy stretched out her crooked foot.

"Watch out then, the sea witch will make you drown," Sandra said. "Let's wake Mum up. Dad will be home soon, it's eight o'clock. Let's make Mum a cuppa tea in bed. It'll cheer her up. Come on Amy, you can help."

Sandra could reach the cups, if she stood on the bottom drawer. She put a cup carefully in a saucer. The tea caddy had pictures of Big Ben and London Bridge on it and she counted the spoons of tea; one spoon for Mum, one spoon for Dad and one spoon for the pot. Carefully she tipped the boiling water in, put the lid on and tucked the orange woolly tea cosy, the one she'd knitted, around the pot.

"You've got to turn the pot around three times before the tea will be ready," Amy said. "It's a magic spell."

"Don't be silly, Amy."

Sandra turned the pot around three times.

"And you have to put the milk in first, and the sugar."

"How come you know so much about making a cuppa tea? You've never done it."

Sandra put the milk in first, then the sugar.

She led the little procession to their parents' bedroom at the end of the hallway, carrying the cup of tea. Her tongue protruded just a little, to keep the cup steady. Amy, dragging her eiderdown, pushed open the door.

"Mum," Sandra said. "Mum, we made you a cuppa tea."

She couldn't see her mother, only a lump under the covers. She carefully placed the cup of tea on the bedside table, only a little of it spilled and caught in the saucer.

"Mum, wake up," Sandra said.

The two girls stood next to their mother's bed. If Dad was home they would have jumped into the bed, jumped on him and he would have rubbed his unshaven chin on their soft necks and they would have run, squealing, to lock themselves in the bathroom, but he was still at work.

"Mum, we made you a cuppa tea," Sandra said.

Their mother blinked and reached for her cigarettes. The cup of tea, so carefully placed on the bedside table was in the way. The cup upended.

"Gawd, what was that?" she said and pulled herself up on her elbows.

The tea was spreading on the bedside table. The Pall Mall cigarettes had taken most of it and the red packet sat in a puddle of brown tea that dripped down the side of the table on to the floor.

"Oh, crikey, me fags. Oh no, that's me last packet."

She reached over and picked the packet up, shaking it. Tea drips scattered on the sheet. She looked inside, threw the cigarettes back into the puddle of tea, lay back on the pillow and closed her eyes. Sandra pulled Amy out of the room, shutting the door.

Sandra and Amy spent the morning playing in their room and their father gave them two sixpences for being so good and so quiet, suggesting they go to the pictures. Later that afternoon they were standing in a queue with Maria and Robert outside the Rec Hall, with sixpences clutched hard. It was the girls' turn to choose the film and this week Sandra was hoping they could watch *Sleeping Beauty* again.

It was murky inside the big corrugated iron building. There were no windows and the light came in through the nail holes in the walls. Children sat on wooden chairs with metal legs. Fifty children with a play of sun fragments lighting up one here, one there. Now you see them, now you don't. At the end farthest from the door was a screen made from sheets. It flapped slightly in the draught. The noise of fifty children, talking as loudly as they could, scraping chairs on the concrete floor, bounced off the high iron ceiling, hit the floor and broke into a thousand shrill sounds.

Amy and Robert sat cross-legged on the floor. Amy patted Sandra on the knee.

"Sandra, we forgot the cushion again," she said.

"Only sissies bring cushions," Robert said. "My brother said so."

"But Mum said I'll get piles."

"Piles of what?" He was looking around the exposed rafters. "There's piles of rats up there. I'm going to see four today, that would be a record."

The projectionist was on the platform at the top of the ladder. He was an old man with white hair and he could climb up and down so easily, even with a big belly. The platform was where the projector was and the fat old man was the boss of it. He was waving his arms and saying something, his mouth opening and closing, like a drowning mermaid. The noise swirled and swelled and lulled a little. The next thing he shouted was so loud it pierced through the nail holes.

"Och, shut your gobs, the lot of you."

A small silence then fifty voices echoed it back to him.

"Shut your own gob."

Fifty children laughed.

"We've got *Donald Duck* or *Mickey Mouse* for starters. Who wants *Donald Duck?*"

A half-hearted yes.

"What about *Mickey Mouse*, then?"

The yes was louder.

"All right then, *Mickey Mouse* it is and we've got *Cinderella*."

A groan from the boys.

"Och, come on now, it's the girls' turn. You boys can have *Hopalong Cassidy* next week."

A cheer from the boys and the projector went on.

Sandra scrambled to her feet with fifty other children as *God*

Save the Queen was played. It was very loud and she could hear it over the noise of scraping chairs. Amy pulled her down and whispered in her sister's ear.

"It's the sea, Sandra. The queen's floating, like the mermaid in the story."

"Don't be silly, Amy."

"God will rescue her, Sandra, don't worry."

Sandra had to stop herself from looking up in the rafters, just in case.

Cinderella, with her perfect feet, fitted the slipper, got her prince, and lived happily ever after. The film over, children jostled to leave, crowding out on to the footpath, claiming bikes and shouting at each other.

"That's a sissy story," Robert said.

"Well, you didn't have to come," Sandra said. "Where's Lenny today, anyway?"

"He's over there, I'm not big enough to have a bike yet. I'm going to tell him it's *Hopalong Cassidy* next week."

Over the road, on the soccer field a group of boys were racing up and down on their bikes. Robert ran towards his brother and the sign that shouted in red capital letters: DANGEROUS RIVER. ADULTS WARN CHILDREN AWAY. The sign the children ignored.

Sandra, Amy, and Maria had reached the fire station when Robert came running up behind them.

"Here you are, Amy," he said. "My brother said you'd like this. He found it in the river."

He held out a wet bundle. It was a rag doll with a china head and china hands and feet. One cheek was cracked and the crack had spread like a spider web across the snub nose and one blue china eye. It was naked and its cloth body was streaked in mud. Amy took it.

"Yuck, its all wet and dirty," she said. "I don't want a drownded doll."

She threw it on the concrete pad in front of the fire station.

The face lost its shape. The spider web seeped across the other eye, disturbing its blue stare forever.

"You can't leave it there, Amy," Sandra said. "We'll take it home and throw it in the rubbish."

She carried it home, put it on the woodpile next to the back door, and forgot about it.

It was Monday. As Amy pulled her head through the neck of her jumper, her breath caught in the cold air, smoking the space between her and Sandra. She'd wet the bed again.

"Don't tell Mum, please Sandra, don't tell her. Just let her find out when we're at school."

"I'm going to pretend I don't know. I'm sick of getting into trouble because of you. How come you still wet the bed, anyway? You're nearly eight. You're too big."

Amy sighed. "There was an earthquake last night," she said.

"I didn't feel it."

"It was from way down, way beneath the house, down in the middle of the earth. You didn't wake up."

Sandra opened the wardrobe door.

"Watch out, that's where she hides!"

The distress in Amy's voice pulled Sandra around. Her sister looked really frightened. She closed the wardrobe door and sat on the edge of the bed.

"She's still here," Amy said. "In the wardrobe. She was pointing at me and she's got a long pointy finger and it was sticking into me."

Amy was staring at the wardrobe as if she couldn't see Sandra.

"She's got long hair, like it was weeds, like the mermaid's hair and her hair was going to wrap me up and take me away."

"Amy, I'm sick of this. You know there's no old lady there," Sandra said.

Amy was staring up in her direction, her focus on some other place and her normally blue eyes drowned in deep black holes. Sandra pulled herself out of them, and away from her sister's fear.

"It's all right. You need to get out of bed, Amy." She tugged her sister out of the wet wreck of sheets and started to undo the buckles on her boot.

"She told me something, Sandra. She said to me 'This is where you belong' like I had to go with her."

"Oh, stop it," Sandra said. "Come and get breakfast."

In the kitchen their mother was putting apples into paper bags of sandwiches.

"You girls don't play down by the river do you?" she asked.

Amy shook her head.

"No, Mum," Sandra said. She was thinking about the wet bed and wanted to get out of the door as soon as possible.

"Good. You two be good girls now and hurry, it's going to rain," their mother said, closing the door behind them.

"Look," said Sandra. "The mountain's disappeared."

There was dark cloud, not just over the mountain but also over the small mound at its side. There was a heavy smell, a faint odour of sweaty socks and dead rats coming from the mill. On a fine day the smell leaked towards Onepu, where the Māori children lived; on a wet day it wrapped itself around Kawerau, permeating into bedrooms, infusing food and impregnating clothes. It made Sandra feel slightly sick.

"It'll rain today," Amy said.

Amy saw it first, up the street from the school. It was a big black car stopped outside a house. She and Sandra, Maria and Robert hurried to see what was happening; the rain spotting their dark raincoats. They joined a small crowd of children that swirled, like leaves caught in a dam.

"What's that noise?" Maria said.

It was a single voice, a woman's voice, rising and falling, riding long, and clear into the coming rain. Behind it was a wailing, a high-pitched cadence of misery that carried the woman's clear voice. The hair on Sandra's neck prickled. Amy was holding her hand and she pulled Sandra closer. It was as if the sound was pulling at Amy, like a rope that was only for her. She pushed ahead of the other children and stopped at the front of the small crowd. The two of them were shoved aside, roughly, as two men came, carrying a small white box. On the box lid was a cross in gold. The box was so small that it didn't need two men to carry it, one could have managed. Amy started to sob.

"What's the matter?" asked Sandra.

"The baby. It drownded. Like the doll, like the drownded doll."

Sandra pushed Amy's hair away from her wet face. The men had disappeared into the front door of the house, leaving the old woman, the one whose voice had carried the coffin into the house. One arm was raised, pointing.

"She's looking at you, Amy," said Sandra.

Chapter Seven

Kawerau February 1959

A shaft of morning sunlight on her eyelids woke Sandra up. Today she was going to a christening for her friend Maria's new baby brother, in the Catholic church. Cliff Richard was smiling down at her. Elvis Presley and Bobby Darin were either side of him. They were refugees from the *Valentine* magazines that had arrived from Aunty Kath. Sandra looked Cliff straight in the eye. *I'm fourteen, I'm fourteen and I still have to wear my school shoes to go to the christening.* She felt it again, that wanting, desperate, deep and diffuse. Cliff, half way around the world, looked unconcerned.

When she walked into the kitchen for breakfast, Amy and Robert were arguing over whether it was better to crunch up weet-bix or leave them whole, her father was reading the three month-old Daily Mirror that came by post from Kath and her mother was stirring sugar into her cup of tea. The discussion between Robert and Amy heated up.

"I still think they soak up the milk and go soggy."

"You can just use more milk."

"But they go soggier if you crunch them up."

"So what, then the sugar sinks in better."

"Why are you here this morning, Robert?" Sandra asked.

"We're practising having breakfast together," Amy said, "for when we get married. We decided we have to be able to have breakfast together."

Sandra snorted. Amy stuck her tongue out.

"Hey, hey, stop fighting you two," their father said. "Your mother's got some news."

Sandra looked more closely at her mother. That's what was different this morning, her mother was smiling. Sandra looked away and rubbed her wet hands on her skirt. *Was mum pregnant (she didn't seem to be), were they going to have a baby in the house like Maria did (how embarrassing) and then would her mother be going back home to England (could they manage without her?) or would they all have to go too …*

"Kath's coming, your aunty," her mother said. "She's coming to stay with us."

"Where's she going to sleep?" Sandra asked. (*Thank goodness, no baby*).

"Oh, we'll work that one out," her father said and went back to reading about mining strikes in Wales.

To Sandra, Aunty Kath lived in blue aerogrammes, in parcels of out of date newspapers and in the magazines with Cliff Richard and Elvis Presley pinups. Aunty Kath was her mother's upset every time the blue aerogrammes had some piece of news about 'home.' She was very far away.

"Yeah. Are you going to the christening tomorrow?" Sandra said. "Me and Amy have been asked to go to the church for the christening. Are you going to come?" "Aren't you pleased?" her mother said. "Your Aunty Kath's coming. I thought you'd be pleased."

"Course," Sandra said. "I hope she brings some more *Valentines* and I hope she stays a long time."

"Oh, she's talking about a couple of months. Won't that be lovely? She's saving up and she says she thinks she'll have enough money by Christmas. She might even be able to have Christmas with us."

Sandra didn't want to give up her bedroom. She liked having her own room, not having to put up with Amy reading under the blankets and her nightmares.

"Dad," she said. "Can I have some new shoes? I need some for going out, you know, for getting all dressed up."

"What's wrong with your school shoes?" her father asked.

"I'm fourteen, Dad, and my friends have got sling-backs and suspender belts and nylons."

"What do you think, Betty? Our girl's growing up. You might need to talk to her about, you know."

He waved vaguely at his chest and turned back to the *Daily Mirror.*

Sandra's body ached for a moment, for when she was little and she would squeal from his rough chin when he hugged her goodnight and for the memory of leaning into his strong, wiry frame.

Inside the church it was dim as the wood paneling absorbed the light. As she came in the door Sandra moved from the bright of the day to a cool, dark cave. It took some time for her eyes to adjust. She sniffed the sweet, strong smell from the flowers. It was heavy and it floated her on its surface. She stood at the doorway with Robert and Amy, unsure what to do. There was a sea of hats and a bulwark of solid Catholic backs in front of them and a narrow passageway between the seats.

"Maria and them are at the front," said Sandra. "Shall we go up the front with them?"

"My mum said watch out for lightning," Robert said. "I don't know what she meant."

"Well, it's Catholic so it'll be in a foreign language," Amy said. "Just don't talk English and the lightning won't come."

"Be quiet you two," Sandra said. "I'm going to sit down here."

From the empty back seat she waved at Maria, who was sitting next to her mother. The baby, a froth of lacy gown in his mother's arms, was crying loudly and Mrs Simpson was jiggling him. Maria put her white-gloved forefingers in her ears, grimaced, and turned back to look at Jesus.

"We're going to sit up close," Amy said.

"What for?" asked Robert.

"Because you and me are practising for when we get married."

"Oh, Amy!" said Sandra but she allowed herself to be pulled up the long carpet to a pew near the front of the church where they pushed past the man who ran the butcher shop, his wife and their five children. They sat next to a large bunch of flowers.

There were rails with cushions for penitent knees and Amy pulled Robert down to kneel. Her crippled leg couldn't hold her weight and she leaned on him. She put her hands together in front of her nose. The organ was droning softly, bottoms were shuffling on the hard benches, the new baby was crying and Amy was whispering.

"What are you doing?" Sandra said.

"We have to pray," Amy whispered. "Like this."

"What do I pray for?" Robert asked.

"Pray for the baby to shut up," Amy said.

She bent her head. The baby kept crying.

"Anyway, that's enough," she said. "I'm only an Anglican."

The organ music got louder. The broad back with the tweed jacket was standing up, so were all the hats. Sandra stood up and Amy copied, pulling Robert up beside her.

The priest had reached the front and was standing with his back to everyone. His white robes hung like sheets on a washing line from his upraised arms and he was talking to someone in a foreign language. He seemed to be addressing the pictures up the front; Jesus with his heart glowing and the Virgin Mary, in her white dress and blue cloak.

Lulled by the priest's words and the heavy scent of the flowers, Sandra leaned back. Amy had gone very still beside her.

"Look, Sandra," she whispered. "It's Mary. She's looking at me."

Amy's face was tipped upward and it seemed to Sandra that her sister's whole self had flowed out, out towards the haloed picture above the altar. She looked very small and lost, lost in some world that Sandra could not comprehend.

"I'm coming," Amy whispered. "Mary, I'm coming."

When the line formed to go up to the man in the white robes, Amy got up to join, pushing her way past the hats and the grey trousers to the pew near the front that had held the Simpsons. She stood next to Colin in the line. Over the droning of the organ, Sandra heard the hissing conversation.

"Go away."

"Why?"

"Because you can't come and take the Blessed Sacrament."

"Why not?"

"Because. You're not Catholic."

"But Mary told me to come."

"Don't be stupid. Go away."

He pushed her as he moved forward in the line.

Amy hit the edge of the empty pew, her crooked leg collapsing under her. Grabbing at the wooden arm of the pew, she pulled herself upright. Her head tilted upward to the picture of Mary reaching out, and she nodded. Back in the pew next to Sandra with her mouth set in that determined way, she folded her arms.

"She did tell me, Sandra, she did," she said.

When the baptism happened, the Simpson family clumped together at the back of the church hall. Amy insisted Robert and Sandra come with her to the front of the people gathered so she could see. Mr and Mrs Simpson were standing right next to the wooden block with its basin and Mrs Simpson was holding the lacy baby. Sandra tried to listen to the man in the white robes but Amy's prayers still hadn't worked, and the baby was crying loudly. Mrs Simpson was bouncing it up and down. She held the baby out, over the basin. The man in the white robes poked his fingers in the baby's ears and dabbed something in the baby's wide-open mouth. The baby cried harder. Then he poured water on its head.

On the way home Amy said that the priest had made a magic spell over the baby's head. Sandra told her he was just making a cross. Amy said that it must have been magic because the baby had stopped crying and it had worked better than her prayers. Sandra had to agree.

Sandra got home just as her parents were leaving for the party next door. Her mother twirled around so that Sandra could make admiring noises at her freshly ironed dress, the petticoat lifting the full skirt. The roses on the fabric were stark red on the white background; her lipstick a matching red. Her newly washed hair had dried around plastic curlers and now the dark curls bounced as she walked.

Her mother smiled.

"Fancy us. Look at us all fancied up, Ian. Kath would like this party, bet she doesn't get to go to parties in a garage, bet she doesn't have a garage. In her new house I mean. We never had a garage in the old house, did we, but then we'd never have a car back home, would we? I suppose we'll need one, a garage I mean, won't we, when we get our car? What kind of car do you think, Ian? If we can get it before Christmas, we can take Kath out. She'd like that. Do you remember how we all used to go on the train, down to Brighton? She used to love those little holidays we had together. We could take her to Rotorua to see the geyser, what do you think, Ian?"

Her father smiled back.

They arrived at the garage, with the tables covered in white paper. It was 'women a plate please,' so her mother put the curried eggs down on the table. She turned to carry on the conversation.

"Where's your father, Sandra? He was here a minute ago."

Sandra pointed to the back garden where the beer keg was balanced between two sawhorses. She'd wanted to talk to her mother about buying her sling-back shoes so she wouldn't have to wear her school shoes but she hadn't been able to interrupt the Aunty Kath bubble that seemed to be holding her mother up. It felt too tremulous, its edges fragile. She looked outside where her father was with a group of men standing around the keg, holding glasses of beer. Her mother started towards the men, hesitated, and came back to stand next to Sandra. Women were coming in and out of the house, with plates full of food and one of them came over. It was Jill, Robert and Lenny's mother. Jill used to be very friendly with her mother but now Sandra thought maybe she didn't like Robert being at their place so much.

"Hello Betty," said Jill. "How are you? Haven't seen you for a while, where you been hiding yourself?"

"Oh, you know, what with the girls and Ian working so hard."

Her mother licked her red lips, smoothed the roses on her dress.

"You remember me talking about Kath, my sister Kath?" she said.

"What? Kath? No, I don't think ... hold on, I know yes, I know who you mean, your sister Kath, she's back in England."

"That's right. She's still back home but she's coming out to visit, maybe this year. She's coming for Christmas."

"That'll be nice. It's such a long way for people to come, innit? How's the girls? Oh, there you are Sandra. Look how big you've got. You're turning into a real young lady. My Robert keeps saying he's going to grow up and marry your Amy, and he's only nine, aren't kids a laugh?"

Her mother nodded. Sandra smiled. The words kept flowing over and around her and her mother. At the edge of her vision, Sandra could see her mother's smile stretch, the bright lipstick a redness, raw.

Jill's words stopped, in the middle of a sentence about new curtains she was making. Sandra looked up to see why. Amy was standing at the door, still in the clothes she had worn to church: her neat pleated skirt, her white cardigan, and her long socks. She was holding the hand of a large, shambling boy. His shirt was ragged and his shorts hung lopsided, hitched up at one side. He was barefoot and dirty.

"Ooh, look what your Amy's got in tow," said Jill. "Who's that?"

"That's Richard, that awful Māori boy who lives across the road.

She's always bringing him home. I suppose some kids bring home stray dogs. She brings home Richard."

Her mother stalked over to her sister, grabbing her by the arm.

"What do you think you're doing?" she hissed.

Richard was the same height as her mother. His eyes were out of focus, like a drunk man trying to fixate. His mouth hung open. He wiped the green snot away with his free hand. Sandra could feel it—lost, every part of him said—lost. He was in a bubble, a bubble that kept him away. Like her mother, who was also floating, in another bubble, held up by her bright skirt, separate, isolated.

"Get him out of here, Amy, get him out of here ..." her mother said.

"Richard go home now," the lost boy said and he turned and ran.

"What's the matter with you, Amy? Sandra, what's the matter with your sister?"

Chapter Eight

Kawerau March 1959

Sandra heard Amy leave the house every morning in summer. By five-thirty Sandra would already be awake, with the light coming through the curtains. From her bed, she could pull her curtains and lie watching the sun creep down the shoulder of the mountain. This morning there was a blackbird, chink-chinking in the wattle tree next door, like the shuttle in the old sewing machine she shared with her sister. The blackbird, sewing the quilt of the morning, without the people, without their breakfasting and their yawning; just the sun leaking through the tree, the sun claiming the mountain, and the blackbird.

Sandra heard the cat protest as Amy nudged him off the bed, stretched and swung her feet on to the floor.

"Talipes," Amy would be saying as she straightened her club foot out as much as she could. Sandra had written the word down for her. "Talipes—I've got talipes." To Amy, it sounded exotic and romantic.

Sandra's bedroom was crowded. Yul Brynner and James Dean had joined Elvis and Cliff on the walls. There were always clothes lying in piles, no matter how much her mother complained. But Amy's bedroom was empty except for her bed, a chair, and a chest of drawers. Her father had built a wardrobe in one corner. There were no visions of old women from this wardrobe. It held her two school dresses, her one pair of shoes (one smaller than the other and built up three inches at the heel) and a large cardboard box full of books. When Amy wanted to be alone, she would take her pillow and a torch, sit in the corner of the wardrobe, and read.

Every summer morning, Amy would creep very quietly out through the hallway, take a towel from the hall cupboard, wrap her knickers and a dress in it and let herself out the back door. She would pull her bike out of the lean-to next to the shed, springing the carrier holder over her towel and set off for the swimming pool. Only Sandra would hear her go.

Sandra knew that Amy would be at the pool by six and, as she slipped off her clothes and stowed them in the cubby holes, the other members of the swimming squad would be slipping into the water, trying not to shriek at the coldness, thrashing around to warm up. The training schedule up on the blackboard always said:

Junior squad:
2 × 220yds freestyle warmup.
4 × 100yds flutterboard.
2 × 100yds backstroke.
2 × 100yds breaststroke.

Amy's hair would go up into the tight rubber bathing cap, she'd take a deep breath, and jump in the water.

Amy tried to tell Sandra how it felt, when she was in the water. How the feel of the water had never changed. First the cold shocked the breath from her and the bubbles from her warm body enveloped her face, holding her in the world of breath and air. As she emptied out her lungs, she felt the water insisting at her nostril edge and at her ear canals, forcing her eyelids open—*Look, see, this is the real world.* The old woman from the cupboard, the one that Sandra never believed in, this was where she lived now, in the world of water where there was so much space, where the light was spread to eternity and where the world outside became far away and insignificant. She was too big to resist, that old woman, and she was always there. A moment to decide, Amy said, that's how it felt; did she dissolve, and become the water, give in to weedy hair and pointing finger, or did she fight it and join that outside world again? For that long moment her arms floated, weightless, and her crooked leg curled, unbidden, to wrap itself around her strong, straight leg. Without any effort on her part, her body slid to the surface, to the meeting place of air and water, and she broke that membrane, the one that had held her submerged. She filled her lungs with air, and her ears with the sounds of splashing and the coach yelling "Watch your turn, you didn't touch then". She swam, up and down the pool, with the water moving as she pushed it, holding her as she needed it, flowing past her as she moved through it.

Sandra would be out of bed by the time Amy came home, leaning her body to push her withered leg hard down on the pedal. Richard was often sitting on the swing, in and out it moved, in and out. He'd be in the same shirt and shorts he always wore; torn, thin, the hem of the shorts hanging, some of the scabs on his legs cracked and bleeding. Amy would slip off her bike, lay it down and hold one of his hands. Sandra would watch them from her bedroom window.

It was often the same conversation.

Richard's eyes, slightly unfocused would wander around Amy's face. He'd hold out an old Christmas card, with a fat Santa in a red suit standing next to a big bag of presents.

"I love you, Amy. Got a present for you," he'd say.

"Thanks, Richard, you're kind."

"Marry me today, Amy?"

"Not today, Richard. Come on."

She'd take his hand and lead him over to the roundabout, on the sunny side, gently turning into the shadow and out again into the climbing sun, the world moving past them slowly.

"Richard," Amy would say. "You know I'm going to marry Robert. I told you that. When we're sixteen."

Richard would sniff and wipe his forearm across his face again.

"We're going to live in a house and you can come and live with us."

"Richard come? Not Richard's dad?"

"Do you want your dad to come?"

"Not Richard's dad."

"Not your dad. Not your mum, she's dead. My mum's not dead. She just seems to go away somewhere else, sometimes. But not your dad either?"

"Not the belt. Not Richard's dad. Richard go home now."

He'd stop the roundabout, climb off and run over to his house. Richard's dad was often out on the front lawn, pulling engines out of the old cars that slumped in the grass. He'd yell at Richard—his already red face almost purple with anger— "Dumb hua, bloody idiot, if you had half a brain … I'll set the bloody dogs on you …" The dogs were two big pig dogs, chained up at the side of the house. They were thin, kept hungry and had slobbering mouths and deep, fierce barks. Their heavy chains clanked and rattled when they ran at Richard and pulled taut just before they reached the front steps. Richard would stop half way up the path and stand with his arms flapping and his body jerking. Then he'd run for the front door.

Amy always watched to make sure he got there.

When Amy came into the kitchen Sandra was reading, twenty pages for double English this afternoon. *Great Expectations* and Miss Haversham was sitting in her cobwebs.

"I wish you wouldn't do your homework over breakfast, Sandra," her mother said.

"Yes Mum."

"And I don't like you talking to that boy, Amy. He should be sent away. He shouldn't be roaming the streets the way he does."

"But he hasn't got a mum."

"So what? He's got a father. That O'Neill man. Like I said, he should be sent away."

"Yes, Mum."

"And I don't want him around here, Amy."

"Yes, Mum."

"Don't you yes mum me, young lady. I know you, you'll say yes mum then just go ahead and do whatever you want. You pay more attention to your sister than you do me. You'll come to a sticky end one day, young lady, just mark my words."

Sandra leaned on one elbow and raised her eyebrows at Amy. Amy gave her a lopsided smile and left the room. Sandra had a sudden vision of her mother, in the old dressing gown her grandmother had sent, sitting looking at something in the mirror, in her dark bedroom, and of the cobwebs growing out from the mirror, enveloping her mother so she couldn't move.

Robert's voice came from outside the kitchen window.

"Is your mum all right, Amy?" he asked.

"No. But she's no different. She's always like this."

"Is your Aunty Kath coming this Christmas?"

"I don't think she's ever coming. Come on. We'll be late for school."

As Sandra walked home from school that afternoon, she was thinking about the discussion they'd had about Miss Haversham's cobwebs and what Dickens had been trying to say with the old woman in her wedding dress, in her ramshackle old house, being weighted down by dust and spider-webs. How it had been about not being able to let go of old dreams and being weighed down with lost desires. How when Miss had asked if anyone could think of someone like this, Sandra didn't say it made her think of her mother.

She shifted her bag from one hand to the other. She was nearly home. At the roundabout outside their house the swings were moving. There was no wind, just the swings going in-out, in-out. Strange, and on such a still day. Then she was running her bag dropped on the pavement because Amy was lying in the dust, near the swings, and she was very still.

"Amy!"

There was no response. Sandra reached her sister who was lying on her back, spread out in the sandy ash. Her eyes were open, staring somewhere distant.

"Amy!"

She was shaking her sister, to wake her up, to get her to come back and bring the world back to normal.

"Amy!"

Amy blinked, took a breath from deep in her being, and turned a dazed face to her sister.

"What happened? Did you fall off the swing?"

"In the clouds. She's in the clouds."

"What are you talking about?"

"This morning she was in the water. She's always in the water but now she's in the clouds too, Sandra. She looked the same as this morning, the angry old woman, you know, the one with the eyes like whirlpools. Then she turned into Mary with the white dress and the kind eyes and she was reaching out to me. With her two hands, she was reaching out to me, then four hands, then eight hands, then sixteen, then more and more so I couldn't count. She was reaching out and wanted me to come."

"It's all right Amy, you must have bumped your head. You don't have to go."

"But Sandra, I wanted to go. I wanted her kind eyes and all her hands. Then, then her face changed and she turned into mum and her eyes were all empty and behind her eyes was the water where the old woman lives. The water was going to swell up and swallow me. I was scared, so scared."

Sandra held Amy as she cried. Or rather, she whimpered, like a little animal lost in some dark place that was not safe. Pushing the damp curls of white hair away from her sister's face, Sandra rocked, gentling her little sister back to this world, with the roundabout scorching in the sunlight and the paspalum drooping in the heat.

"Hush," she said, "hush, it's all gone now. It's all gone."

Dinner was late again that night. Her mother banged around in the kitchen, slamming the cupboard doors and when they sat down at the table, she pursed her lips as she dished up. Sandra sneaked a look at Amy. One that said; "They're not speaking. Be careful." Their father's eyes wandered from Amy to Sandra, to Amy and back again. The smell of beer said why dinner was late and mum was in a bad temper.

"We been learning about tidal waves at school," Amy said.

"Have you now, and what did you learn?" her father said.

"We been learning about a great big one that nearly came from South America, all the way to New Zealand."

"Well, it wouldn't come here," said her father. "We're miles away from the sea."

"Yes but what if it did come, Dad? What if all that water did come? You would've been drowned and Mum would've been drowned. Me and Sandra would've been orphans."

"Don't be silly, Amy," her mother said. "Are you going to eat that cabbage?"

"Yes, but what if we did? What if you and Dad were killed, then what would happen to me and Sandra?"

"What's the point of me cooking you good vegetables if you don't eat them?"

"Och, lassie, your sister's old enough to look after you. Aren't you, you're my big girl now. Speaking of which, I was talking to Pat today, at smoko, he's worried about his girl, your friend Maria. He's worried about her hanging around with that Lenny. He's a bad one, that one. He's always with those forestry boys, you know, those Māori fellas, and they're drinking. You're not getting about with them too, are you?"

Sandra shook her head.

"You know what happens, don't you, a bit of drink and a girl will have her legs wide open. You know what I mean."

"Our Sandra's a good girl, Ian. You know that. Now give us your plate. I need the housekeeping money, if you haven't drunk it all away. You girls, get on with the dishes."

Sandra could see that Amy wanted to ask about the tidal wave again, she wanted her parents to tell her that the earth would stay still and the tidal wave wouldn't pull their whole lives away and leave her floundering, orphaned. Amy was staring at her mother, her shoulders slumped, her forehead wrinkled into a frown. Sandra squeezed her sister's hand under the table.

The next day they were standing on the edge of the creek, Sandra, Amy, Robert and Colin, where someone had chopped manuka branches down and laid them across the cold water. The water was so clear that the bottom looked only two inches away and the sand was speckled, white pumice and black rhyolite, sparkling when the sun was on it. The weed on the creek bed, like the old woman's hair, went from lime green to black. It waved with the eddying water that swirled, like so many eyes, in the bends of the rushing water. This was where Amy had almost drowned, when she was little, when the water claimed her, when the old woman whispered to her.

Look. See. This is the real world. This is what eels, trout and koura see. And you. Now, you. Surrender. This is who you are. You are the creek. You are the water.

Sandra remembered it with a shiver.

They hadn't told their mother where they were going. It was Amy's expedition. She'd helped herself to the string and safety pins and said she would be home for tea and her mother had looked at her blankly. So she'd told her sister, who said she'd come because she didn't want to stay home when their mother's eyes were only windows on to nothing.

"I've got some rotten meat," Robert said. "It's the best thing, my brother Lenny said so."

"And I've got some string and some hooks," Amy said. "Well, some safety pins, we can bend them to make hooks."

"Don't be stupid, Amy," Colin said. "You can't catch an eel with

a safety pin. I got some fishing nylon, real fishing nylon, and I got
a real fishhook."

His tongue was protruding as he tied a big fishhook on to the
thin, almost invisible nylon. He threw the line into the creek where
it was pulled by the current. It was hard to see, swallowed as it was
by the water. He yanked at it. It snapped up into the air and sank
again, back into the dark water.

"What do we do if we catch one?" Amy asked.

"I can kill it," Colin said. "Look."

He pulled out a pocket-knife and flicked out a blade with one
practised hand. It had a serrated edge.

"What for? What're we going to do with a dead eel?" Amy
asked.

"Oh, I don't know. We could eat it, I suppose."

"My brother would," Robert said. "They eat eels all the time, up
the forest, for smoko and that."

"Who's going to cook it?"

Sandra tried to imagine her mother cooking the eel. She got
as far as coming in the kitchen door with it, and the screaming.

"Mum won't," she said.

There was no more talk for a time. The water flowed over the
broken manuka in its bed, pushing at it, whispering that it was time
it moved too. It shushed the grasses that bent at the bank side, pulling at them. Sandra felt it pull at her, lulling her into its movement,
dissolving her until she and the water would become one.

The line was hauled in, without an eel, and without the hook.

"Damn," Colin said. "Hope Dad doesn't find out."

"Did you pinch it, Colin?" Amy asked.

"Nah, just borrowed it. I was going to put it back," he said.
Colin decided they should move on to another bend in the creek.
They left the noise of the water behind, pushing their way through
blackened manuka that held the memory of a rain of hot ash. The
only sound was the cracking of dead branches and the crunching
of dry ash underfoot. The lichen stuck in Sandra's hair. It was

stringy, like so many ribbon skeletons, bleaching slowly from bright yellow and bright green to white. It crumbled in her hand, leaving a lurid yellow stain. There were no birds or wind, no time here, no life to measure its passing. It was an in-between place. Sandra sniffed. The air smelt mostly of dust and sulphur, and desolation.

Colin yelled from somewhere ahead of them and when the others caught up with him, he was squatting in the dry ash.

"What's that?" Amy asked.

"Dunno," Colin said. "It's been dead a long time. It's like those Egyptian mummies we been talking about in school."

"It's got no head. Prob'ly something ate it," Robert said.

"Look, it's got a tail, it's all curled up," Colin said.

"Might have been a possum," Sandra said.

"It's still got a bit of fur, reckon it was a rabbit," Robert said.

Colin poked at the body. It was hard and leathery with skin stretched taut over tiny ribs. The soft insides had rotted long ago. On its long ears some small tufts of brown fur still clung. Like the lichen on the trees, they were reluctant to let go. It was an essence of rabbit, pared down to its least presence, leaving a memory of the smell of rot.

"I reckon we'll look like that when we're dead. We'll be like the mummies, all dried up," he said.

"No, we won't," Robert said. "They only get like that because they're all dry. Like it's dry here so it made the rabbit all dry up. We'll be all full of maggots and sloppy."

Amy held her nose as Colin turned the body over to show a still furry underside with grey ash clinging to it, claiming it.

"It doesn't matter, anyway," Colin said. "When you die, you go to purgatory where horrible things happen, specially if you've done a sin and not confessed it."

"So are you going to tell your dad about the fish hook?" Amy asked.

"And when you're in purgatory you have to ask Mary or one of the saints to help you," Colin said.

"Does she help you?" Amy asked.

"Only if you're a Catholic," said Colin. "She only helps Catholics."

"I'm going to be a Catholic," said Amy.

"Don't be silly, Amy," Sandra said.

"You can't anyway," Colin said. "You have to go to mass and do confession and learn all this stuff and be confirmed and all that."

"I can do all that."

"Only if Father Searle says you can and your mum and dad don't like church."

"They won't care. I'll ask Father Searle. Whose father is he anyway?"

"He's a Catholic father. That means he's like everyone's dad."

Sandra watched the decision being made. She remembered Amy's vision of Mary of the white dress and the kind eyes, how much kinder Amy said Mary's eyes were than those of the angry old woman, and, especially, how much kinder they were than the emptiness of her mother's eyes.

"I am so going to be a Catholic," Amy said.

The sling-back shoes with the tiny gold buckles stayed in the shoe shop window. Sandra still wanted them, but the wanting had become more diffuse, a sort of longing for something she didn't understand. Maybe she'd never get the shoes. She walked past the dairy and across the road, thinking about how stupid she'd look in her school shoes when she was sixteen. She was passing the Catholic Church when Amy and Robert rode up on their bikes.

"What are you two doing here?" she asked.

"We're looking for the Catholic father," Robert said.

They stood outside, on the footpath. The wooden building sat in a field with no gardens or trees. Amy had already lain her bike down on the pumice.

"Do you think he lives in the back of the church?" she asked.

"I don't know," Robert said. "The Anglican minister lives next door to the church he's the boss of, but there's no house here."

"I don't think Catholics have a minister," Sandra said.

"Colin said they have a father," Amy said. "A Catholic father for all the Catholics."

The front door of the church was open, inviting them inside to the empty, cool darkness. Candles flickered in one corner, around a little statue of Mary. In the darkness, Sandra could see a white dress catching the candlelight, glowing.

"Do you think I could light a candle too, Sandra?"

"You can't," Sandra said. "You're not a Catholic."

"I think they're Catholic candles," Robert said. "You have to ask first."

"There's no-one to ask except Mary and she wouldn't mind," said Amy.

"She's prob'ly not the boss of the candles," Robert said, "and anyway, she's not real. We better ask the Catholic father."

"Let's go round the back, maybe he lives in the back," said Amy.

As they walked out, Amy stopped and looked at Mary. She didn't move, just stood there in her white dress looking at the ceiling. Amy gave her a wave.

Around the back of the church a horse leaned over the fence, trying to reach the longer grass. Sandra went over to help, pulling the grass and offering it to the horse. Amy and Robert went up to the door that stood open, showing an empty kitchen. Amy climbed the two steps, one foot at a time, and knocked.

A man in dark trousers, with braces over his white shirt, came out of a back room, blinking at them through his little round glasses.

"Well, hello there," he said. "And what can I do for you two?"

"We're looking for Our Father," Amy said. "Do you know where he is?"

"Well, no, did you think he came by here? How long ago?"

"I don't know."

"What's his name then and what does he look like?"

"I don't know."

The man came down the steps, scratching his head. He put one hand on Amy's shoulder.

"Do you think we could start again, little miss? I'm Father Searle and I'm the priest for this church. Would you like to tell me your names?"

Over the horse munching on the grass, Sandra could hear a soft song in Father Searle's voice. She knew it wasn't Scottish, her father was Scottish and his voice made a different song. Amy seemed to like the warmth of his hand on her shoulder. She took him to be the father of all the Catholics that she was looking for.

"Do you know about Mary?" she asked.

"Which Mary do you mean, little miss. Don't tell me you've lost a Mary as well as your dad," he said and he laughed.

Amy stared at him. Sandra was about to go over and help; to tell him that her sister had peculiar ideas about a terrifying old woman who'd got mixed up with their mother, and that Amy seemed to think that Mary from the Catholic Church could help.

"Sorry," Father Searle said. "Now, little miss serious, what's your name and what's your little friend's name."

"I'm nearly ten," Robert said, pulling himself up, "and my name's Robert."

The man put out his hand. Robert looked at it then put out his own and the two of them shook hands.

"Well, Robert, pleased to be meeting you," the man said. "Maybe you and your friend would like a drink of orange?"

"Yes please," Robert said. "Amy's my friend. She wants to ask you lots of questions."

"Well then, sit down. I'll be right back."

They sat on the step. Amy waved at Sandra. She seemed to be managing, waiting for a Catholic father who laughed about Mary with his eyes wrinkling up behind his round glasses.

He came out of the kitchen with two plastic cups of orange cordial, handed one to Amy and one to Robert and sat down. His eyes were at the same level as the two children and he wriggled on the narrow step as he waited. Amy turned her cup round and round.

"And what is it you want to know, Amy?" the Catholic father on the concrete step said.

"I want to be a Catholic, Our Father," Amy said.

"People call me Father Searle, Amy, just so I don't get mixed up with Our Father, you know, the one which art in heaven. Our Father means God, Amy."

"Good," Amy said. "Because I've got a father already and I don't need another one."

"What about God, Amy? He's your Father, too."

"Well, my father's all right. He just drinks too much beer sometimes. I want to be a Catholic because of Mary, Father Searle, Mary with the white dress. You know, the one in your church, with all the candles."

"Mary, Mother of God. Yes, Amy, I do know who you mean. But tell me, what church do your parents go to?"

"They don't go to church. Mum used to go to Anglican church and I used to go to Sunday school when I was little. They have Mary too but she seems to like you Catholics more."

"And what do your parents think about you wanting to be a Catholic?"

Sandra bit her lip. She thought she knew. Maybe she should interrupt. The horse moved its rubber lips on her hand. It tickled.

"Oh, they don't know. I want to be a Catholic but they won't mind. I came to a christening and they didn't care and I came to church on Christmas Eve once."

"Who did you come to our church with, Amy?"

"The Simpsons. They live next door to us."

"Oh, yes. Bea Simpson. She's a strong woman in our church. I'm coming to her place for dinner this week, I believe."

"That's Mrs Simpson. Colin's our friend, well, sometimes, and Maria used to be my sister Sandra's best friend, before she got boys."

Sandra buried her head in the horse's neck. Maria had sling-back shoes. Father Searle didn't say anything about Maria and boys.

"It would be a good thing for you to come to catechism classes, Amy, if you want to be a Catholic. Then you can learn about the Holy Roman Church and all about Mary and the meaning of the Blessed Sacrament."

The horse shook its head and snorted—*Yes, that's what I thought*—and Sandra stroked his nose.

"Would you teach me about Mary and how she can help?" Amy asked.

"Well, you would learn about all sorts of saints, as well as Mary. Is there something you need help with?"

Amy looked at her feet. Sandra waited for Amy to tell him about swimming training and the old woman with the long weedy hair and the terrifying face who lived in the swimming pool; about the dreams in the middle of the night and, just lately, during the day when the old woman in the clouds got all mixed up with Mum's empty eyes and that made the old woman even more scary; about how Mary with the white dress and kind eyes was the only one who seemed to be able to calm the old woman and fill up the emptiness. Sandra hoped Amy wouldn't tell this kind man. What would he think of their family?

Instead, Amy finished her orange drink and handed the glass back to Father Searle. She looked intently at his face, peering to try and see behind his glasses and he smiled, a long, soft smile and nodded his head.

"Mary makes me feel good," she said.

"Tell you what, Miss Amy, you can come to church with the Simpsons if you want to. I'm sure Bea would be happy to have you tag along, maybe with your little friend here. Then, if you really want, I can have a talk to your parents one day. How does that sound?"

Amy nodded. Sandra hoped Amy would find a way to tell their parents before 'one day' arrived.

"And what about you, young man?" Father Searle asked.

"Well, I'll see," said Robert. "Me and Amy, we're going to get married and she wants us to get married in this church. I'll just see how Amy gets on first, with being a Catholic and that."

"Thank you for coming with Amy, Robert. I'm sure she appreciates having a good friend like you."

He shook hands, gravely, with each of them.

Before they collected their bikes from the side of the building, Amy went back into the church. Sandra kissed the horse gently on his nose and left it to find its own long grass. She waited with Robert by the door as Amy walked up the red carpet, one leg striding strong, one leg tentative and unsure. She reached the corner with the plaster statue of Mary, the candles a small ring of flames around the folds of the white dress. Carefully taking a small candle, she lit it from one of the many on the metal frame, placing it in an empty spot. Amy took a deep breath and looked up at the still, blank face and the blue eyes gazing at the ceiling. Nothing happened. The hands that reached out from the sleeves of the white dress stayed still. The little finger of one hand was broken, the end of it missing. Amy put a kiss on her forefinger, and carefully placed it on the broken plaster. As she came back out of the church door her mouth was set in a determined line.

"Happy now?" asked Sandra. "Can the dreams go away?"

"It'll be better when I'm a Catholic," Amy said.

Chapter Nine

Kawerau September 1975

There's a car already in the driveway, at the house where her mother is. Through the fog where the old memories live, she registers she doesn't want to be here; with Robert and her mother, and the past that is pushing cold fingers into her very being. She hugs the spine of her course book hard against her belly.

"The doctor's here," Robert says. "That's his car. It'll be Betty."

He's in the house before Sandra can get her door open. She moves slowly, out of the car, along the footpath and to the open front door with its mother duck frozen in glass. She stands in the lounge, under the Virgin Mary's red heart and wonders what to do. She can hear voices in the bedroom. Where her mother is. She has a nagging feeling that this is not going to be a few days. She pulls out a cigarette, finds her lighter, breathes the smoke in and lets it flood her lungs.

The door of the lounge opens and an older version of the doctor Sandra remembers steps into the room. He's talking over his shoulder and doesn't see her. She slams a door inside herself. The door to the last time she saw him. The doctor. Who knows so much of who she used to be. She takes another deep drag of her cigarette.

He's carrying a doctor's bag and pushing a pen back into his jacket pocket.

"You must be Sandra," he says. "My, how the years fly."

She's unsure what to do, what to say. She feels very young.

"Your mum had a fall," he says. "She's all right. She's in bed now."

She clenches her teeth.

"You'll be wanting to spend as much time with her as you can," he says. "She's very frail."

"Yes," says Robert from the doorway. "You'll want lots of time with her, won't you, Sandra?"

She feels the panic coming up—that blank face, those empty eyes—she doesn't want to spend time with that. She sits down on the sofa and stares at the carpet and the pattern moves up to swallow her. She closes her eyes. Bea's weight sinks into the old sofa next to Sandra. She offers her man-sized handkerchief. Sandra is floating somewhere else, watching her hand reach for the handkerchief. Watching the bits of her body as it sits, very still on the edge of the sofa; the two feet on the floor; the two hands clutching a large handkerchief; a dirt stain just above the knee of her track suit. Chaos swirls inside, a long arm is pointing at her, trying to pull her back.

Why me, why do I have to look after her again?

"Robert," says Bea. "Sit down. We're going to pray for Betty. Come on dear, you can join in if you want to."

Sandra's head jerks up. She's trapped between the picture of Mary on the wall beside her and Bea, her hand moving up, down, across.

"Let us pray. In the name of the Father, and of the Son and of the Holy Ghost."

Then there are two voices.

"May Blessed Mary, ever virgin, pray for us and all …"

Sandra's chest tightens, her breath is coming in small gasps and the handkerchief is now a hard ball in her hand. The bursting heart of Mary is threatening to leak its red pain over her and drown her.

"Shut up, shut up!"

There's a small silence. She looks from one surprised face to the other. Bea has been caught with one hand raised to her heart and her mouth open. Robert swallows the sinner he was praying for and his mouth clenches.

"Jesus. I can't believe you people. All that happened. I can't believe you think that a few words to a picture on the bloody wall will make any difference! What's the matter with you?"

She throws the balled up handkerchief and it sits on the swirling carpet. As Bea bends to retrieve it, Robert frowns at her over his folded arms.

"We're 'you people' now, are we?"

"Well, what use is it? Prayers? What did they do in the past?"

"What else have you got, Sandra?"

"I've got a life. More than you have. I've got a job and prospects. I'm successful, Robert."

Bea put a hand on her knee.

"And you've got a past, too, Sandra, and a very sick mother who needs you."

She doesn't want that need. She wants her flat with the dirty hippy and her stoned flat-mate. She wants the boss with his old school tie and his smooth face. She wants to be there, where she can live her own life. She stares down at her legs, her two feet on the floor. She rubs at that mark on her knee, clay from the mountain, she can't get it off.

"I need to be back in Auckland. I've got commitments. In fact, I think I'd better ring the office."

What else have you got?

The question follows her into the kitchen.

What else have you got?

It persists as she dials the office number. The phone beeps insistently at her.

"Hello? Is that Melanie? It's Sandra. Yes, I'm in Kawerau. Just ringing to see how that deal's going."

The phone beeps.

"Needs to close immediately? They're insisting?"

The phone keeps beeping.

"Yes, I understand. I'll see if there's a bus tomorrow."

She puts the receiver back in the cradle. From the lounge come two voices. "Hail Mary, full of grace …" The words sink into a murmur. She can't go back into that. She clutches her course book and waits in the kitchen, the one that looks so familiar. Outside the kitchen window, through the thin branches of a wattle tree, the breathing body of the mountain sighs.

What else have you got? it asks.

She's pulling the book out from her waistband and flicking fast through its pages when the murmur of prayers stops.

"I'll make us a cup of tea, shall I?" says Bea.

Sandra smiles at Bea as she comes back into the kitchen, with her bottom teeth just showing, pushing her book back into its hiding place.

"I need to be back in Auckland tomorrow. I've got commitments. There's a deal about to close. And I'm expected back. I'll have to go tomorrow …"

She runs out of words and slumps on the kitchen chair. The lump in her throat is back.

"I'll just put your cuppa here, shall I?" Bea says.

The table wobbles and the tea spills a little. Sandra wills herself not to cry as Bea sits on the chair opposite. She wants to look away, go away, not be involved.

"Your mum needs you, Sandra."

She doesn't want these words either. She wants Melanie, who never minds her own business and even Brendan who never stays the night, not the weight of her mother's need. She picks at that mark on her knee. The vortex is swirling again, pulling at her. She will not go there.

"You're all she's got."

"Shame she doesn't recognise me then, don't you think?"

These words escape, like refugees, from her tangled, knotted belly.

What if she did? Recognise you? What then?

As she pulls her cigarettes out of her pocket, her hand unsteady, the lighter jumps from her hand and lands at Bea's feet. Like an offering. A burning offering. She stares at it. Bea bends down to pick it up and turns it over to where the initials curl on its silver surface: *I M.*

"Your dad's."

Sandra nods, the unlit cigarette still in her hand.

"We miss him."

Sandra nods, the lump balled in her throat.

Bea sighs and hands over the lighter. Sandra lights the cigarette, the flame wobbling slightly, crosses her legs and inhales, pushing the smoke past the barrier in her throat. As she blasts it back out again, the smoke screens her from the concern in Bea's face.

"Not sure I can be of much help, actually. As Robert said, I've been away too long."

Bea squints into the smoke. She nods her head, slowly.

"Well," she says. "That's up to you, dear. Just remember, no matter what, she's still your mum. And you know, I don't think she's long for this world."

A shiver goes up her spine.

A goose just walked over my grave, if not mine, then someone else's.

Robert is at the door of the kitchen and he's standing with one hand reaching out.

"Sandra, you need to come," he says.

Bea gets up, puts her hand down and holds Sandra's arm. She wants to shrug it off; she wants to snarl at the elderly fingers holding her arm; she wants to burst into tears. Bea pulls Sandra up off the chair and she's compelled by the pulling and pushing, drawn by Robert's reaching. All these hands—she just wants them to leave her alone. Sandra walks over the swirling carpet and follows Robert back down the hallway and through the open door into the bedroom.

She heads for the window, she can manage to stand by the window, but that hand on her arm guides her to a chair, near the pillow, near the white head and the closed eyes of her mother. She sits. The door shuts as Robert leaves her. In the room that smells of English Leather and of some old woman.

I have more courage, I have more courage is repeating itself in her head.

She keeps her eyes on the pink candlewick bedspread. A snoring sound comes from the bed, where she will not look. She counts the squares, starting at the bottom of the bed. She's reached forty-seven when her eyes meet a hand. It's thin, clawed, the fingers bent, the skin loosening from the bones—an old woman's hand. The fingers twitch and she jumps. They begin to jerk, as if pulled by some puppeteer, pulling strings to lift first the fingers then the whole hand up and off the bedspread. Enthralled as the jerking intensifies, the randomness of it startling her with each new movement, she can't look away. Her breathing jerks, the old woman's breathing groans as the hand jerks. Her body, almost in a dance, joins in, fighting for breath. Sandra and her mother. Then, as if some crescendo has been reached, the hand drops back on to the bedspread and is very still. Sandra sits in that stillness, in a space that time has vacated, in a space that suspends.

The arm is now immobile. There's a stain on the sleeve of the cardigan, there, just near the elbow. The sheet covering the old woman's chest doesn't move. She stops in that stillness, takes the breath the old woman doesn't want and forces herself to look at the face, her mother's face, with the widow's peak that forever denotes mourning. The emptying eyes; an emptying that's unique, yet … Sandra's seen it so many times. All those times when the promise and the life that was her mother would drain away. This emptying is not so new. Its familiarity lies heavy. Almost involuntarily, she steals another breath and jerks her head away. On the dresser is a photo. It's a copy of the one in her handbag; of her father, cupping a cigarette, and smiling with hope and enthusiasm. Across one corner is written 'Love Ian xx.'

What happened to that hope? What use was that love?

Chapter Ten

"Maria, I just wanted to ask you something. Don't you think … you know, your mum and dad, they must've done it, you know. They must've, to get a baby. Don't you think that's yuck?"

"You think so?"

"Yeah, and they're so, you know, old."

"I just don't think about it. I've got some new stockings to wear. Nylons. And mum gave me my birthday present early. Look, it's sling-back shoes, we bought them last week."

Sandra was at Maria's house, helping her pin up the hem on the dress she'd made in sewing class at school. The shoes had a little heel and tiny gold buckles. Sandra sat back on the bed, slumped against the wall, thinking about the long socks and school shoes she'd have to wear. She wanted a suspender belt and nylons and sling-back shoes. She wanted them so badly that it hurt. Maria was twirling in front of the mirror.

"I think it's straight now, what do you think?"

"Hmm, it needs a petticoat," Sandra said.

" I just want to go and show the boys, see what they think …"

"What do you want to do that for?"

"Oh, um, just to see what they say."

The boys were all in the garage, working on the old jeep that Lenny had picked up at the dump. Peter and Lenny were leaning over the engine and Colin was sitting in the driver's seat, pretending to turn the steering wheel. Sandra stood at the garage door and Maria walked carefully past her, in her new shoes. When Lenny poked his head out, Sandra could see a big pimple on his cheek. It was red and swollen. He'd probably been picking it. His eyebrows went up, really high, and his eyes moved from Maria's feet to her face, very slowly. Maria blushed, raised her chin and slid a look out of the corner of her eye. A surge of blood went through Sandra's body. She folded her arms tight over the prickly warmth and bolted back to the sanctity of Maria's bedroom.

Maria came back in, flushed and smiling. She was carrying her sling-back shoes. Sandra flicked over the page of the old *Valentine* magazine she'd brought over. She'd already read it three times.

"Did you see that, Sandra? Did you? What did you run away for?"

"Did I see what?"

Maria sat on the stool next to her dressing table and pushed her chin up and opened her mouth, like a soft invitation.

"I think I'd let a boy kiss me the first time he took me out."

Sandra turned over another page.

"Depends who it is, of course. What about you? Would you let a boy you really, really liked kiss you the first time?"

She wanted to say no, she also wanted to say yes. She wanted a boy to look at her like Lenny had looked at Maria. Mostly she wanted shiny, black, sling-back shoes.

"The boys are going possum hunting tomorrow night, with Lenny's gun," said Maria. "They need us to hold the torches. What do you think, Sandra? Do you want to come?"

"S'pose so."

The next night Lenny drove along the road to the lake. A rough road, never meant to be permanent, the soft ash moving with every wheel that traversed it— hillocking in the middle and the sides, leaving potholes and corrugations. The jeep bounced. Beside him, Peter held the twenty-two up in the air so it wouldn't jab either of them. The safety catch was on but it was loaded. In the back on a hard wooden seat, Maria and Sandra were holding on, trying to keep their balance. Colin had wheedled his way in on this trip. He was wedged between the dog pen and the wooden seat.

They drove on to the turnaround at the lake edge. Here teenagers parked up at night and beer was drunk and virginity was stolen, or given away. The brightness from the jeep's headlights caught the bent tops of reeds darkening the deep water. The jeep jerked to a stop and Sandra lurched. Lenny, the first one out, pulled his swandri over his head. Sandra wondered why he still bothered with his brothers and younger neighbours. He was working now, on a forestry gang and his swandri still looked new. It might have something to do with that look, the one he gave Maria last night.

"Come on," he said. "We're going up to the speedboat hut. Reckon we'll get some possums up there. Me and Peter are gonna shoot."

"Can I have a go, too?" Colin said.

"Nope, you're too young. You two girls, you're gonna use the torches, one each, big ones, shine them on whatever makes a noise out there."

"What about us? What do we get to do?" Colin asked.

"You watch out for noises and tell the girls, then they point the torches that way. Someone has to go out and get the possums we shoot, too. They may need finishing off. I've got Dad's hunting knife."

"Yeah, that'll be me," Colin said. "I can do that. Slit their throats."

He reached for the sheath and pulled out the knife. It glinted, catching the moonlight. He pulled it through the air in front of his neck.

"Where's the torches, Lenny?" Maria asked.

"I'll show you," Lenny said and he and Maria bent into the front of the jeep. Sandra could hear giggling.

Maria and Lenny led the hunting party up the path. Maria played her torch upward and its beam, narrow and far-reaching, caught the blackened manuka and pierced the dark that wrapped around the hill. Sandra came behind, directing her torch beam on the feet of the climbers. Ash shifted. Her heart was pounding; it was a steep climb. The hunting knife was jammed into the back of Colin's pants, just in front of her. He was using a scrubby manuka to pull himself up the last steep slope and it whipped back in her face. When she grabbed it to haul herself up, its shallow roots came away in her hand. The torch fell and its beam drilled into the ash. Blunted lava pieces absorbed the light, the tiny fragments of rhyolite glinted like so many small eyes watching. She scrambled for the torch, scrambled for her balance and the ash shifted again.

The door was hanging off the speedboat hut where the judges sat on racing days. Brown bits of glass from beer bottles littered the floor and the shutter from the front window lay on the ground. The hunters crowded into it, moving along the length of the wooden bench; Maria jammed up against Lenny, Sandra in the doorway, shining her torch into the narrow space. The beam caught the graffiti carved into the bench; 'Joe got a big dick' she read and 'Susan fucked me.'

"All right, everyone," said Lenny. "I need you, Maria, with a torch in here with me. Peter, you can help Sandra outside with the other torch then we can swap over when you get a turn to shoot. Colin, you sit outside with Peter and Sandra and listen for possum noise."

Maria giggled. Sandra shone her torch through the open front of the hut, out into the bush. The edge of her beam caught Maria's slightly open mouth as she tilted her face towards Lenny and Lenny's hand as he pulled a bottle out from under his swandri.

"Got some supplies, in case we get cold," he said. "Except you're not getting any, Colin."

"Oh, go on Lenny."

"Nup, you gotta be a teenager to drink Blackberry Nip, eh Maria?"

He put an arm around her as she reached for the bottle,

unscrewed the lid and took a swig. Sandra jerked the torch beam at her.

"You want me to shoot first, Lenny?" Peter asked. "Seeing as I've got the gun and you're busy."

"Na, mate, gizzit. You need to be quiet everyone. No talking, no noise. Come on, let's get some possums."

Sandra sighed. She stationed herself at the door of the hut with the torch off. Peter sat down close by and wrapped his arms around himself. Colin worked his way to the other side of the hut. They waited in the dark, fidgeting, wary. The moon came and went through the clouds and the manuka was silvered, then darkened. At the bottom of the hill the lake sat, waiting, absorbing the light, the water still. The thick reeds held dark silt and the bodies of drowned speedboat racers, still wearing their colours, sinking softly in surrender into the blackness. They had names known to everyone. Anything else held in that lake did not.

In the shadows Sandra heard a hissing, like her cat when he was startled. She shone the torch beam into the fork of a tall manuka to the right of the hut and the beam caught the bushy tail of a possum. The animal turned, its eyes glowing in the light, glinting like the rhyolite in the ash.

"Peter, Peter," she whispered.

Peter put his head in the doorway of the hut. Sandra heard a shot. The possum jerked and tried to climb higher. Another shot and it fell out of the torch beam.

"Woohoo! I got the bugger."

Lenny came out with his arm around Maria, the twenty-two waving above his head. The arm around Maria was tight, possessive. Sandra wanted an arm like that, one that held her. She hurt for the wanting of it.

"Have you put the safety catch on?" she asked.

Colin went crashing through the bush. Sandra shone her torch towards the waving manuka. The beam showed Colin's progress as he swung down the hill, held on to manuka, slipped on the ash.

The crashing stopped.

"Found it," he yelled. "Kill, kill!"

He emerged from the bush, holding the possum by the tail. He threw it to the ground and its head fell back, almost severed. Colin wiped the blood on the knife blade on his shorts.

They stood around the dead possum and passed around the Blackberry Nip. When it came to Sandra she took the smallest sip she could and then choked as it reached her throat. Colin grabbed at the bottle as it came past him and Lenny lunged. Some of it spilled on the possum. The dark fluid splashed on the almost severed head, mingling with the blackening blood. The sweet smell intensified. Sandra covered her nose.

Lenny poked at the corpse with his foot, turning it on to its back. The furred belly moved. A small head emerged from the pouch, fur-less, rat-like, its whiteness catching in Sandra's torch beam.

"Jeez, what's that?" he said.

"Oh," Maria said. "She's having a baby. It's a baby possum, look, it's getting born."

"Kill, kill!"

Colin slashed at the pouch, the hunting knife digging deep, past the foetal possum, into the bowels of the mother. Lenny grabbed Colin's arm and took the knife. The intestines oozed from the possum's body, spilling from the confines of the fur, engulfing the tiny bones of the dead foetus.

"Yuck," Maria said and buried her head in Lenny's shoulder.

Sandra kept her torch beam rigid. The smell of warm blood, of punctured gut and sweet Blackberry Nip, was making her sick but it was the coils of intestine, greenish, streaked with red veins that overwhelmed her. She felt herself being smothered, obliterated, like the small, white foetus.

She was still feeling sick when the jeep stopped in the driveway. Peter and Colin took the corpse, gloating over their kill. Sandra stayed in the back of the jeep, hoping she would feel better soon when the noises started from the front seat. Sloppy, saliva filled noises; Lenny grunting and groaning "Come on Maria, you're not scared are you?" his breathing, ragged and heavy as he humped his body up and down; Maria giggling and the giggling turning to moans.

"You're disgusting," she yelled but they didn't even notice, even when Sandra slammed the jeep door.

Safe in her own bed, it took a long time before she went to sleep. The noises kept coming back and she felt as if she was being engulfed by Lenny's flesh, and his tongue. She could feel her own body tingling, heat flushing through her and her nipples aching. She crossed her legs, very hard.

Tomorrow Maria would have to go to confession. What would she say, in the dark, to the priest?

Bless me father for I have sinned. It has been one month since my last confession. These are my sins; last night I kissed a boy and he put his tongue in my mouth.

Would she say: *I let him touch my tits?*

Worse still would she say: *and I really liked it.*

Chapter Eleven

Kawerau July 1959

Sandra woke before dawn. Her dreams had hung like formless, nebulous spirits, stolen from some other place and when she tried to pull them back, they'd dissolved, leaving her shivering and crying. So she pulled her duffel coat on over her pyjamas and, leaving her shoes untied, went walking into the cold dark. The wind was coming straight off the snow on the other mountain, the distant one, Tarawera, the one that was unpredictable, the one that blew its top nearly one hundred years ago. The wind was sharp, cutting at noses and making throats dry and shriveled, stealing the moisture of breath, smoking it and suspending it in the air. As she walked, lights came on in some houses, babies cried in others. There were people living ordinary lives but she couldn't shake a sense that something wasn't right. It followed her round the sinuous streets and back up her own driveway. The feeling persisted as she dressed. It was still with her when she went into the kitchen.

When Amy came in with her white hair tangled and her eyes focused on some distant place, Sandra knew that the dreams had not just been hers. Amy hunched over the heater and Sandra turned back to the stove. The porridge bubbled and exploded small gouts of air, the kitchen clock ticked and the kerosene heater hissed.

Amy broke the inhuman quiet.

"Can you help me with my homework, Sandra? I want to take

some photos and Dad won't let me take the camera. He said I could if you come."

"Where do you have to go?"

"I need to go up to the steam bores. It's for a project about power."

"Can't Robert come with you?"

"He hasn't got a camera."

"It's a long walk. Will you manage it? I've got homework to do too, so we'd better go this morning."

The frost had mostly gone by the time they left the house, its remains retreating deeper into the shadows. Their hands were cold, even with gloves on.

"Do you know which way to go?" Sandra asked.

"I think we have to go up the road next to the mill, towards that noise."

In the distance was a sound whose rhythm had become so familiar it was no longer heard. It was the steam bores muttering to themselves, gathering momentum until, hissing and rumbling, they released great gouts of steam, only to quiet again to their fractious mumbling. The sound got louder as Sandra and Amy crossed the loopy road that surrounded the town and headed towards the bridge. A wood-chip truck came past, its high sides rattling, its gears graunching. The wind of it almost swept them into the river. As they turned towards the noise of the steam bores and the mill, the blunt head of the hammerhead crane lurched, its load tipped and, in slow motion, the load of logs fell.

Sandra thought of her father going into the mill with its wide doors and sulphur steam, walking in with his hard hat on and his steel-capped boots for protection. There was the smell, up close the smell of the boiling pulp was almost palpable. She knew he would be blasted by the noise, it was loud enough out here. His insides must be vibrating all the time with the rumbling of the paper machines. Sandra could feel it, almost like a conversation between her body, the machines and the deeply fissured rocks underneath it, the ones that shook with earthquake from time to time as they shifted and resettled. For a moment she could see the unstable earth opening up, and swallowing the mill into a deeper inferno.

They walked on past the mill gate with its security guards to where the road dipped down towards the river. Ahead of them were thin curls of steam. They hurried on, with dampness on their faces, sulphur on their lips. The river-bank stopped them.

"We're on the wrong side," said Amy. "I think we should've gone along the other road."

Across the river, close to the bank, was a shallow lake, its dark mud and grey-green water steaming lazily, as if to say the hot earth was not in a hurry, it could wait. It cooled itself, the mud belching its poisonous fumes. Behind it the steam bores slept. A big, angular form sat in the middle, covered in mud.

"What's that?" asked Sandra.

"Did you know," said Amy. "That when they tried to dig the steam bores the first time, before we moved here, they blew up?"

"Was anyone killed?"

"No, but it threw all the bulldozers in the air. They all went kaboom, right up high, all the bulldozers. It just made a big mess."

"So, that thing's a bulldozer? How did they build the steam bores then?"

"They made the river go through the hot muddy bit, to cool it down. It made the old woman really, really mad."

Before Sandra could reply, the dribbles of steam became a raging blast of hissing white as the bores released. The steam cleared and they could see the lake again. Only this time there was someone standing at its edge. It was an old man, with a hat on, and a stick. He was standing very still. He seemed to have appeared from nowhere.

"Who's that?" asked Amy.

"It's the old man who came for the bone. Remember, Amy? He came and got the bone and said all that stuff."

"But what's he doing?"

"I don't know. He does a lot of prayers, that's what he did that day when he came for the bone. Mrs Simpson said he does lots of prayers in their church. His house must be near here, over that side of the river."

"He must be talking to the old woman. He probably knows her."

There was something about the stillness of the old man that stopped Sandra. She'd heard the old man's lilting voice and, although she had been quite young when she had taken him around the back of the Simpson house to collect the stolen bone, she'd known, in some way she could not explain, that he was healing something and that maybe she should not be watching.

"We should go," she said.

"No, wait. Look, there's someone else coming."

"Where?"

"Look, by the big manuka. Maybe it's the old woman."

A figure emerged from the bush that fringed the hot lake. They watched, fascinated, as the woman moved deeper in the sticky mud towards the rejected bulldozer, the hem of her dress pulling her in. She seemed to be part of some dreamscape where the lake was entrancing her, enticing her. Maybe she would walk into the mud and water and disappear—sink into its warmth and dissolve.

"That's Mum," Amy said.

"No! It can't be. Why would she be here? How do you know it's her?"

"That's her cardigan. I recognise it. What's she doing, Sandra?"

The figure that was their mother lifted her face up and an unearthly howl, too loud for their mother's slight body, pierced the sulphurous steam. There were words in there, words that defied sense. Sandra, one pointing finger reaching out towards their mother, took one, two, three steps into the dark water. Black water, stinking from its time in the bowels of the paper mill. She sank in the soft sand up to her knees and the swift blackness almost pulled her in. She couldn't swim the river. The steam bores raged again and the steam coursed across the two figures at the other side of the river, blotting them out. Sandra stared into the white steam but could see nothing. She turned back to her sister.

"Amy, we've got to help Mum. Come on."

Amy hadn't moved from the riverbank. She was staring into the steam, her face immobile, her eyes unblinking.

"Amy!"

Sandra's hand on her arm made no difference.

"Amy!"

Sandra shook her.

"Don't worry. The old lady's come for her."

Sandra stared at her strange sister: the matter of fact words, the calm face, the eyes focused on some other place. *What should I do? Stay here with Amy, in this other world that Amy had slipped into? Or help mum? Who should I choose?*

She took one last, desperate look across the river. The steam had been sucked back into the mud and at the edge of the lake two figures were heading into the manuka. Both very muddy. Both going very slowly. Like some portent, she could feel the old man's hand as if it was on her own arm. His voice with its soft cadence, drifting and falling as if he was trying to mend her mother, or save her from something.

Walking home seemed to be the only thing to do, so they went back past the mill with its buildings emerging and sinking into the smoke. Now you see it, now you don't. Back over the bridge and along the road snaking home.

They stepped over their father's steel-capped boots at the door and came into silence and the cat licking up sugar from the kitchen floor. By tacit agreement, they kept the silence. Neither of them wanted to think about where their mother had gone or where the old man had taken her. If they pretended it hadn't happened, maybe it would be all right and if they kept busy, they wouldn't have to think about it.

The two of them were on their hands and knees, sweeping the sweetness from the green lino when the loud voices seeped down the hallway. Sandra looked up at Amy and, like mirrors one of the other, they sat very still, each holding her breath. One of the voices became a high-pitched sobbing.

"Home," it insisted. "Home, home, home."

There was a sharp crack and silence. A low insistent keening welled up from the bedroom, bubbled and flooded the house, swallowing every other feeling that may have been. It filled the kitchen and condensed on the windows, tearing on the glass and flowing down to the windowsills, splashing down on Amy and Sandra and threatening to sweep them into the torrent of it. It rose up in pitch, up until it spat.

"Get out," it said. "Get out!"

Sandra helped Amy up off the floor. They crunched the sugar underfoot as their father came into the kitchen.

"Your mother's had a funny turn," he said. "Look after her, will you, I'm off out."

He was met with silence, two pairs of eyes looking blank.

"I found her on the road, with some old man, covered in mud. God knows where she'd been."

He threw a crumpled blue aerogramme down on the table.

"Get your own tea," he said and slammed the back door behind him.

Sandra unfolded the damp, crumpled aerogramme. It was from Aunty Kath but the handwriting was spidery and difficult to read. She read the first sentences: 'I got cancer and I can't come to New Zealand and I know you can't come home.'

Sandra and Amy finished sweeping up the sugar, tipping it in the sink. They tip-toed down the hallway, opening the bedroom door very carefully. Their mother was a lump in the bed. She seemed to be asleep.

Chapter Twelve

Kawerau August 1959

The frost had just retreated from the asphalt when Sandra's basket-ball game started. She stamped her feet and hugged herself, crossing her arms over her breasts, wrapping them around her white shirt-sleeved arms. Her new bra was a bit tight around the back and it cut in when she breathed but Sandra had wanted to get out of the shop in a hurry.

"I haven't seen your mum around the shops for a long time, is she all right?"

"She's fine thanks," Sandra said. "I'll have this one, it fits." She'd been thinking, nosy cow, it's none of your business.

She didn't want the woman to know that, since the letter from her Aunty Kath, her mum was living in some other world more and more of the time.

She prowled the edge of the white line that defined her small territory, blowing on her hands. The final whistle went. Her team won without any contribution at all from their captive goal-keep. As she pulled a jumper out of her bag and got her head stuck in the neck, Maria came bounding up, flushed and sweating.

"Neat, eh? We beat the pants off them," she said.

"Thanks to you. I didn't even get to touch the ball."

Sandra pulled hard at the jumper and shoved her arms into the sleeves.

"What're you doing tonight, Sandra?"

"Nothing."

"Can I tell Mum I'm with you?"

"Why?"

"Dad and me had a big bust up last night. He said someone at work told him he should keep me away from Lenny 'cos him and his mates are into the booze. They drive around in Lenny's car drinking. So Dad said I can't see him anymore."

"So what do you want to tell your mum?"

"Oh, just that I'm hanging out with you at another girl's place. Your mum won't tell, will she?"

"She won't even notice. Where're you going to be?"

"Well, you know, we'll just park up somewhere."

No, thought Sandra, I don't know. She imagined Lenny, in his green Mark One Zephyr, cruising down the road to the lake (except it would be bumping rather than cruising), bumping down the road to the lake. She imagined the car sitting on the bare patch next to the dark eye of watching, waiting water. Lenny turned the key off. He reached out, not for Maria but for Sandra, pulling her across the slippery car seat. He leaned forward and his lips forced her mouth open, his breath hot, his tongue pushing hard. He slipped his hand up her dress, pulling at the edge of the elastic of her knickers. Sandra arched her bum up from the seat. Then she stopped herself.

"Are you and Lenny, you know, are you doing it?" she asked.

Maria looked away, a little smile on her face.

"You are, aren't you? You are doing it. You're going the whole way, aren't you?"

"What if we are?"

Sandra bit her bottom lip.

"Maria, what if you get pregnant?"

"I won't. He, you know, he takes it out," she said.

Sandra shivered, her nipples hurt. She crossed her arms and squeezed her breasts in their new bra.

"Come on, let's go and get an ice-cream," said Maria.

That night Maria told her mother she was at Sandra's house

and Sandra sat in her bedroom, wrapped up in a blanket with a hot water bottle and the radio on, listening to the hit parade. She pushed drawing pins into her wall. Right next to the two posters of Elvis, she hung up her latest poster—Elvis Presley again—carefully pulled out from the centre of the last *Valentine* magazine, sent by Aunty Kath who was never going to come. Three pairs of Elvis eyes were looking out of the window, at something far away.

By Monday, Sandra had decided she wasn't going to lie for her friend anymore and what's more, she would tell her so. Right now, she had something more urgent to do. She hurried along the corridor with the black and white tiles marching ahead of her and a cold wind coming in from the open doors at each end of the school block. The corridor always seemed so long, especially when you were in a hurry. She lengthened her step, so she only landed on the black squares. For luck.

Geography had just finished. She needed to investigate her stomach cramps and she was clutching her brown paper bag, the one that brought the comments from the boys in class if they saw it: 'Got your lunch in there? I know where you're going. Sandra's got her rags on.' She had to go now, between classes. She paused at the door of the girls' toilet, listening to the conversation inside.

"What do you think about French kissing?"

"I think it's disgusting, I nearly choked last week. Lenny nearly had his tongue right down my throat."

"Yeah? I like it. My little sister thinks that's how you get pregnant. Give us a light, my fag's gone out."

"I really copped it from Dad, he saw the big love-bite on my neck."

"Use toothpaste, as soon as you can. That gets rid of it. Colgate's best."

"Give us a drag, yeah, look at my neck. Back seat of the pictures and he had his hand on my left tit but only on the outside of my clothes."

"Eh? Don't you care if people can see?"

One of the voices was Maria's. Now would be the time to tell her there would be no more alibis. Her stomach cramps worsened as she pushed the door open. They stopped talking when she came in. The tall, blonde girl holding the cigarette took a drag and drew the smoke up her nose. A smoke coil tried to escape and was pulled expertly in. Sandra wished she could do that but it'd only make her choke and feel sick.

"Hi Sandra," Maria said. "Oh, you got the curse. Just finished mine. I tell you I was praying, it was a bit desperate for a week or so!"

"We'd better go, bell's just gone," said the blonde. "We've got English."

"Don't be late, Sandra, Miss'll get you," Maria said.

The door hissed back on itself after they left, closing with a whump.

Once in the toilet cubicle, Sandra pulled out the sanitary pad, the belt and the safety pins. The empty toilets echoed. Gingerly she pulled down her navy blue school knickers, sat on the toilet and sighed with relief. Her period hadn't started yet so she wouldn't leave a stain on her school uniform. She'd escaped more jeering from the boys in class.

She fumbled with the pins. At least she didn't have to worry about whether she'd get a period or not, that was some consolation. The hard part about not having a boyfriend was that she never got to go out anywhere anymore. It seemed you either had the going out and worry or you stayed at home. She reached for the toilet chain. It clanged and rattled, the noise bouncing off the walls. She felt another cramp in her belly. Maybe she could go home, Miss would understand.

She was late for English class. The only seat left in the room was next to the new boy and she stood looking for some alternative.

"Sit down, Sandra, and hurry up. I'll give you two minutes to get yourself settled, otherwise it will be a detention," said Miss.

Sandra slid into the seat, pulling the chair as far away as possible from her neighbour. She took him in with small sideways glances. He was sprawled with one leg long under his desk. His elbows were spread and he was drumming on the table top with one hand.

"Stop that noise, will you?" said Miss. "In fact you can be the next to read. What's your name again?"

He sniffed and looked down at his offending hand.

"Rewi, Miss," he said.

"Rewi, you can read Macbeth, he's a dark king. We're on page ninety-three, scene seven. You pick up from 'If it were done.'"

Rewi started reading, faltering over the rhythm, his voice soft.

"If it were done when 'tis done, then 'twere well it were done quickly."

"Come on Rewi, speak up. This is a man who is troubled, he's being pushed by his lady wife, by Lady Macbeth, to kill his king. He wants to, but he doesn't want to. Why does he want to? Anyone?"

Sandra stared. He was squirming in his chair. Rewi, that was his name, he'd only come to the school last week. His black hair was standing on end where he'd been running his hand through it. Under the wide nostrils of his flat nose were the beginnings of a moustache. Sandra could almost feel his thick lips softly, gently opening her thin English mouth, his tongue probing. He turned his head, glanced, looked down and was caught by her stare. His brown eyes fixed on her green ones. He smiled.

"Rewi, pay attention, you might be going to be king, but stop ogling the girls. Come on, start again—'If it were done.'"

Sandra watched a deep flush come up from Rewi's neck. She didn't know a Māori could blush like that. She blushed too, fixing her stare down on her textbook, trying to concentrate on the Scottish king. Rewi stumbled through the passage, his voice still soft.

"Right, everyone. I want you to spend ten minutes discussing with your neighbour. One of you keep notes. I want you to write a list of the influences you think there might have been on Macbeth to kill his king. The influences can be from outside of him, or they can be from his own thinking. Understand?"

The class settled, murmuring and rustling. Sandra didn't hear the questions that several people asked because she was stuck on one thought; she would need to talk to Rewi, the boy who had smiled at her and whose blush was a deep brown blush, not a bright red like hers. She bent down to get a pad of paper out of her bag, pulling up her long grey socks as far as she could to hide her bristly knees, in case he noticed she hadn't shaved her legs in the last few days. Paper found, she started fiddling with her fountain pen. It fell between the desks. As she bent down to get it so did Rewi and their shoulders brushed. In the confusion of sorries, the pen was left on the floor. Sandra felt her face flame up again and she took a deep breath. As she gathered herself to try and retrieve her pen, Rewi leaned down and picked it up. He quietly put it on her desk and started writing his own list. Sandra bent over her work, sneaking looks out of the corner of her eye. She stopped when one of her sly peeks was intercepted by Rewi. Her list had only one item on it. It said: 'He loved his wife and she wanted him to do it.'

After the class had discussed their lists, the reading continued. Rewi stayed as Macbeth and Sandra read Lady Macbeth. When she read 'I have given suck, and know how tender 'tis to love the babe that milks me', there were titters around the class. She kept her head down, to hide her red face. So did Rewi.

At last the class was over and Sandra packed her bag ready to walk home. She pulled out her beret and carefully placed it on the back of her head. Maria had already gone with the blonde girl, probably to sneak a smoke in the toilets. Sandra lifted her heavy bag, full of homework, and turned to leave the room. Rewi followed her and he was still following her when she walked out the gate. He was stopped by the prefect on duty, told to tuck his shirt in, pull his socks up and put on his cap. She discovered she needed to swap hands with her bag and adjust her own socks. By the time she'd done that, he'd caught up.

"Walk you home, eh, Lady Macbeth?" he said.

She nodded, looking at the footpath, at the letterbox of the house across the road from the school, at her bag, at the cat running across the road, at anywhere other than that brown face that blushed when she did.

"Carry your bag for you?" he asked.

She blinked, focusing on his outstretched hand. Their hands touched as she passed her bag over. As if her hand was burned, she pulled back and folded her arms.

"I'm going to visit my aunty, she lives down Atkinson Street. Where do you live?"

For one moment Sandra couldn't remember. They set off towards River Road and plunged into the labyrinth that snaked its way to Weld Street. Her thoughts were running down every intersection, every dead end street they passed. Words seemed to have emptied out of her, leaving a vast, embarrassing silence. Rewi filled it up.

He told her he'd been living with his grandparents in Taupo since he was a baby and that he'd come to stay with his parents so that he could get to know his mother's family. He told her he was only here until the end of the year, then his koro wanted him to go to boarding school—to St Paul's which was a Catholic boarding school because his family was Catholic. Except that he didn't go to mass and his parents thought he should.

Sandra nodded a lot. She was listening with every part of her body. She could hear his words, his Māori way of speaking, his pride in his future. Her body could hear his maleness, the depth of his voice reverberating somewhere in her belly. She could smell him, this morning's Lifebuoy soap overlaid with the salt of sweat and a flat smell of different food having been eaten and digested. Her body electrified when they accidently, or maybe not so accidently, bumped each other. She noticed he was looking at her and that he'd stopped talking.

"Sorry, what did you say?" she asked.

"I said has Miss talked to your parents yet? She talked to my koro when he was up last week, about me doing more subjects for School C. She's talking to all the parents of kids she thinks will do well. That means you, doesn't it?"

"Um, I suppose so."

"What're you good at? English? That Shakespeare stuff is real hard. I think I'm better at Maths than English. But we all have to pass English, eh?"

"Um, yes."

Sandra didn't seem to be in control of the next words she said. Maybe it was Lady Macbeth who embodied herself and interrupted Sandra's silence; *But screw your courage to the sticking place.*

"I can help you with English. We could study together and maybe you could help me with Maths."

They'd reached the corner with the sign that said Atkinson Street.

"See you tomorrow, Lady Macbeth," said Rewi.

When he passed her bag back, their hands touched again, just lightly. Sandra decided to shave her legs and stop biting her fingernails. She smiled back at Rewi with her whole self lifting as the corners of her mouth curved.

That evening, Sandra was doing her homework on the kitchen table. Some days she had to get dinner ready because her mother was lying down but tonight her mother seemed a bit better. The chip heater had been going all day and the kitchen was warm. Her mother reached for another potato and pared off a long dark peel into the sink.

"I got a letter in the post today, Sandra," she said. "From a teacher. She wants me and Dad to go into school, she wants to talk to us. Have you been in trouble?"

"No, Mum. She wants to talk about School Certificate, about how many subjects I should be sitting. She wants me to do an extra one, do six exams but it cost more."

"What you want to do that for?" asked her mother. "You don't need all them exams to get a job. You could work in the Four Square, that's good clean work."

She blinded the last potato with her sharp knife, filled the pot with water and put it on the stove.

Sandra wrote in her exercise book. 'C'est cinq Août, aujourd'hui, et il fait froid. It is the fifth of August today and it is cold.' She considered the next question: 'Quelles sont les personnes importantes dans votre vie? Who are the people who are important in your life?' 'J'aime,' she wrote. Who? She wondered if Maria would be writing Lenny's name and if the blonde girl from the toilets this morning would be writing the name of the boy who made toothpaste on the neck necessary. Inside her own head she let herself finish the sentence 'J'aime Rewi,' the boy with the Māori eyes and the Māori hair and she wrote down the names of her mother, father and sister.

Chapter Thirteen

The breath has gone and now the lines are going: the crumpled skin is smoothing: the eyes close and are sinking back into her face. The pillow is swallowing her. She's shrinking, shrinking. Sandra's eyes stall on the widow's peak, the hair pointing from her mother's forehead, and travel down her nose to her mouth. The same hairline, same nose, same mouth. From some distant place, somewhere inside that is far away, she watches her mother leaving. She waits, drifting in that far away place, as if there's some end to this leaving, some experience that will end something but there's just her and this body that is nobody now, that used to be her mother. Still she sits. Numb. Waiting.

A sound interrupts the waiting, pulling her attention to the window. There's a large blowfly caught against the window. It's hurling itself at the pane, again and again. The sound is loud and insistent. She stands up and moves slowly, drifting to the window. The catch is stuck. She pulls at it, gently at first, then harder, desperate for it to open, for the window to be wide and the blowfly to leave, forever. Try as she might it will not budge. The buzzing intensifies and she can feel it making room for itself inside her head. She smashes her hand on the windowsill, the fly escapes. Intent on catching it, on shutting it up, she tries again. Smash. Escape.

There it is, the next thing. Escape. She turns the round, black doorknob, pulls the door open and steps out into the hall. There are muffled voices coming from the kitchen and the radio is playing 'No Woman No Cry' and the sound pulls her down the narrow hallway into the lounge, to stand on the swirling carpet. The Virgin Mary, eyes turned up to the ceiling, is watching her mother leave. Just as she's watched others in the family leave.

They find her standing there, in the lounge, Bea and Robert. It's Robert who pulls her down on the sofa, Bea who hurries off, wiping her hands clean on her apron. Sandra waits again; for Robert to say something, for the Virgin Mary to say something, for anyone to break in with the next thing to do. His hand is on her shoulder and she jumps with the weight of it.

"She's gone." Bea is back and she starts to cry with her apron up at her face. Robert's hand moves and the two of them hold on to each other.

"Maybe it's for the best."

"She went peacefully."

"Poor old Betty, what a life she's had."

She wants to scream. *What about my life? What about me?* A cold, hard raft of resentment gives her the next thing to do.

"Well, that's that. I'll be heading back to Auckland then."

"What?" Robert says. "What do you mean you'll head back to Auckland. Who do you think's going to bury her, Sandra?"

Not me, she thinks, *definitely not me*. What she says is, "Well, you can. Can't you? I need to go."

"Now, dear," Bea says. "You've had a shock. I can understand. You didn't expect your mum to pass away when you've only just got to see her again."

Sandra shrinks back from the outstretched hand.

"I mean it. I need to go. As soon as I can."

"You callous bitch," Robert says. "You can't face it can you? This is all you can do, run away."

He keeps a protective arm around Bea and Sandra aches for that arm, any arm. Maybe her dad's arm, he used to hold her then she grew up and he died. She didn't come to that funeral and she's not coming to this one.

"Sandra," Bea is pleading. "Please, Sandra. Don't go. Don't run this time."

Those faces are needing her, needing something she can't give. Panic, look around blindly for cigarettes and the book, must have the book. Grab them from the sofa and out the door.

Sandra runs. The street is empty, there's no-one to see her. Only the mountain holds witness with its heavy clouds, they're back to press their weight on her. The footpath winds around corners, its white ribbon pulling her. She runs until she's gasping, breath difficult to wrestle from the still, heavy air, leaving it behind, all of it. Absorbed in the sensation of escape, she crosses the road to the sign—DANGEROUS RIVER it says. ADULTS WARN. *Adults warn.* The words are stuck in her head, round they go. *Adults Warn.* If only they had.

Breath gone, she stops at the edge of the river where the path goes. Gasping, pulling in the heavy air with its sauerkraut taste and the smell of the weed that looks like green hair in the current. Stopped by the river where the children who never listen to the adult's warnings still swim on hot days and are carried by that current, pulled to freedom or to the bottom where the eels are and the weeds will not let you go. The current swirls, whirls in vortices like so many eyes, eyes pulling her into the depths. As it slides her down it says

Shlep, shlep, here, come, come here, this is the real world, she knew.

Sandra fights for breath, she will not go under.

As she pulls out her cigarettes from her pocket, she's trembling so hard that the cigarettes spill, slipping from their silver paper home to scatter on the pumice. Each individual cigarette is stark on the sandy pumice, not touching any other. She reaches for one, puts it into her mouth and … and what? She reaches into her pocket for her cigarette lighter and finds the spine of her book, jammed into her waistband. She pulls it out and it falls open. *Identify your habitual SSS; self-sabotage-sentences.* She knows the answer to that, always knew it, just didn't want to. In red letters she can see it emblazoned on the page. *It is always my fault. Always.*

It's been drawn in every breath, held in spidery webs across her skin, trapping her in memories she does not want.

Shelp says the water, here, come, come here, she knew.

She will not go under.

She reaches for her lighter again and the letters I M glint on the silver. It takes her three goes to get her cigarette alight.

There's a bus tomorrow, she knows that. She knows when every bus leaves this town. It goes at 10.00 am. She could be home tomorrow night, back in her own flat, her own life. She'll ring the bus depot this afternoon. That'll keep her away; from this river that's pulling at her, from Robert and his need and from her mother's still body. She takes a deep drag of her cigarette and the ash drops into the pumice.

Sandra doesn't hear him coming. He just appears. He used to do that when he was a child, just turn up, everywhere there was Amy. It's him she needs to get away from. She grinds the cigarette out, leaving the brown filter butt mashed into the riverbank.

The pumice crunches as he sits down. He doesn't say anything. He stares straight ahead at the river. The river pulls again, pulls the two of them, down into its green depths. There's just its voice.

Shlep, come here, to this world.

His voice startles her.

"I get great comfort from being a Catholic, Sandra," he says. "I converted, after, you know."

She stares down at the cigarettes, the escaped cigarettes, and begins to pick them up slowly, putting them back in order in their packet. He carries on.

"It was a great comfort. Father Searle, you remember, how he was so good with, with us all."

The last cigarette won't fit back in the packet. Maybe she should just smoke it. Robert leans over and takes it from her hand.

"Bea's arranging for your mum to go to the chapel at the funeral home, the one in Whakatane. You know, the one where your dad went."

He's fiddling with the cigarette, turning it round and round in one hand. It breaks and she can see the bits of tobacco coming out of the split in the paper. Sandra doesn't remember the funeral home. She never went there. She doesn't even know where he was buried. No, he wasn't buried, someone told her he was cremated. His thin body, with its big splayed nose and a memory of hair, became a thin coating of ashes, to be swept up and put in a box, and that box, where was it? She doesn't even know where his ashes were put. She almost asks. Her eyes are drawn back to that cigarette going round in Robert's hand, leaking itself out, bit by bit. She knows she won't ring the bus depot this afternoon.

"Bea's worried about you, Sandra."

The cigarette sags, the two bits held together with a tenuous piece of paper. She can't hold on any longer. It's not the earth that trembles this time, beneath her, it's who she built when she left here. It's the men who only stay for a month at the most, it's the weekends working to pull together deals, it's the empty wine cartons that clutter the back step, it's the red trouser suit. It all shakes and slumps into just so much ash. She takes a breath with no count to it, a breath that is years long. She's back in the desolation that she tried to run from all those years ago.

"You will stay, won't you?"

She nods. No words. She just nods from her emptiness. At the water and at Robert.

"We should get back."

Robert pulls himself up and holds out his hand. She hesitates, takes it and he hauls her to her feet. One foot has gone to sleep and she staggers. He grasps her elbow to steady her and there's an echo, deep inside.

Before she follows him back across the field, to the road, she crouches in the pumice. She pulls her course book from under her sweatshirt and places it carefully in the shallows. The water seeps into the porous pages, smearing the words. From beneath the willow roots, an eel slides. Big and black, like the one Rewi said was bad luck, what was it called?

"Take it," she says. "Take it, whatever you are."

They have to wait for the traffic from the mill. Cars mostly and a few workers on bikes with their swandri jackets and steel-capped boots, all on their way home from the four o'clock shift. The ribbon of pavement winds back along the streets. Robert points out who lives in which house. Most of the names mean nothing, she's been gone too long but there's one house in Atkinson Street where Rewi's aunty lived. The name is the same. It's like looking through the wrong end of a telescope to a distant, almost life. She can't say anything, can't ask Robert.

Then it's gone.

Sandra stops at the Simpson's letterbox. It seems a lifetime since she stood next to it, this morning, with her suitcase and her platform shoes. The head of her shadow merges into the high hedge, the one that hides the house next door where she used to live. This time she lets herself look at it. She can only see the green roof and the chimney with its television aerial pointing in all directions at once. The paint is peeling from the corrugated iron and rust is showing through. She helped Dad paint that roof, one sunny Sunday morning.

That's enough. One step at a time. She walks back up the path to the glass mother duck in the front door. She takes a breath, ready to walk down the long hallway to the empty bedroom and at the edges is—another life. One she ran from, one that could have been.

What else have you got? What else?

Chapter Fourteen

Sandra sighed as she packed her French text book away. Behind her Maria was giggling with her new friend, the one she sneaked smokes with and shared ways to hide love bites. Sandra seemed to have lost that friendship. There were girls who knew the secret language: a certain lift of an eyebrow, a look from the corner of half-closed eyes with a half smile, a tongue run slowly along slightly parted lips, backs arched to show breasts under gym frocks and the top of a thigh as a suspender was adjusted. Sandra had watched them do it but she just did not have the password for that club.

She headed for the classroom that doubled as a library; trying to think about the English essay on Macbeth that she was working on, trying to ignore the fluttering in her belly and the flush coming up from her neck. Shakespeare came on her dates, or geometry, or algebra and they came with Rewi.

He was already there when she went in. Two desks were set up, side by side, facing the book-lined wall. He smiled. Sandra tried lifting one eyebrow and gave him a look from the corner of her half-closed eyes. She dumped her bag, arching her back and smoothing her gym frock as she sat down, to a puzzled look on Rewi's face.

"You all right?" he asked. "How was French?"

"French?" said Sandra, sighing. "We've got to do a translation for Friday. You need to do it too. How was cadets?"

During French, Sandra had sat by the window. The class was

small, girls only, and most of them had done the same thing as Sandra, looked out the window at the boys. Up and down they marched with sticks over their shoulders and their socks pulled up tight. The Corporal was the oldest boy in the school. He was about to turn twenty and this would have to be his last year and everyone was hoping this time he'd pass School Certificate so he could join the army. He marched precisely and his voice carried right over the football pitch. He'd make a good soldier. Rewi wouldn't. His shirt was hanging out again and one sock kept slouching down to his ankle. Sandra had counted three skips in a row as he tried to get himself back into step.

"Attendez-vous, mes mademoiselles," demanded the teacher.

Five minutes later the mademoiselles' eyes drifted off out to the make-believe soldiers again. It had been a long French period.

"Cadets was boring. I don't want to be a soldier."

Rewi's shirt had sweat stains under the arms. Sandra could smell the salt and the heat of him.

"Want to do that algebra?" he asked. "It's due tomorrow."

She nodded. The letters, that could become numbers with enough imagination, settled themselves on the page. They added and multiplied, almost automatically, in orderly progression under Rewi's pencil. His explanation marched with the letters, this drill precise.

"Then you can substitute the b with that number, eh? And if you know that number, then you know the answer," he said, leaning back in his chair.

Sandra's imagination was looking for another answer. His calf was leaning on hers, that sock slouching down his leg was resting on her shoe. His shoulder was pressed against hers so they leaned one against the other. She held the pencil up to her mouth, tracing her bottom lip. Out of the corner of her eye she watched Rewi's lips moving and, with just a bit more imagination and a substitution or two, she felt their softness on her neck.

"D'you get it?"

"Think so."

"Try the next one."

"How do I start?"

"You haven't been listening, Lady Macbeth, have you?"

Sandra blushed and Rewi laughed, pressing his leg against hers.

"Got to go. Got rugby practice. See you tomorrow after work experience. Meet you at the gate."

He was out of the room, his shirttail flying behind him. Sandra looked down at the letters on the page. Somehow they wouldn't transform themselves. The magic had gone.

The next day Sandra waited outside the doctor's surgery. She was to accompany the Public Health Nurse for the day, visiting new babies and sick people in the community. The nurse was a stout woman, with her hair pulled back in a bun and she wore a navy suit and a sensible pair of flat shoes. She was based in Whakatane hospital, where Amy had to go for her foot.

"When we go to a house," the nurse said. "You're to stay in the car and I'll ask the patient if you can come in."

Sandra nodded.

"I don't want you talking to the patients, either. You're not to intrude."

Sandra frowned. It didn't look as if the day would be much fun.

"In you get, in the back. We've got to check on some meds and change two dressings in town first, then we'll be off out to Onepu. There's a new baby and a man who's just been discharged from hospital. Any questions please save until the end of the day, I need to be able to concentrate, is that clear?"

Sandra wondered if the nurse was related in any way to the Corporal, the old man of the school, he was good at giving orders too. She thought nursing was looking after people, not being this bossy. She looked out of the window as they drove off from the surgery. There were six little children playing on the swings on the traffic island. One of them was stumbling along, just new at walking, and fell on a nappy-clad bottom. An older child came over and lifted him up, almost collapsing with the weight.

"Where's the mother, I ask you? Look at that, no supervision at all," snapped the nurse as the car bunny-hopped down the road.

The first three visits the nurse made were not suitable for young ladies, she said, so Sandra stayed in the car. The next visit was to clean a leg wound. The tusk of a wild boar had left a long, deep gash. She looked away when the nurse started going on about how the pus was reducing.

The thick smell of sulphating pulp followed them as they drove out past the mill to Onepu.

"I don't know how you people put up with that smell. It can't be healthy," said the nurse, winding up her window. "Now, we're going to visit a young mother with a new baby. She's not married and she's probably about your age. Māori girl, of course. Pay you to take a lesson from this."

They pulled up outside a small shed that sat on the edge of the river. Sandra got out of the car. She could see the river from where she was standing, it wasn't the luminous green of the water that flowed under the bridge in the town, it was black. On the surface were rafts of brown foam, like the dirty suds from the washing machine when her dad's work clothes were washed. She gagged on the stench. There was the stink of the mill, with its sulphur tang and its rottenness and intertwined in the miasma was the putrid smell of dead fish. Two of them floated between the foam islands, white bellies bloating towards the sky.

"Terrible how some people live. I'll just pop in and see if you can come," said the nurse.

She pushed the door of the shed open.

It sat in a field of yellow ragwort, a green rusting shed made of corrugated iron, with paint clinging to the wood of the windows and door and a barrel at one corner to collect the rain from the roof. There were no power lines or phone lines coming in, just a lean- to on one side, full of firewood. Someone called it home. Lace curtains were carefully tied back and a rag rug with bright colours sat on a concrete step, to welcome visitors. A pair of gumboots had been neatly placed together in front of the open door.

"Come on," the nurse called.

Sandra stepped over the concrete step. Inside the house was one room, with a curtain to make another. There was a makeshift bench with a small pile of dishes on it and a big plastic bowl full of water. An old wood stove, with pots piled on it, took one wall. A sofa, its flowery pattern rubbed and stained, was covered in a blanket of grey and brown patches stitched together with bright wool. On one of the chairs at the red formica table sat a young mother with a baby wrapped up in a towel. Above her was a picture taped to the bare wood wall. Jesus with his ambiguous eyes had one hand pointing to his flaming heart.

"Baby's had her morning bath," said the nurse. "I'm just going to fetch the scales to weigh her."

The mother's dark head bending over the baby and the hands softly patting the swaddled bundle looked familiar.

"Hello Iripeta," Sandra said. "I know you. We went to primary school together, remember?"

Iripeta nodded and beckoned Sandra closer. She pulled the towel away from the baby's face and Sandra looked into eyes that were neither blue nor brown, eyes that were waiting for the world to happen. They focused, wide open and unguarded, on Sandra as if inviting the possibility of who she could be. The possibility of all consuming love, of holding and shielding, of always. A smile slipped across her face and she reached to stroke the damp, black down on the baby's head. She thought of Rewi's soft, beginning moustache.

"Her name is Anihera," said Iripeta.

"What do you think you're doing?" said the nurse, coming back with the scales in her hand. "I specifically asked you not to talk to the patients. You can go and wait in the car, Miss. Now, give baby to me, we'll get her weight."

Iripeta wrapped the towel securely around her baby and passed her carefully to the nurse. She pointed at the navy suited back and made a face at Sandra—crabby old bitch it said. Sandra pretended to cough to hide the giggle, gave Iripeta a wave and went back to the car, cloaked in the smell of the dead river.

At the end of the day Sandra didn't have any questions. She was thinking about the stink of the river and the little curtains in the windows of the shed. The odd word from the nurses' lecture surfaced belly up in her thoughts:

"Shame,' the nurse said. "Pregnant, not married."

It was the look on the face of the baby's mother and Rewi's soft, black moustache that carried the dirty, brown words like foam on the water in Sandra's mind.

She walked back to school. At the gate, she watched the prefects on duty insisting on berets and caps and socks pulled up. Rewi was late. She was about to give up when he arrived, sneaking up and grabbing her arms from behind.

"Ho, Lady Macbeth, you nearly knocked me over," he laughed when she turned and flung an arm out. "Stroppy woman, eh? Come for a walk by the river, Sandra. We don't have any home-work tonight."

Rewi had one hand on his chest as he spoke and Sandra had a flash of Jesus with the eyes that invited or accused, giving his heart away. She nodded.

They walked along the riverbank. She was revisiting the same river but here it was green and swirled over rocks with clear, light foam that dissolved back into the water. The air, cleaned by the river, carried a slight spice of trout and eel. Forget-me-nots were a blue drift across the pumice banks. Young willows draped into the water, branches like hair drifting with the current.

Rewi and Sandra sat down under a plantation of willows, the canopy of twigs with a beginning of bright green budding, the roots drowning in the water.

"How was the railways today?" Sandra asked.

"Waste of time. I didn't even get to go on the train 'cos the driver wouldn't let me. Uncle just got me to make them cups of tea in the office. Did you know some dumb hua built the station round the wrong way? They had to make new windows and a new door on the side the train comes. Dumb eh? How was your day?"

"I met a girl I went to school with. She's got a baby and she's the same age as me. She lives out in a shed, by the river, on the other side of the mill. It's just a shed. She doesn't even have a tap for water or any electricity."

"What's the baby called?"

"Annie Heeda, I think she said."

"Anihera. That's Iripeta, the mother. She's my cousin on my mum's side. Lives with my koro and nan. Cute baby, eh? Don't you think it looks like me?"

"But why does she live in a shed?"

"That's Māori land, belongs to my mother's people. They been there a long time. My koro told me that before Tarawera erupted, this was all swamp. Good eels and kumara because of the hot pools. Then the mountain went up and most of the people left. Not many here when the mill got built. They want to stay but you can't get money to build a house on Māori land."

Sunlight slipped over an eel nosing at the edge; fatter than the sinuous willow roots, its fins flicked under the surface.

"Look," said Rewi. "Eel. That's a big one, must be a paewai, not a good one to catch, those black eels are bad luck."

The eel disappeared in a gap in the roots.

"So why doesn't she move into town?" asked Sandra.

"My koro says you can't leave the land. It's like your whole family, the land, can't just leave it."

"But the river stinks down there."

"Yeah, hard, eh? Like my koro says, you can't leave your whānau when it's sick, Sandra."

Sandra stopped asking questions. If she had a baby like Iripeta, one she loved as much as Iripeta did, she would want to live in a house with a bathroom and running water and a heater. Not in a shed in a paddock with a stinking river.

"Sandra," said Rewi.

He put an arm around her and pulled her close. She shuffled over and one of her arms draped itself over his knee, as if it belonged there.

"Lady Macbeth, eh? Will you hit me if I kiss you?"

A fantail flicked its erect tail close to their faces, chirping at the feast of insects disturbed by the two of them, melting each other into the pumice bank. The gritty pumice bank, warmed by the sun, shifted under their weight, remembering eruption and the lightness of flying. Their bodies pressed, softness holding and yielding to urgent hardness. His big, soft lips landed on her smile that moved to meet the sweet sensation of being kissed and kissed again. Almost. Almost.

Uninvited, a small white shape formed itself under Sandra's closed eyes. Fur-less, rat-like, a half formed possum foetus being smothered by coils of greenish intestine.

"Stop. Stop."

Sandra disentangled her legs from Rewi's, pushing at him and scrambling up off the warm bank. She ran. Away, from the soft lips and the pulsing of her whole body, from the hardness pressing against her leg, from his dark flushed face.

In the river, the eel called paewai snaked off from the roots of the willows, carrying its omens to another darkness.

Chapter Fifteen

Sandra had suggested to her father that, for her mother's birthday, they all go to the pictures in the new picture theatre. He'd agreed to come home from the pub in time for the dinner she'd help her mother cook. Meanwhile, there was the dirty washing that had piled up and needed sorting. She pushed her arm down into the sleeve of Amy's blue cardigan. The warmth of the wool against her skin stopped her.

Warmth, her body said, closeness, being held, Rewi's arms wrapping her, his legs twining with hers, his body pushing into hers and the heat from her belly bringing their fingers, knees, ears into one pulsing singularity. Us, her body yearned, us.

"Penny for your thoughts, Sandra?" Amy said from the floor, leaning on her elbow and turning her face up to her sister.

Sandra startled. For a moment she felt Amy look straight into her and she knew that Amy could read every sensation, every wicked thought. She shook the jersey out and shook her sister's sentience away with it.

"Nope," she said. "Not for sale."

Amy smiled as if she knew what the thoughts were anyway and went back to spreading colours on the white puddle of paper on the floor. The cat tapped at the moving pencil and she blew in his face. Shadows showed through the frosted glass at the front door and the doorbell croaked.

"Someone's at the door, Mum," yelled Amy.

"Well answer it then," came a voice from the kitchen.

"I'll get it," Sandra said.

She couldn't make out who the two figures wavering through the glass were and hoped it wasn't Miss from school. Mum hadn't gone to school to keep the appointment about extra exams. She opened the door. It was Mrs Simpson from next door and a small man all in black: a black suit, a black hat, a black shirt, with a white band around his neck. It was the Catholic father.

"Hello, dear," Mrs Simpson said. "Is your mother in?"

"Yes, I'll go and get her," Sandra said.

She poked Amy with her toe as she went past, mouthing "What are they here for?"

Amy rolled over, pulling herself up from the floor.

"Oh, it's you, Our Father, I mean Father Searle," she said. "Have you come to talk to mum about me being a Catholic?"

Sandra stared from the lounge doorway. Goodness knows how Mum would deal with this. Father Searle removed his hat.

"Well, yes, we have Miss Amy," he said. "Your father too, if he's home."

"Oh, no, Dad's not home. He doesn't come home much. He's working, you know, or he's down the pub with his mates."

By the time Sandra came back into the room with her mother, Amy had swept all of the washing into a pile on the sofa and Father Searle and Mrs Simpson were sitting awkwardly on the edge, damp towels and crumpled underwear beside them. Sandra stood close to her mother.

"Mrs McLeod," Father Searle said. "You have two lovely daughters here. I haven't really talked to your biggest girl yet but I've met your Amy, she came to see me."

Sandra watched her mother as she wiped her hands on her apron. That look was tiding into her mother's eyes, the one that came when the world was too big and threatened to engulf her. She kept wiping her hands, the apron pulling tight as her fingers clenched and unclenched. The cat wove its way between her legs.

"Mum's a bit busy, right now," Sandra said.

"Oh, it's all right Sandra," Mrs Simpson said. "Father Searle was wondering what Amy meant. She told him that she wants to be a Catholic, you see, and he was wondering what your mum and dad thought about that."

"Dad's not here," Sandra said.

"Mrs McLeod, your lovely little girl here wants to come to our church and I was wondering, I been thinking maybe it would be a good idea to talk about your whole family. Would you all be interested in coming, to St Gerard's church I mean. God welcomes all-comers you know."

"No thank you, I don't want any, thank you. Thank you for coming. No, I don't want any today," her mother said and, with her hands still twisting her apron, she backed to the door, held the door frame for a moment, then bolted for the kitchen.

In the silence that followed her mother's retreat, Sandra shifted her stare to Father Searle's shiny black shoes and blinked, hard.

"Are you all right dear?" asked Mrs Simpson.

Sandra nodded.

"Oh, dear," Father Searle said. "I'm sorry, I didn't mean to upset your family. Your little sister's so clear, you see, she wants to come to the Catholic church. She's welcome, but she can't become a true Catholic without the teaching of the catechism and we can't do that without your parents' permission, preferably with them coming too."

"I don't think Mum can give that, Father," Sandra said. "I could ask Dad and see what he says, if you like, except he's not here right now."

"Well, Bea," Father Searle said. "I think if Miss Amy wants to come to church, she can come with your family. I want to know about you, young lady, what about you, how are you keeping your spirit strong?"

Amy was still on the floor. Coloured pencils were placed neatly in their tin next to a large sheet of newsprint. Looking up at her from Amy's picture was a woman in a blue and green flowing dress, with enormous eyes, ambiguous eyes that invited and accused. She was holding a very small swaddled baby. Sandra could feel the hugeness of the woman and how she was flowing in and around the tiny body.

"I'm all right," she said.

"Well, we won't keep you any longer dear," Mrs Simpson said. "Looks like you're really busy. Don't see you so much these days. Don't you forget, we're just next door if you need us."

Sandra opened the door to let them out. Father Searle was almost the same height as her. As he went past, he put one hand on her shoulder and she could see herself in his little round glasses.

She shut the door behind them. She could just hear what they would be saying as they walked back to the Simpson house, about her father being at the pub or at work all the time, and especially about her mother's strangeness. A deep sense of shame soured her belly.

"Get your stuff up off the floor, Amy," she said. "Look, it's a real mess. I don't know why you keep drawing that same stupid picture all the time anyway."

Amy carried on drawing. With her red pencil she drew a heart in each of the corners of the paper, colouring them in hard. They sat like bright red blood on the page.

"I'm going to be a Catholic, Sandra," she said,

"You can't always get what you want, Amy, remember that."

"Even what *you* want, Sandra?"

Sandra didn't reply.

"I'm going to be a Catholic. Even if Mum and Dad don't say I can. I don't think they care anyway."

Sandra sat down on the dirty clothes. She tried to bring back the feeling of warmth that Rewi imprinted on her body, the hard strong arms and the heartbeat that promised the same rhythm forever.

I don't think they care anyway, oozed into her. The dirty little words rubbed themselves inside her, smudging and soiling. She grabbed at the washing, her careful sorting for nothing, pulled it into one big heap and stamped to the back door. She stood there with her arms full of the everyday dirt of her family, stopped by the impossibility of turning the door handle. A small hand came up from behind her.

"Here," Amy said. "I'll open the door for you."

Later that day Sandra sat her mother down in front of the dressing table. She looked at the two faces in the mirror, both with the same green eyes and ran the tail comb through the thick, dark hair that was just like hers; hair that came to a widow's peak on the forehead, forever denoting mourning. Hers was straight and long and tied back; her mother's permed with chemicals that smelled of ammonia, from a box bought at the chemist. Her father used to help his wife apply the lotion and rinse it off in the kitchen sink. Now it was Sandra who cared enough to put on the rubber gloves and guard her mother's eyes from the caustic chemicals. It was the least she could do.

"Let's give your hair a bit of a tease up, Mum," she said. "Give it a bit more height."

"Ooh, I don't know dear," her mother said. "It makes it all tangled and the knots are hard to get out."

"Oh, come on Mum, it'll look real nice. I won't do much. We'll make you real glamorous, look, I'll put some of my hairspray on too."

"I hope your father hasn't forgotten," her mother said, and her face in the mirror began to pucker and the frown lines settle in. Sandra hoped he hadn't, too.

"He won't," Sandra said. "It was his idea, anyway. Now, look, let's get your hair all done, then you can get changed after we've had tea. Dad will want a wash anyway. He said we'll take the car."

"Sandra," her mother said. "Sandra, love, you're fifteen now, you're a woman. You need to watch yourself. With boys I mean. You'll be getting a boyfriend soon, I suppose. They'll have their hand up your skirt quick as all look out. And you know what that means."

Sandra could feel that heat in her neck. It would creep up into her face any time now and she would be hotly, redly exposed. She held her breath. She didn't want her mother, or her father either, to know about her and Rewi and the kisses and the hands. She pulled a strand of her mother's hair tight and pushed the metal comb back against its natural growth. It tangled under her fingers.

"I don't know, love," continued her mother. "It all seems so exciting when you're young then it all seems to change. The babies come and men need, well you know, and if you don't feel like giving it, they seem to just not love you any more."

Sandra breathed very quietly, allowing the blood to settle back from her face and neck. She smoothed the top layer of her mother's hair over the tangled teasing she'd caused. She picked up the hairspray can, shook it hard and sprayed the light, buoyant curls so they sat rigid. She checked her handy-work in the mirror, avoiding looking in the eyes that were like hers, that were oozing tears again.

"Mum, you're making your powder run," Sandra said. "Here, here's your compact. Do your face again. I'm just going to check the dinner."

The pie was on the table and the knives and forks laid out. Still in his work clothes, minus his boots, her father stood by the fridge with a beer bottle in one hand and a bottle of lemonade in the other. When her mother came in, Sandra pulled out a chair for her. Her mother's face was freshly powdered and held rigid to match her curls. Her party hair, teased and lacquered, looked out of place with her old house- dress.

"Well, Betty, happy birthday, love," her father said. "Thought you might like a shandy, and the girls too. We can all drink your health."

"Your hair looks really good, Mum," Amy said.

"Do you like it?" she said, touching it gently.

Sandra wiped her hands on her mother's apron. She nudged her father.

"You look beautiful, my bonny lassie," her father said.

He placed a pale glass of half beer, half lemonade next to her plate and bent to kiss her. She lifted her head, hesitantly, her lips trembling into a pucker. He dropped a quick peck and turned to fetch another glass. Her mother's face stayed uplifted for a few seconds longer, the lips still puckered, the face expectant. Then it started to slide into the folds and lines of sourness. Sandra saw the decision point when her mother pulled her back straight, took a breath and made a smile.

"I'm going to church tomorrow morning, with Mrs Simpson," Amy said. "Does anyone want to come? Father Searle asked me last week if any of my family were interested."

Sandra kicked her under the table.

"What's this?" asked her father. "You going to the Catholic church? What do you want to do that for?"

"I want to be a Catholic, Dad, and Father Searle said I could go to church but he would rather we all went."

"There's no way I want to be a Mickey Doolan," her father said. He frowned at his wife.

"Did you know about this?"

She shook her head and one hand crept up to pat at her hair.

"Oh, it's just that Amy wants to go because her friends go, Dad," Sandra said. "She thinks it's neat because they do stuff together, picnics and socials and things. Can we have ice-creams for pudding, please Dad? I didn't make a pudding. Me and Amy will do the dishes because we're already dressed. You need to get your good dress on, Mum. Are we walking or are we going in the car?"

"Now hang on," her father said. "Let me get this clear. Noone in this family is becoming a Mick. If you want to go to church Amy, with the Simpsons, that's all right. I know them, they're good people, but there'll be no more talk about becoming one of them."

"Give me your plate, Amy," Sandra said, interrupting the breath that Amy was taking. "Come on, we're going to do the dishes. You can borrow some of my lipstick, if you like, the pink one."

They were early for the film and sat in the best seats, at the back, as the cinema filled up. The leather was cold against Sandra's stockinged legs. She slumped in the seat, trying not to catch the eye of her classmates who'd come with boyfriends and friends. She seemed to be the only one in the cinema with her family. Finally the lights went down and everyone stood up as the *National Anthem* played. The Queen, sitting straight on her horse, had her lipstick precisely applied and it glowed red to match her neat, military coat. Sandra stole a sideways look at her mother and frowned at the blurred red lipstick that smudged into the lines around her mouth. She'd refused to let Sandra repair it, saying her hair was enough. Sandra ran her tongue around her own pink lips. The lipstick tasted soapy and unpleasant. She so wished she hadn't come.

The film was *South Pacific*. 'Make happy talk,' said the mother of the brown girl. 'Make it to the white American.' When the lights in the cinema came up and the screen showed "Intermission" in loopy writing, Sandra looked around. There were three girls from her class, leaning against their boyfriends and one blonde girl was smoking a cigarette. Sandra wondered if her parents knew.

"Can we go and get ice-creams now, Dad?" Amy asked.

"Not for me, lass. But I'll get some for you three."

They were standing out in the foyer, carefully holding soggy ice-cream cones, when Miss came over.

"Hello, Sandra," she said. "This is lucky. This must be your mum and dad – hello Mr and Mrs McLeod, I'm Sandra's English teacher."

She held out her hand. Her mother swapped her ice-cream over, fumbling with her handbag. Her father's forefinger went up to touch his hat, he corrected himself and shook the hand that was offered, clearing his throat.

"I'm so glad I ran into you," she continued. "We tried to make an appointment to see you both at school. Never mind, I can tell you briefly what we would have discussed. Your Sandra is doing very well, she's a clever girl. The school has registered her to sit an extra subject in School Certificate so she'll be doing six subjects instead of five."

There was no response from her parents.

"Thank you, Miss," Sandra said.

"You should do well, Sandra," she continued. "I expect a university career for you. Just you keep studying, don't let yourself be distracted by that boy Rewi."

She smiled and walked away. Sandra's high collar hid the red flush but it was well on its way up her cheeks. When the bell for the end of interval played, she was the first back to her seat.

In the second half of the film the white man sang about the importance of learning to hate all the people your relatives hate. He didn't have a happy ending, neither did the brown girl he was supposed to learn to hate.

As soon as their father started the car, Amy started the questions.

"Why couldn't he just marry that brown girl?" she said. "He loved her, didn't he? And her mother wanted them to get married."

"A mixed marriage isn't a good idea, Amy," their father said.

"Why? You came from Scotland and Mum came from England and you got married."

"If there's a mixed marriage the children don't know where they belong. They don't know if they're from one race or the other."

"I know I'm from New Zealand," Amy said.

"That's enough. I don't want you girls marrying anyone with a bit of the tar brush in them. It's not right. It's not good for the children when you have them."

Amy made a face at Sandra and whispered.

"So I can't be a Catholic and you, what aren't you allowed Sandra?"

There it was again, that feeling that those blue eyes saw straight into her. Sandra sat back on the leather seat, its plastic covers cold and slippery, and looked out at the black road, its white markings stark under the street lights.

Chapter Sixteen

Kawerau October 1959

"Mum," called Sandra down the hallway. "Do you want bacon and eggs?"

She listened for a moment but there was silence. She could open the door to the bedroom where her mother had been when she got home, probably asleep. Sandra didn't really want to wake her up. It was too hard to know what kind of reaction she'd get. Sometimes her mother was a vague person who barely seemed to remember where she was, as if she was living in another country. Last week, when she got home from school, she'd walked into the bedroom and her father was lying between her mother's legs and he was grunting as he pushed up and down. He hadn't seen her, but her mother had—or at least, she might have. Her mother's face, already turned towards the door, seemed to be pleading 'rescue me,' as if she was drowning. Sandra had left the door ajar and gone right to the other end of the house. As her father left for work, he'd said goodbye but she'd pretended to be looking for something under the sofa.

Someone needed to get Amy some tea because swimming club started promptly at six and it was after five already. Amy had her togs on, with her school dress over the top, and she was crouching on the kitchen floor, wrapping up her underwear in a towel.

"She prob'ly doesn't, but can I have her bacon and some baked beans too?"

"Ooah, Amy, look at those knickers. When did you last have clean ones?"

"There aren't any clean ones."

"Didn't Mum do the washing on Saturday?"

"I don't know but there's no clean knickers in my drawer."

Sandra sighed. She'd been doing the washing more often lately.

"I'll do some washing tonight, when I get home," she said, "and hang it out in the morning. You'll have to help me hang it out, Amy, or I'll be late for school again."

"Where are you going tonight and why're you all dressed up?"

Sandra blushed. She leant down to get the frying pan out of the cupboard.

"I'm not dressed up," she said. "I just finished making this in sewing so I want to wear it. Anyway, I thought I'd come with you to swimming club. I need to talk to Rewi about the homework Miss gave us, and he said he'd meet me by the swimming pool."

"Rewi'll like your dress. Are you going to marry him, like I'm going to marry Robert?"

"Don't be silly, we just help each other with our homework," Sandra said.

She reached for the tin of fat from the fridge.

"Do you want your eggs all runny?" she asked.

"Is there any bread to dip in them?"

Sandra looked in the cupboard. The bread was mouldy on the edges. She could cut it off.

"I'll make toast," she said.

They left the dishes in the sink. Amy promised she'd do them when they got home. She wobbled out of the driveway on her bike and there was Robert, carefully pushing his foot back so the back brakes didn't lock and stepping off his bike next to the letterbox.

"I never noticed before, Robert," Sandra said. "You've got a girl's bike. Don't your brothers tease you about it?"

"I have learned to take no notice of my brothers, Sandra," Robert said. "They are so immature. Are you going to win tonight, Amy?"

"I'm full of baked beans," Amy said. "Maybe I can blow off lots, like a jet boat, and be first."

Robert nodded, his face serious.

"You need to be careful, Sir says you get cramp if you go swimming straight after eating."

They wobbled off on their bikes and Sandra had a sudden glimpse of the two of them, middle-aged, going shopping for groceries together, discussing what colour curtains to put in the lounge.

The smell of sulphur got stronger as Sandra came closer to the fence around the swimming pool. Sulphur Hill was steaming quietly, its blackened manuka hiding the Boy Scouts sitting on the patchy grass outside their den, promising to do a good turn every day and to always tell the truth. Life should be that simple. She wasn't telling the truth, but she was doing her parents a good turn by not telling them about Rewi, especially her father. She crossed the road, following Amy and Robert to the bike stand.

"I have to go and get ready," Amy said. "It's my freestyle race first. Can you look after my things, Sandra, someone's been stealing from the changing sheds again."

"Oh yeah, they'll really want your dirty knickers," Sandra said.

"You shouldn't say things like that," said Robert. "You make Amy feel embarrassed."

Married twenty years, thought Sandra as she watched the two of them go in the entrance. Out of the corner of her eye she could see Rewi peeling himself off the concrete wall, keeping his hands in his pockets. This was the first time she'd seen him out of school uniform and he looked much older, even though his white shirt was still hanging out.

"Nice dress," he said.

Sandra glowed at the way his eyes went from her face, to her feet, and back to her face. She smiled.

"Shall we go and watch your little sister in her race?"

He was standing very close and his hand brushed hers. Sandra remembered Amy's question. The answer was that her parents wouldn't agree to her marrying Rewi.

They sat on the scrubby grass at the far end of the pool, away from the starting blocks and parents looking official with their clipboards and stopwatches. Some discreet sense had informed Robert that he should sit a distance away. Amy teetered alongside the pool, her towel fat with her belongings, with her mismatched shoes in one hand.

She dropped her shoes and used one hand to balance herself as she knelt down on the pool edge. She unrolled her towel, pulling out her bathing cap. As she stood up, she staggered and Robert was at her side catching her elbow, catching her balance for her. He bent to get the bathing cap.

Amy stood against the evening sun, the gold fingering her blonde hair and it haloed around her small, intent face.

She's thin. She's so thin she looks as if she could just fly off, any time. Sandra felt a shiver go from her hairline and feather its cold prescience down her spine. The cold lodged itself deep in her middle. Robert handed Amy her bathing cap. *Thank goodness for Robert, he's holding her here.*

Amy stuffed her hair into the cap. She looked even smaller.

"You're shivering, Amy," Sandra said.

"Here, you need to wrap yourself up in your towel, keep warm," Robert said.

He grabbed the end of the towel and pulled. Amy's underwear went flying. Sandra tidied quickly, hiding the not quite clean knickers from Rewi. She and Rewi weren't an old married couple. Amy and Robert walked back along the side of the pool, to wait for the beginning of the race.

"Your little sister," said Rewi. "She's like patupaiarehe."

The word floated, not easy to catch.

"She's what?"

"She's patupaiarehe. She's a fairy child, like a spirit of something."

Sandra frowned. The cold in her core deepened.

The whistle sounded and the under-thirteens stepped up on the diving blocks. Amy was at the end where the shadow of the hill was reaching. She stood half in its dark. The starting gun sounded and six bodies threw themselves into the water.

"She's staying under the water a long time," said Rewi. "Is she all right? Look, all those others are up and swimming, can you see your sister?"

The last of the sun was catching the fractured surface of the pool, glinting back its light. Sandra squinted, trying to see below. There it was, a white, shrunken leg, paddling the water away, then it was gone again. Now you see it, now you don't.

She pushed herself up from the ground, just as Amy surfaced. Amy had stayed under the water for almost a quarter of the length of the pool. Sandra's heart pounded, she could hear it, like water surging in her ears. Rewi's fingers interlaced hers and he held her hand tight.

Amy came last in her race. She had to try three times to pull herself out of the pool. Robert wrapped her up in her towel. Sandra watched him fussing and he walked close to her as they came back along the pool edge. Amy was shivering.

"Amy, you need to get yourself dressed, you're freezing," Sandra said.

"She's still there," Amy said.

Amy took her clothes and limped into the dressing sheds.

"What's she talking about?" asked Rewi.

"It's a ghost," Robert said. "Amy's got a ghost, an old lady who lives in the water."

"Don't listen to him," Sandra said. "Amy's got a vivid imagination."

"Well, I believe her," Robert said.

Sandra and Rewi sat on the grass. Sandra smoothed her dress down over her knees. The surface of the pool was settling again, smoothing itself before the next onslaught of swimmers.

"My koro had Father Searle come and see him the other day," said Rewi. "He said there's a little girl who sees an old lady, Father said it's a spirit. He said the little girl wants the Virgin Mary to help her. Is that your sister he's talking about?"

"Oh, probably. She's decided she wants to be a Catholic and I bet she's told Father Searle about it. She's been seeing ghosts for a long time, since she was small. It's embarrassing, all these people knowing about her silliness. I'm sick of her nonsense."

"I think Father Searle took her seriously," said Rewi. "He and my koro were talking about coming round to your house and doing special prayers."

Sandra put her head down, she didn't want to meet Rewi's eyes. She poked at an ant nest at the edge of the concrete. The ants scattered randomly, scrambling to get away from her stick, from the threat of something that was beyond their comprehension. When Father Searle had visited their house, her mother had backed out of the room, her eyes wildly looking for some reference point to anchor her.

"Here she comes," Rewi said. "Look, she is like a patupaiarehe."

Sandra felt the coldness grow. Her mother had enough ghosts, without having to deal with Amy. She dropped the stick on top of the ant nest.

They walked home into the coming dark. The shadows crept up the mountain, eating the light, pulling the weight of its solidity into the night. By the time they reached the corner, the dark was almost complete.

"See you at home," called Amy as she and Robert pedalled fast to get the dynamos on their bike lights to work.

"Don't forget the dishes," called Sandra.

Rewi and Sandra walked the long way, past the deserted garage, moving on to the pumice road when the footpath ran out. There were no sounds, no people, and they walked quietly. Sandra shivered.

"You cold?" asked Rewi.

"No, just a shiver up my spine. My mum would have said a

goose just walked over my grave."

"That doesn't make sense. You haven't got a grave, or a goose."

"Neither does Amy being a, what did you say, a patu something."

They were silent again. Their footsteps were absorbed by the pumice, which gleamed white in the last of the light.

"That's a flash dress you're wearing," said Rewi.

"Mmm. I made it, in sewing. Miss made me undo it three times, to get the zip in straight."

"Looks nice."

Maybe she should have said, 'Glad you like it,' or 'Oh, this old thing,' or… anyway, he probably wasn't interested in how dumb she was at getting a zip straight. He took her hand. He ran the soft underside of his thumb on the inside of her palm. She breathed him in, soap, sweat, sweet. She swallowed. She could feel every part of her body, her bra strap cutting into her back, her hair heavy on her neck, the pumice sticking in her sandals. The night air pushed against her, tingling her. They reached the old pines where the darkness was thick and the air was heavy with a sharp pungency.

There were no words. The soft pine needles made no complaint as they sat, or even as they lay. A tentativeness of hands and lips began. Sandra wanted his lips on her neck, she arched her back and his hand reached and held her breast. His leg was over her hip and he was hard against her belly. Her dress was up over her hips, her knickers around her ankles. She kicked them away and reached for his belt. Her hands were urgent and the blood was beating in her ears. It carried away the flash of her father, humping up and down, and her mother's mute plea. It carried away the flicker of green, coiled intestines and a small, very small white baby possum. A fierce wanting pushed her whole self towards him, meeting him. He rolled her on her back, and arched his body over her as he pushed into hers. It hurt. A piercing hurt that went from her core, engulfed her and carried her with it to a place of such intensity that the pain didn't matter. She was drowning but, she didn't want to be rescued.

Then it was done.

"Are you all right?" asked Rewi.

"I think so."

"Did I hurt you?"

"Yes, but …" But what, but she'd wanted it as much as he had? That it was a pain that was worth it?

"But I'm all right."

"Lady Macbeth, at this rate we'll have to get married and have ten kids."

Sandra caught her breath. Married with ten kids. This was soft melding into each other, a finger stroking the down on the baby's head. It was Amy, staying too long under the water, afraid of what she found there, also needing protection. That was when the ghostly cold crept in. The cold that took over the warm pain in the core of her, sat heavy and solid, more real than the red heat of him deep in her body. She shivered.

"Another goose, Lady Macbeth?" he asked and kissed her gently, his soft black moustache tickling her nose.

She lay in bed that night, with a sanitary towel pinned between her legs and a dull aching warmth in her belly. She touched her lips, softly, and ran her hand over her neck, to get to know this new person, and smiled at Elvis, who was still gazing out the window, longing for something far away.

In a hollow of pine needles, bark oozed sticky resin to mix with the blood and semen. A light dust of pollen drifted down from a stamen in its nest of sharp needles and caught in the open edges of a pinecone.

Chapter Seventeen

Kawerau October 1959

A letter for Mrs E. McLeod had sat on the table for two days. The queen on the stamp looked down her nose at the address. So she should, Kawerau had been mis-spelt—it said Kawarau and the letter had travelled the length of the country before finding its way to this town. Sandra put her porridge plate down and a little milk slopped on to the envelope. She wiped it off and turned the letter over. A letter with an address typed on the back was unusual, the address even more so; Heffernan and Sons from somewhere in London.

"Do you want jam and cheese on your sandwiches?" Amy asked.

"No thanks." *Maybe I should open it.*

"What about marmite and cheese?"

"No thanks." *Maybe I should take it in to Mum and make sure she opens it. Maybe if I took a cuppa tea in.*

"Well, what do you want?"

"No thanks." *Maybe I should wait until Dad comes home and make sure he makes sure Mum opens it. Maybe....*

"What do you mean, no thanks," Amy said. "You're not listening. You're away with the fairies these days, Sandra."

Sandra propped the letter back up against the sugar bowl. She looked down at the porridge in her plate, grey lumps floating in milk looked back up at her.

"You'll have to make your own lunch," Amy said. "I'm on road patrol duty, I've got to go."

Sandra waved vaguely at Amy. She didn't feel much like eating breakfast this morning. Slimy dollops stuck in the drain holes when she tipped it down the sink. A knife was poking out of the jam, its handle sticky. She wiped the thick redness on to a piece of white bread. It smelled strong and rich. That would do for lunch.

She decided to open the letter.

It was only one page with an address in the top right hand corner. A formal address for a lawyers' firm. The full stops and commas were all in the right place, just like in the textbook. The words were correct too: 'we regret to inform you' it said, and 'as the next of kin.' It seemed to be about someone called Mavis Katherine Stokes. Sandra frowned. *Who was Mavis Katherine Stokes?* She'd leave the letter for Dad, he'd be home tonight, probably, after the pub. She took her jam sandwich with her to school. Double geography beckoned.

"You'll need to be able to draw in the features of one map," said the geography teacher. "You'll have the outline in the exam paper and it depends what the question is, it may be about geology, for example. If you're asked about geology, what will you be marking on your map?"

A piece of chalk hit the blackboard. There were titters around the room. Sandra turned to the noise that was growing in the back. Two boys were pushing at each other and a chair fell over, delivering one of them to the floor.

"Not again," said Rewi "Why's it always in geography?"

"You. Smith. Out. And you, what's your name, out you go," the teacher said.

"It's not fair, Sir, what's his name started it," said Smith.

The class laughed.

"I don't care, you're upsetting the whole class and it's only six weeks to your first school certificate exam. Some people want to pass exams, you know. Out, out, both of you."

He pointed at the door. The two slouched forward from the back of the room and left by the other door. The class laughed again.

"That's my cousin, the 'what's his name' one," said Rewi. "My koro will be mad at him. He's always in trouble."

His hand brushed her cheek as he whispered. Sandra felt the tingle warm her and moved her leg over to lean against his.

"Now, where was I?" continued the geography teacher. "If you're asked a question about the geology of the United Kingdom, you'll be putting in the rock types. You'll need to memorise at least two maps, the other one is the climate map. We've done both of these. I want you to find them in your notes, come up and get a couple of map stamps, and practise filling them in."

"I'll get your stamps, Rewi," Sandra said. "You find the notes."

She queued at the front of the class.

"Can tell what you've been doing," said a voice behind her. "You and that Māori boy, you've been sleeping together."

Sandra recognised the voice. Maria was standing behind her in the line, her eyebrows arched. Sandra looked around to see if anyone else had heard. Once she would have blushed a deep red but not now, not now because she was part of that club, with the password.

"So what?" she said.

She leaned down to press the curve of the United Kingdom on paper, tilted her head and smiled a little half smile.

"You know who the father of Iripeta's baby is, don't you?" Maria said.

The map stamp slipped but when Sandra looked up, Maria had gone. The map was smudged. Sandra was sure he would have told her. They're cousins, that's why her baby looked like him. No other reason.

In English they were revising letter writing: business letters, letters of complaint, informal letters. The textbook was boringly exact and there seemed to be a lot of people writing complaints about shoes that didn't fit well. Rewi was scratching his head, making his hair stick up even more.

"How do you remember where to put all the full stops?" he

muttered. "Look, one after E S Q—what's an esk anyway? Dumb language, English. Should just call everyone matua, doesn't need a full stop."

Sandra leaned down to get her ruler out of her bag. The floor slipped sideways and, like when she used to go round and round the washing line then lie on the grass, she lost direction and any sense of where she was rooted. Spinning in some other world, somewhere with no solidity with a deep pulse pulling at its edges, a heartbeat world, pulling her into its darkness. She closed her eyes and leaned her head against the wooden edge of her desk.

"Sandra, are you all right?"

The floor was being anchored by a pair of black shoes. Sandra looked up past the stockinged legs. It was Miss, standing next to her desk. The world settled back into its curves and lines.

"Um, yes. I think so. I didn't have breakfast this morning."

"Well, that's not very sensible. Gather yourself together, I want to talk to you about next year. Rewi, we've had the paperwork for your scholarship for St Paul's. I'll be sending it off today. It looks good. Your exam results have been excellent, and a vast improvement in English. I think you can be thanked for that, Sandra, am I right?"

"Yes, Miss," replied Sandra.

"What about you, Sandra? I really want you back here next year for sixth form. What do your parents think?"

"I don't know, Miss. They want me to get a job, I think."

"Well, get them to come and see me. You've got a university career ahead of you if you apply yourself."

It all seemed too hard: Rewi would be going, she'd have to talk to her parents about visiting school. She stared at the page in front of her, with its correctly punctuated address and the letter she had read at breakfast repeated itself in her head: *We regret to inform you as the next of kin of the death of Mavis Katherine Stokes....*

"It's Aunty Kath," she said. "My Aunty Kath's died."

"What?" said Rewi.

"The letter, I opened it this morning. It said someone had died. It's my Aunty Kath, in England."

"What do you mean, didn't it say her name in the letter?"

"No. I mean, yes. It did, with her other name, she's got another name and I forgot. I forgot. I haven't seen her for years. I forgot her name."

"You need to go home? Be with your whānau?"

"No. Dad will need to tell Mum." *And I don't want to be there when he does.*

The letter was missing when Sandra got home. She went down the hallway and the bedroom door was shut.

"Mum, Mum," she called, knocking quietly. "Mum, are you all right?"

There was silence. She opened the door gently. The room was dark, its blinds drawn. It took a moment for Sandra's eyes to adjust. The bed was empty and its rumpled sheets showed it had recently been occupied. Her mother was sitting at the dressing table, staring into the mirror.

"Mum, are you all right?" Sandra said.

Her mother kept her eyes on her reflection. One hand came up. With her forefinger, she pushed a stray curl away from her face. Her eyes focused on the world beyond the mirror. She was smiling gently at this place, beyond the glass.

"Mum?" Sandra said.

On the dressing table were doillies crocheted with fine cotton, by her mother; a brush and comb with hair strands captured and entwined; a hand mirror with a crack across the surface; an ashtray with a half burnt cigarette, the smoke drifting, insubstantial and, a single page with a perfectly punctuated address.

"Mum, it's Kath, isn't it? It's Aunty Kath, she's died," Sandra said.

"You can't borrow my red dress, not tonight," her mother said.

"Mum, Mum, stop it!"

"You think you look better in it, don't you Kath? Well, you don't.

I do. Ian thinks I look much nicer in it than you. You always wanted him, didn't you? Well, you can't have him, he's mine."

"Mum, what're you talking about?"

"Look, look, just have a look at this."

Her mother pulled open the drawer in front of her, hunching over, scrabbling with one hand amongst the underwear. She turned away from the mirror, narrowed her eyes and pushed a piece of paper at Sandra.

"You just have a look at this. He liked my letters. He kept them. Look, he read them, all the time. Go on, read it. Go on."

The goose had slipped across Sandra's grave and was shivering up her spine. She reached out and took the piece of paper. It was worn, its edges ragged where it had been folded and unfolded many times. She stood with it in her hand, impaled by her mother's eyes.

"Now, get out of here, get out."

Her mother turned and put her hands up to her ears, her elbows on the dressing table. There was a smell of singeing hair. Sandra gently took the cigarette from her mother's fingers, put it in the ashtray and left.

She closed the bedroom door, her hand shaking. In the hallway she opened the fragment of paper.

One day soon there will be no goodnights
Just settle down hold each other tight
Our love will grow stronger through the years
We shall know laughter kindness and tears
But when we are old bent and grey
We will keep loving each other every day

Sandra folded it carefully. There was no punctuation, she noticed.

Chapter Eighteen

Kawerau November 1959

She checked the calendar in her homework diary and counted the days again. Nine. She checked her underwear in the toilet again. Nothing. She poked a finger inside again. No blood. She frowned at the mirror on the bathroom cabinet. She looked pale. She felt sick. She was shaking, all of her was shaking.

She unlocked the bathroom door, put her diary back in her bag and went into the kitchen. Amy had left bread and a jar of jam sitting on the bench, plum, Sandra's favourite. As she screwed the lid down on the red jam, her stomach heaved. She filled a glass with water and sat down at the kitchen table.

"What's for dinner?" Amy asked.

"Bread and pullet."

"Ha, ha. No what's really for dinner?"

"I don't feel well. I think I've got a tummy bug. You can cook your delicious eggs for you and Mum."

"You mean the scrambled ones or the double fried ones?"

"Shut up, you're making me feel sick."

Sandra opened her French text book. There was a translation to do before the end of the week. She could concentrate on that.

"Where's your boyfriend tonight?"

"You mean Rewi? I don't know. He didn't turn up at the library. We were going to do this translation together."

"Not a good sign, Sandra. You need someone you're going to

marry to be punctual. Robert is."

"Are you going to make those eggs or not? If you are, I'm moving to my bedroom. The stink will make me really sick."

Sandra gathered her books up. She'd waited for half an hour for Rewi. He hadn't said he was coming to the library but then he never did, it was just assumed that he'd turn up and today he hadn't. Not a good sign, as Amy said.

The cat was asleep in the middle of her bed, in a puddle of sunshine. Sandra thumped down next to him, folded her arms and stared out the window. There was a lavender bush outside her bedroom. Her mother had planted it, to remind her of home. Tiny purple flowers were breaking out along the length of its plumes. She pushed open the window, catching a branch and it spilt its thick, heady scent. A bee had been industriously working the purpleness and was catapulted into the room. It buzzed against the glass, as if trying to drill its way through, throwing its stripy body at the barrier again and again. Sandra stared at it. Suddenly she was crying, sobbing.

For the frustration of it.

For the blind, unknowing persistence.

For no clear reason she could think of.

By the time she looked up, it had gone. She wiped her face with her hand and got on with her translation.

She must have gone to sleep, slumped against the wall. When she woke up it was almost dark and the streetlights were already pushing away the shadows outside. Across on the traffic island she could see two people on the swings, Amy and Richard. As one swung forward, the other swung back and for several breaths they were synchronised, in and out, in and out they went. Somewhere in the middle they amalgamated to make one figure. She reached for the bedside light, pushed the switch and they were gone. There was just her own reflection staring back at her. Now you see them, now you don't.

She stretched. Her neck ached from her awkward position on

the bed. As her body woke up she felt the nausea again and the shakiness inside.

"Sandra, Sandra," Amy called. "Come outside a minute."

Maybe a walk outside would help. She stood up. One leg had gone to sleep so she shook it. She left the front door open, shivering a bit as she stepped out of the porch, pulling her school cardigan close. One of the swings was still pushing its burden back and forward and now there were two figures sitting on the roundabout. There was Amy's white cardigan and someone else.

"Hello, Lady Macbeth," said Rewi.

Sandra's heart pounded. She tightened her folded arms protectively over it. She wanted to hit him. She wanted to kiss him. She wanted to run away.

"Oh, it's you," she said.

"Sorry about today," he said.

She looked down at the scuffed grass around the edge of the roundabout. She sniffed.

"Sorry about not coming to the library," he said.

She looked over to the swings, in and out they went, in and out.

"My koro turned up, at school," he said. "The one from Taupo. He's the one I grew up with."

She looked at his face. It was shadowed, dark. She wasn't sure she knew this one, the Rewi who grew up in Taupo.

"What did he come to school for?"

"To talk to Miss, about the scholarship," he said, "and to make sure I'm working hard. He had a big talk to me too."

He sat down on the roundabout, patting the section next to him. She leaned on the iron bar between them and he put his hand over hers.

"My koro said I have to get this scholarship," he said. "He told my mum and dad that I have to stay home every night and every weekend to study. He asked me if I had a girlfriend, too."

Sandra caught her breath. That song went through her head: the one about needing to be taught to hate the people your family hate. A wave of nausea radiated out from her belly.

"What did you say?"

"I told him about you, of course," he said.

Of course. She hadn't told her parents about Rewi.

"What did he say?"

"He just said that I had to get this scholarship," he said. "So, Lady Macbeth, we'll have to stop doing seeing each other so much, just until after School C."

"You'll come to the library tomorrow?"

"Can't," he said. "My koro's still here."

He kicked the concrete pad of the roundabout. They drifted gently round in a circle, light, floating.

"Who's that fulla with your little sister?"

"That's Richard. He lives over the road. He's not the full quid."

"He's what?"

"He's not the full quid. You know, one sandwich short of a picnic. Don't you know what that means?"

"Na. I'd say he's pōrangi."

"Anyway. His dad doesn't look after him, and his mum's dead. Amy looks after him quite a lot."

"Poor fulla," said Rewi. "He needs a whānau, everyone needs a whānau."

Richard jumped off the swing and headed across the traffic island to home. His shadow slipped past the letterbox and the dogs started to bark.

"Holy! What's that racket?" said Rewi.

A white cardigan hovered, materialising into Amy.

"That's the pig dogs. They nearly eat him every time he goes home," she said, and disappeared again towards her unlit house.

Rewi kicked at the concrete base. Round they went again, into the dark. On the shoulder of the mountain sat a thin moon. It was either the last of the old moon, or it was the beginning of the next. It was hard to tell if the tiny sliver of a moon was held in the arms of the old, or if the new was holding the old.

"Can you answer the door?" Sandra said.

"It's probably only Robert," Amy said. "He's early, it's only quarter past eight."

She scraped the last of the porridge from her plate, put it on the bench and went out of the kitchen to the back door.

Sandra poked the bottom of the pot. The porridge had stuck, it was slightly burnt. At least she'd eaten some today. Murmurs came from the back doorstep. It can't have been Robert, Amy would have just let him in. The back door slammed, shaking the kitchen window. The acrid smell of burnt milk jarred Sandra's nose and her mouth filled with saliva. The porridge in her belly shook itself upward. She pulled her hair back and bent over the sink as she vomited.

"Oh dear, you're not well," Mrs Simpson said.

Her voice floated in from the kitchen door as Sandra heaved up a second installment of her breakfast. Leaning on the kitchen bench so that she wouldn't fall over, she scooped some water into her mouth and rinsed out the sourness. Mrs Simpson put a hand on Sandra's back. Sandra blinked back tears and took a shaky breath.

"What's wrong, dear?"

"She's got a bad tummy bug," Amy said. "She's had it for two weeks and she can't eat much without being sick. She gets real sick when she eats porridge."

"You're trembling, poor little love," Mrs Simpson said. "Come and sit down."

Sandra was crying, tears trickled down her face, without any effort on her part. The vomiting had been getting worse. It left her cold, cold and shivering. It was hard to concentrate at school when she was hungry and feeling sick at the same time and she was tired to her very core. She'd almost fallen asleep in French yesterday.

"How long has this been going on, Sandra?" asked Mrs Simpson.

Sandra sniffed, the sour smell of recycled porridge in her nose. Mrs Simpson handed her a handkerchief, a big man-sized handkerchief.

"Sandra. How long?"

"About two weeks."

"What else is happening?"

Sandra worried the handkerchief into a ball. There was a matching hard lump in her throat and she was cold. What was happening was that she was heavy with fear, and worry, so heavy that she wished she could just sink through the floor. A tear tickled the end of her nose. She dabbed at it. She'd checked the calendar last night. Fifteen days. Today would be the sixteenth day, long days, days full of trying not to think about it.

"Well, I think I'm getting my, you know. I'm sure I am. My breasts are sore."

"How late is it?"

"Two weeks."

"Sandra, look at me. Come on, look up. You know, don't you?"

Sandra nodded. Yes, she knew. She stared at Mrs Simpson, willing her not to say it. If it wasn't said, it may not be true. She stopped breathing with the effort of getting Mrs Simpson not to say it.

"I know about pregnancy and it sounds to me as if you are. Can your mum take you to the doctors? He can do a test to confirm it."

Sandra slumped in the chair. She put her head down and shook her head, and kept shaking it. Another tear and another tear and another crawled down to gather on her chin. She'd have to tell her mother.

"Betty's not been out much lately," Mrs Simpson said. "She's taking your Aunty Kath's death quite hard, isn't she?"

"Mum's gone to live in her bedroom," Amy said. "We've been doing the washing and making the dinners, except Sandra's been sick so we have to have my special eggs a lot."

Sandra took a jagged breath and looked up.

"You and Rewi will just have to get married," Amy continued. "When you and him are sixteen, next year. Like me and Robert are, when we're sixteen."

"It's that Māori boy, is it Sandra?" Mrs Simpson said. "Oh dear.

Look, I'll get an appointment with the doctor for you. You promise me you'll tell your mother today. Then if she isn't up to taking you, I will. Your dad should be home tonight, he's not working is he?"

"Dad goes to the pub after work," Amy said. "He doesn't come home for dinner anymore. I don't think he likes my special eggs."

"Well," Mrs Simpson shook her head. "I'm picking Pat up at four, so I'll get your dad to come straight home. Now, promise me you'll tell both of them, won't you Sandra?"

Sandra nodded.

"Right, that's settled then," said Mrs Simpson. "Now, you two get yourselves off to school. Oh, and Amy, what I came for was to tell you that Father Searle's going to visit with Mr Watene. He said something about coming round to do special prayers for you."

After Mrs Simpson had gone, Amy and Sandra sat at the kitchen table in silence, staring out the window. The mountain had on its morning sunshine, the long, sleek slopes proud against a blue sky. The world still existed out there. The sun finally caught the small mound at the side of the big solidity.

"Look," Amy said. "The mountain's got a baby, like you. I'm going to be an aunty. Do you think you're going to have a girl or a boy? I want a little niece. A nice little niece."

Probably the day had no more hours in it than any other. Probably the sun shone all day. Probably Sandra managed to make sense when she talked. She didn't remember. She was only partly present to that sixteenth day of her late period. The one that Mrs Simpson called pregnancy. Most of her was worrying at what to do. *Should I make a cup of tea and take it in to Mum? Would I get Dad to get Mum out of the bedroom and sit them both down in the lounge? Should I say congratulations, you're going to be grandparents? Should I say your grandchild's got a touch of the tar-brush?*

The words from the Public Health Nurse floated between her and the map of the United Kingdom. *Shame, pregnant and not married*, they said. Maria's words banged around in her head—*You know who's the father of Iripeta's baby?* Rewi asked her if she was all right, but she couldn't tell him. She just said she'd been up late studying and he believed her. The first exam was in two weeks, he'd sat up late too. They agreed not to study together after school.

Amy turned the mince off when she heard their father's bike come up the side of the house. She stood close to Sandra, leaning slightly against her sister's body. As they waited, Sandra could hear the murmur of voices down the hallway. Her heartbeat counted the interminable moments; they stretched longer and longer. This waiting could just be the rest of her life. She could float here, held by the familiarity of the kitchen, not telling anyone and nothing would need to change. She started when her father came into the kitchen with her mother trailing behind him. Her mother was dishevelled, her hair was unbrushed and it was as if she was sleepwalking. She sat on a kitchen chair, perching on the edge.

"Is this about your exams, Sandra?" asked her father. "Pat told me that the teacher's been singing your praises, lass."

He sat down opposite his wife.

"I'm pregnant."

Just like that. The words were out. They were said. They could never be taken back. They were out in the world, heavy words, sitting on the table. Her mother looked over Sandra's left shoulder as if she was talking to someone else.

"Can you get the spuds on, Sandra? I'm just going to lie down for a bit."

"Sit down, Betty, for Chrissake," her father said.

Sandra opened and shut her mouth. Maybe she hadn't said 'I'm pregnant.' Maybe she just thought she had. Maybe she wouldn't need to. Maybe it was a mistake. A sour taste came up to tell her she'd have to try again.

"Did you hear me? Mum? I said I'm pregnant."

Her father's fist came down on the table.

"What do you mean, you're bloody pregnant?" he shouted.

The sugar bowl rattled. Sandra jumped and Amy's arm came round her middle. They leaned on each other. A small island stranded on the cold, green lino of the kitchen floor.

"I heard you the first time, Sandra. I don't know what you want me to do about it. You made your bed, now you have to lie in it. Now I'm going to have a little rest."

Her mother walked out of the kitchen.

"Jesus bloody Christ," swore her father. "This bloody family. You'd better see to your mother, Sandra."

He stormed out of the kitchen and slammed the back door. His bike flashed past the window.

Sandra was looking down a long, long tunnel. At the end of the tunnel she could see a young woman sitting at a kitchen table. The young woman had her head in her hands. She was curling herself inwards, like a possum protecting its underbelly. She was curling herself inward over a handful of cells that were making her feel sick and over a deep, deep hurt. She could hear a heartbeat, lubdub, lubdub. It got louder, until it filled the world and rocked her possum body in its sound. No, it was her, Sandra, she was rocking herself, her curled-up-self on the hard kitchen chair, with the cold, green lino at her feet. The heartbeat subsided, burying itself again in her body.

"I don't know what to do," she told the sugar bowl.

She put her head down in her arms and cried from her soft underbelly. A small hand reached in, under the sheltering arc she'd made for herself and pulled. Amy. She insisted they try again, that Mum would be all right, she really would.

They stood in the doorway of the bedroom.

"Mum? Mum?" Sandra said. "I don't know what to do, Mum."

Her mother squinted at her through the smoke of her cigarette.

"Do?" she said. "I'll tell you what to do. You get a douche, from the chemist. You know the ones? The orange ones with a long nozzle, it's got to be a long nozzle. You fill it up, you fill up the douche bag."

She was talking very fast, in a monotone.

"Then you get a knitting needle, not a big one, about a size eight, one you'd use for double knitting wool and you wrap the knitting needle with a clean bit of old sheet. It has to be a clean sheet, mind. Then you get your sister to help you push the knitting needle up inside. Not just a bit inside, right up, right up inside and you push hard on the douche bag. Then it'll all come out, the whole lot, with lots of blood and you'll have to take the day off work."

She was sitting very still. Her face was stone. Her eyes were glazed. Her cigarette had burned down to the filter. She hadn't noticed.

"Except that sometimes it won't work. Sometimes nothing comes out. Sometimes you stay pregnant and the baby comes out crippled, because you stuck a knitting needle into it. The knitting needle makes the baby have a crooked foot and then you have to look after a cripple all your life and people know and they hate you because of a knitting needle."

The words bruised and bled. Sandra reached out for Amy, softly pulling in the rigid little body of her sister. Cradling her.

"What's the matter now?" their mother snapped. "Oh, it's you two. Sandra, have you put the spuds on yet? The spuds need to go on. For dinner."

They stood in the doorway, holding each other, holding soft underbelly to soft underbelly, staring at their mother. Then Amy reached up and wiped Sandra's face with her sleeve, with her woolen sleeve, knitted on number eight needles.

"Come on," she said. "Come on Sandra."

It was a bad night. In the kitchen, the mince sat congealing in the pan. The only one to eat dinner that night was the cat, sitting up on the stove and licking at the half cooked meat. Sandra cried, wiping her nose on the sheets she'd washed just the day before. Amy curled her body up next to her sister on the bed, folding into herself, silent. The dark swallowed Elvis and crept into the room as if it would never leave.

At nine o'clock the pig dogs started barking and then one of them kept vigilance, barking an intermittent warning into the night. At eleven o'clock the sisters stared into the dark.

"Sandra," whispered Amy.

"What?"

"Sandra, by your wardrobe, look."

"Don't start that again."

"No, look. She's smiling. The old lady, she's not angry any more."

"Go to sleep, Amy. I'll look after you."

When Robert knocked on the back door in the morning, he woke them up. Amy uncurled herself from the foot of Sandra's bed and went to open the door. Sandra tried to blink open her swollen eyes. She must have a cold or something, she had a headache and didn't feel well. Then she remembered. She was pregnant. Her breath caught. She was pregnant and not married. She swung her legs over the side of the bed and stood up. She would try and eat some breakfast. That was the next thing to do.

Robert and Amy were sitting eating weetbix when she went into the kitchen. Their whispering stopped. In the small silence Robert held a spoon half way to his mouth. His face was serious.

"Do you want to have a baby, Sandra?" he asked.

Sandra stared at him.

"It's just that, me and Amy want to have babies, when we're sixteen. You're nearly sixteen, so do you want to have this baby?"

"What if I don't?"

"You have to want the baby, Sandra," Amy said, "You just have to."

The eyes that looked up at Sandra from Amy's eleven year-old face were the eyes of Mary, full of a millennium of sadness.

Sandra opened the weetbix packet. The next thing to do was to eat breakfast, breakfast, and to get rid of Amy and her pleading.

"Just get out of here, will you?" Sandra said. "Both of you. Just leave me alone."

"Well, me and Robert and Colin are going for a long bike ride anyway," she said. "I'm just going to get dressed Robert, I'll meet you at your place."

"Where are you going?" Sandra asked.

"Oh, just somewhere," Amy said. "Why would you care?"

"We're going up to the Falls," Robert said. "We've got to do something there."

Sandra didn't ask what. She'd put in too much milk and the weetbix floated. Like the little thing inside me, she thought, it's floating around inside me, a little bit me and a little bit Rewi. Floating. She was floating herself, not enough sleep and crying did that. She didn't notice when Robert left.

The second bowl of weetbix did stay. Although she spent some time hanging over the bathroom sink in case. Under the sink she found a douche, an orange one. She pulled it out.

Chapter Nineteen

Kawerau February 1975

"Good morning, dear," says a voice from somewhere in the room.

Sandra's swimming just under the surface of sleep, in the dark silt-filled water, with the weeds that brush against her, winding around her legs, clinging, pulling. She pushes them away and a dead fish, released from the dark weed, turns belly up in her hands, one eye staring at her, accusing. Her own dark hair is drifting across her face, winding itself around the fish, around her nose and mouth and she doesn't need to breathe any more. She can just sink down, down.

"Wake up, I brought you a cup of tea."

She keeps her eyes closed and the voice reels her up to the surface, to the meniscus between asleep and awake. She floats there, trying to feel some familiarity. *Where did these fluffy sheets come from? Why are the walls so close and where is the door and what happened to the darkness that is my bedroom, in my flat, in Auckland? Who's that person insisting on tea?*

There's a clatter of teacup in saucer and she knows she's in a single bed, in a bedroom that opens to a hallway and leads to the room where her mother is, no, where she was. She opens her eyes and Bea sits down on the end of the bed.

"How are you, today, dear?"

Sandra can't lie here, on her back. She pulls her pillow up to face that concern, to ward it off. The bed head creaks as she settles and pushes her hair behind her ears. *Today, how am I today?*

A sound pushes in from next door, through the high hedge. It's a child screaming in tantrum, a high-pitched wail of anger, an incoherent rage that winds higher and higher. She tenses with it. It stops as suddenly as it started and leaves her jangling.

"I'm all right."

That's the best she can do.

"The funeral director will be here in half an hour," Bea says. "Pat's home. He did a double last night. Honestly, the man is too old for double shifts but he won't be told."

"Oh, Pat, yes."

"You know our Maria's in Australia now, don't you?"

Sandra didn't, but she nods.

"They've just moved to Western Australia, for the mining."

"Really? That's a long way away."

"Yes. We miss the kiddies. Still, we see Peter's little ones. And Max, you remember him as a baby, don't you? He's living with Peter."

Bea stands up and walks to the doorway. As Sandra reaches for the teacup, Bea pauses.

"I don't suppose you ever …"

The teacup almost tips over. It clatters in the saucer and some of the tea spills. Sandra grabs for the handle, holding it very hard. The question dissipates.

"Anyway, you need to get yourself up, Sandra. The bathroom's free."

The funeral director looks too young to be doing this job. There's Bea, with her greying hair and Pat, with the lines that say the years have not been easy on him. These two were almost family to her, almost. The man in the dark suit says his name is Tom Sharp and he's sorry about her loss in a solemn voice, his movements slow as he gets out a pad of paper and unscrews the lid of a fountain pen. Practising for his own death.

There's a knock at the back door and she knows before he

comes into the kitchen that it'll be Robert. He slips into a chair, with a nod. Almost family.

"I believe, Sandra," says Tom the funeral director, "We helped with your father's funeral. It was a few years ago, before I joined the firm."

She can feel a panic rising. The funeral she never came to. She just nods.

"I'm glad we can be of service again. Now, we have several things to do. First, there's the notice, for the papers. Do you want a notice, if so, which papers do you want us to put it in?"

She looks blankly at his empty page. He's written 1. Death Notice. She doesn't know the names of the local papers. The paper she gets is *The Auckland Star*. That wouldn't be any use. Isn't there a local paper? There used to be. There were headlines that screamed at her once, told her there was a hole in her life that would never be filled.

"Well," Bea says. "Just the local papers, I think. The *Gazette* and the *Beacon*. That would do, don't you think, Sandra?"

She just nods.

"Very well," says Tom. "Now, how much do you want it to say? If it goes in the "Births and Deaths" column, a brief announcement of death and the details of the funeral will cost you ten dollars. A longer announcement with names of family will be around thirty dollars. What would you like to do?"

They look at her, Bea, Pat, Robert and the dark-suited Tom. They want her to make a decision about how much to spend on telling the world that her mother is dead. She coughs, to hide the laugh that's threatening. If she starts laughing, she won't stop. Her eyes water. Bea hands her a handkerchief and pats her shoulder.

"What about a longer notice?" Bea says. "It could say after a long illness."

Yes, thinks Sandra, it was a very long illness. *How about it says after she gave up on life, after she disappeared into her bedroom, after she shut the door.*

Sandra stirs her tea, stares at the teaspoon, remembers pushing food on to a spoon just like this one, coaxing her mother's mouth open to force some of it in. Closed mouth, blank eyes, lost in some alien dream where nowhere was home.

"Can I check Mrs McLeod's full name, please?" says Tom.

"Betty," Sandra says. "She was called Betty."

"Yes, that can go in brackets. But we need her full name."

"Betty McLeod."

"I think he means the name on her birth certificate, Sandra," Robert says.

Sandra blinks at him. The panic is rising again, she's not sure she knows.

"That will be Elizabeth Ada McLeod," Robert continues. "I've had power of attorney for several years. That's the name on her birth certificate. Do you want her date of birth? I have that, too."

This is all news to her. Once there was a stranger who was her mother. She carries the pain of her mother's lostness, and she doesn't know her full name, or the year she was born. It's written down, in black ink, on the blank page.

"And who would you like to have acknowledged in this notice?" asks Tom.

Those eyes are looking at her again. *Who would you like to have acknowledged?*

"Me," she blurts.

"Yes, of course," says Tom. "How about 'Much loved mother to Sandra?'"

Sandra stares at the words he has written down on the page and she searches for a match inside herself. *Much loved ...*

"What about other members of the family, Sandra? Who else?"

They linger unbidden at her edges. There's her dad, sprawled asleep in the chair with his head nodding, the cat curled on his chest. On the floor is a small girl with white curly hair, intent on drawing on a big sheet of paper almost as large as she is. On the paper is a sprawl of green and blue, moving, coalescing to a figure that is absorbing her, this small girl, until she's gone and there's just the drawing on the page. Of the old woman.

Sandra pushes the chair back, it falls on the kitchen floor with a loud clatter. Escape, that's all she can do, escape. Her way is blocked by Robert. He stands in the kitchen doorway, a solid impediment to her flight.

"No," he says. "No, Sandra, don't."

She tries to get around him, to push him out of her way but he won't be moved. He holds her shoulders, pushing his hands down hard and it hurts. She hurts. His eyes are full, of rage, of pain, of the same substance of which she is made. He pushes it down with hard hands, before it can erupt. She goes limp in his grasp, turns to the table and slumps in a chair. They've gone from her edges, leaving a grey emptiness where the ash drifts.

Robert's voice pulls her back from that alien place.

"The notice needs to say 'and Amy. Much loved mother to Sandra and Amy.'" The hardness of his voice grates and she waits in the silence that follows.

"Well," says Pat. "I suppose it also needs to say 'Much loved wife to Ian.'"

She looks out the window into the open door of the garage. There's a rusty skeleton of a bike in there, its pedals missing and its handlebars askew. The cover on the seat still has a bit of green on it. She recognises that bike or, at least, she knew it when it was still intact.

"Where do you want the funeral?" asks the efficient funeral director. They take over, this almost family.

"Oh, it will only be a small one," Bea says. "I think your chapel will serve nicely."

The fountain pen notes that down.

"And who would you like to take the funeral service?" he asks.

"You mum was still an Anglican, wasn't she Sandra?" asks Bea.

Sandra has no idea. All she knows is that her mother wouldn't have converted to Catholicism.

"I'll get the Anglican minister who does services at our Chapel to get in touch with you."

He writes that down, too.

"Do you know if she wanted to be cremated?"

She shrugs.

"I think both her and Ian wanted cremation," says Pat. "What do you think, Sandra?"

She nods and stares out of the kitchen door, the one that goes through to the lounge. On the wall is a mirror and in the reflection she can see the Virgin Mary, looking straight at her, with heart aflame and one hand pointing, accusing. *It's your fault, it's always your fault.*

Chapter Twenty

Kawerau November 1959

On the day before the eruption of Tarawera mountain, on June 10 1886, a phantom war canoe was seen on the lake by a party returning from a tangi. An old woman, her hair long and streaming in the wind, pointed at the canoe and muttered but the ghost warriors kept pulling their oars through the cold, still water. The next day, the earth broke open and the world came to a fiery end. Eventually the lake filled and the water found a new path as the deep, urgent, Tarawera river. A young river, it tried to return to its volcanic beginnings, some of its water disappearing into the rough, tumbled rocks of older eruptions.

This is where they went, Amy, Colin and Robert, on that day. They rode their bikes along the old forestry road and left them at the base of the hill. They climbed up past the falls, where the hidden water plumed out in fierce joy, falling down the steep escarpment, bruising itself on the hardened lava and, pausing, misting the air, hung suspended, then fell again. Wet with spray, they carried on to the disappearing river, where the water seeped into dark places, fathomless, secret places that held and caressed, that ensnared.

Sandra did not stop them.

It was late afternoon when her father came home. Sandra heard him take off his boots and sit down at the kitchen table. She kept her attention on the pot she was scrubbing. She was tired, tired in a way that she didn't ever remember being tired. Dirty water spilt on the bench and splashed on the floor. She stood looking at it, not moving.

"Here, lass, sit yourself down, let me."

Her father put his hands on her shoulders and Sandra leaned into him, leaned herself and all of her younger selves into his strength and his care.

"There, lass, there, there. We'll work it out."

The knock on the front door startled them both. Her father answered it, with Sandra trailing behind him. Standing on the doorstep was a young policeman with his helmet in his hand. Next to him was Robert. His clothes were muddy and one knee was badly scraped. He was clenching and unclenching his fists and his breath was ragged.

"Mr McLeod?" asked the policeman. "Constable Collins, may I come in?"

Her father stood to one side and the policeman came in, one hand guiding Robert. They sat side by side on the sofa, Robert with his head down and one knee jerking up and down.

"Is Mrs McLeod in?" asked Constable Collins.

"Is she Sandra?" her father asked.

She nodded.

"I'll go and get her, Constable," he said.

Sandra stood holding the front door, as if to close it. The late afternoon sun slanted on to the mill felt covering on the floor. Sandra stood and stared at the top of Robert's head. Dust motes caught in the sunlight between them hung motionless, bright, as if they'd been there forever, then they were gone. The policeman cleared his throat.

When her mother came into the room she was in a nighty and a housecoat, with her slippers on the wrong feet.

"My wife's not very well, Constable," her father said.

"I'm sorry to hear that, sir," said the policeman, "and I'm sorry to be here with what might be bad news."

Her mother was clutching her cigarettes. She pulled one out and then seemed unsure what to do with it. Her father reached into his own pocket and lit it for her. She took a big lungful of smoke.

"This young man here turned up at the police station this afternoon. He told us that he, your daughter and another boy called Colin, went up to the Tarawera Falls this morning, on their bikes. He told us that Colin and, Amy, isn't it? were walking on the rocks just under the top falls, the ones where the river disappears underground and that one of them, Colin, slipped. Amy tried to catch him. Robert alleged that they both disappeared, behind the falls. He said he tried to find them, and that he almost fell in himself, but they were gone."

There was silence. Her mother breathed out her lung full of smoke. Out of the open front door, Sandra could see Richard, swinging back and forth. The empty swing next to him was going back and forth with him. It was as if she'd already known this visit was going to happen and these words were going to be laid out, still, immovable words that settled into her cold core.

"They drowned," she said.

Robert looked up. His eyes were looking somewhere far away.

"She took them," he said.

The silence returned. Somewhere in the room a low moan started, a moan that carried so much hurt that it faltered and stopped and sank into the thick molasses of shock. The stillness was broken by her father. He stood up, as if to rush out the door.

"You can't just sit there and tell me Amy's drowned. We got to find her, a search party, that's what we need, get everyone on a search party."

"Sir, we've got the police from Whakatane on their way. They're getting volunteers. We've already got a search party started."

"I'll come."

"With all due respect, sir. You're needed here, with your family. We'll keep you informed. Now, if you'll excuse me, I need to go and tell Colin's parents and get this young man home."

Sandra stood in the doorway, watching the policeman catch Robert's hand and walk next door, to Colin's house, to tell his family. She turned back into the lounge, pushing her hands up under her armpits and holding herself tight so that she wouldn't disintegrate. Her father was talking but she couldn't glue the words together. He was taking her mother out of the room and leaning over his shoulder, trying to tell her something. She couldn't reach that meaning.

She began walking, one foot in front of the other, away from the house and away from the policeman and his words. She couldn't leave her own behind—(left foot) *she* (right foot) *drowned* (left foot) *she* …The words carried her past the shopping centre, past the sling-back shoes with their gold buckles, past the swimming pool. Here she faltered. She leaned on the wire fence. The water inside the pool was still, reflecting the afternoon sun and a cloud, perfectly held in the centre of the pool.

"She drowned," she whispered.

The words caught on the fence, and went no further.

The tar seal stopped long before Sandra did. One step (*she*), two steps (*drowned*), took her up the edge of the old forestry road, alongside the bike tracks that must have been made, when was it? A long time ago. So fresh, they were so fresh. She followed them up the valley, as the darkness bled the colour from the day.

At dusk she reached their bikes. Two bikes, Amy's and Colin's, waiting for them. There were trucks parked alongside the road and a police car. From up the hill came voices and flashes of torchlight. Her feet took her up the track—left (*she*), right (*drowned*). Following Amy and Colin. Holding her hands tight under her armpits. Into the noise of the water.

She was almost at the falls when they found her, two large men with flash lights. They asked who she was and she couldn't remember. They asked what she was doing here and she said she had to find Mary. They said they were looking for another little girl, who was lost and she said Mary would know. *Mary would know.*

They held her gently, even though she struggled and swore at them. When she bit one large hand, they lifted her off her feet and carried her back down the track, setting their teeth against the wail that the black trees absorbed. They drove her home, following the same bike tracks back down the valley, past the still swimming pool.

When Sandra got home, the house was dark, her father gone. The swings on the playground were still.

There were no bodies, no inert arms and legs to be lovingly straightened, no hair to be brushed back from empty faces, no cold, cold lips to kiss goodbye. The only thing the police brought back to the house was one shoe, with a built-up sole, size two. They said they'd found it at the foot of the Falls.

Sandra placed the shoe on Amy's unmade bed. She washed Amy's clothes, trying to remember how the stain on Amy's white cardigan got there. She searched for the lost sock so that the pairs could be neatly lined up in Amy's drawer. Amy would need clean socks. Then, when all of Amy's clothes were clean, waiting for her, she slept, most of the night and some of the day. When she woke up she listened for Amy's voice, for her clumping walk in the built-up shoe, size two. When she came out into the kitchen, she looked for the halo of Amy's white blonde hair in the morning sunlight. She put a bowl out, for weetbix, crunched up so the sugar soaked in.

For two weeks after the police visit, noone came to the house. After one week her father gave up his trips to Fenton Mill Road, to search the disappearing river for his daughter. He sat in the lounge with the curtains drawn and drank whisky, as a sort of wake for his lost girl and, he didn't even get drunk.

Sandra watched hands pick up casseroles that appeared on the doorstep. She watched feet walk up the hallway and one hand push food into her mother's mouth. She supposed they were her hands and her feet.

The house became full of closed doors, Sandra closed the door to Amy's room, her mother closed the door to her bedroom and, everyone closed and sealed the doors to themselves. There was silence, a holding of breath, a waiting: for Amy to come home.

Eventually there was a knock on the door. Sandra let Mr Simpson into the house. He asked if they'd like to be part of a memorial service at the Catholic church, for Colin and Amy. He said that Father Searle had offered to do a service, a requiem mass in memory of the two children. For some completion. Her father said he would see. Sandra said she would come. She said she wasn't sure about her mother.

On the Saturday morning Sandra dressed. She didn't have anything black to wear, so she wore her school uniform. It, at least, was navy blue. She didn't bother looking in the mirror to do her hair, just pulled it back into a ponytail. She went alone to the Simpson house.

Before they climbed into the car, Mrs Simpson took her hand. Her own was shaking. Sandra looked down at the hands and gripped hard, as if to stop both of them being swept away.

"You were as much a mother to little Amy as Betty was, you know Sandra," she said. "It's a terrible loss, for both of us."

Sandra's tongue was stuck. She'd spoken so little this last week that it seemed to have forgotten words. She nodded.

"They're both with God, now. Sandra, remember our conversation, about you maybe being pregnant?"

Sandra took a gulp of air and it shuddered out. She didn't want to think about it. Maybe then it would just go away.

"Are you?"

"I suppose so, I tried ..."

"Let me help you get that doctor's appointment."

Sandra nodded. The rest of the Simpson family came out, one black-clad blur. They squeezed into the car, Sandra jammed between Mr and Mrs Simpson in the front seat.

"Is your dad holding up?" asked Mr Simpson.

"He's all right thank you," Sandra said.

"No, I mean how is he, really?"

"Oh. He's drinking whisky."

"Lots?"

"Yes."

"We need to get him back to work. I'll come over later. I'm going back tomorrow, we both need to get back to work."

"What about your mum?" asked Mrs Simpson.

"She's not doing anything," Sandra said. "She lives in her bedroom."

"Has she seen the doctor?"

"No."

"That's two appointments."

They passed the swimming pool, alive with children's bodies as they jumped and dived, the water splashing up into the sunlight. Sandra sat constrained by the two warm bodies each side of her, staring at the suspended water, feeling the affinity of the cold, cold water with her own frozen being.

Father Searle was waiting for them at the door of the church. Sandra heard him murmur something to each of the Simpson family as they filed inside. She pulled herself forward, one step (*she*), two steps (*drowned*), taking care not to stand on the cracks in the concrete. She felt the hand on her shoulder and looked up into his face. There was a tear on Father Searle's cheek. She stared at it. It was foreign water that she could not comprehend.

Sandra's body sat in the front pew, and her self floated into some other place. Jesus didn't seem to care, with his heart that glowed, showing no shadow. She tried to catch his eyes, the eyes that invited and accused. If only she'd stopped them going, when Robert told her they were going to the Falls, if only she'd said no.

Father Searle was a blackness standing at the altar, with his back to her. He could not accuse. Not from where he was. There was just a ring of candles where the little statue of Mary had stood. Someone had lit one of them anyway. It spluttered and went out, submerged in its own wax. Sandra wondered if Mary was out looking for Amy, maybe they had met already. She would notice that Amy didn't have her special shoe. She closed her eyes. *Send her back*, she pleaded, *I'm sorry, please send her back*. She hurt, all of her hurt.

Words floated into her body and they caught, snagging her attention. Amy. Mary. Father Searle was talking about her sister. She listened. He was talking about Amy's special love of Mary, mother of God, and how Mary was a mother who had known loss and that loss was bigger than the world, bigger than the human soul could hold and that it needed to be given to God.

Sandra stood up. She had to get away from this mother who had not stopped Amy, who had not helped her. She stumbled for the aisle. It was a long way to the open door and each side of the red carpet were faces, faces of people who knew it was her fault.

'You should have stopped her,' they said.

She took a deep breath at the door and sat down on the steps, on the cracks in the concrete and stared at the bare ground in front of her. She clenched her fists and pulled her shoulders up to close them out. Those accusing words. *You should have stopped her.* She put her hands over her ears and rocked back and forth. Someone sat next to her.

"Sandra," he said.

Nothing else, just her name.

"Sandra."

He sat close to her, the warmth of his body seeping into her. He put an arm around her shoulders. She slowed her rocking and let go. A sigh was pulled from deep inside her.

"Your little sister, eh?" he said.

She leaned on Rewi and a tear, foreign water, crept on to her cheek. He wrapped his arms around her and rocked, rocked to the crooning of Father Searle's Latin wafting out from the church.

Exams started on Monday—Geography. Tuesday was General Science. Then there were two exams on Wednesday—French and

Maths. English was on Friday morning. The sixth exam fell off the schedule. They were done.

On Friday afternoon, Sandra came home and went to bed and slept for several hours. She drifted half awake in the dusk. Her window was open, the evening air was cold and with it came the soft smell of lilac. There was a memory with that lilac scent, from a long, long time ago, a summer evening memory from somewhere that was soft and crooned of delicate, tiny cups, and plates of leaves set out for dolls, sitting in a row. Except there was one muddy doll, a rag doll with china hands and one crooked and bent china foot and a thin intent china face, haloed by wispy blond hair, flying away hair. A doll with a cracked cheek that stared ahead through one cracked blue china eye. That stared. Accusing.

The dogs across the road barked.

"Amy," called Richard. "Amy, will you marry me Amy?"

Sandra pulled herself up off the bed, slowly, heavily, pulling her body up through the thick air.

"Amy, I love you Amy," came in through the window.

She lifted the metal stay and pushed the window wider.

"Go away," she yelled. "Go away."

The dogs barked again, a cacophony of barks, vicious noise that jarred.

"She drowned," whispered Sandra in the noise. "She can't marry anyone. She drowned."

The air thickened around the wardrobe.

The toilet flushed. Sandra peeked out of her bedroom door and her father came out of the bathroom.

"Let's get some dinner ready, lass," he said. "I'm starting night-shift tonight, going back to work."

He disappeared back into the bedroom. Sandra went down the hallway to the bathroom and splashed water over her face. She stared at the person in the mirror. Who is this person, pregnant, not married, this stranger with some small alien sitting inside her, using her body to make a new one. She shuddered. There used to be a game called let's pretend. Let's pretend it isn't happening. This stranger couldn't play that game.

"Exams all done," her father said as he came into the kitchen. "Are you happy about that, lass?"

Sandra nodded. She couldn't remember anything about any of them, they were a blur of words that ran into each other and bled on to the page. Sense had seemed nothing but a vague beckoning as her pen made marks and the clock ticked.

"We'll get through this business, Sandra. We'll manage. We'll all miss her, but we'll manage."

"Mum's not managing."

"Oh, don't you worry about your mum. She'll be all right."

"Mrs Simpson thinks she should see the doctor."

"What for? What's a doctor going to do? Tell her she's sad about her sister and her daughter? She'll get over it. It'll just take time."

The butter was melting in the frying pan. The yellow knob got smaller as she pushed at it. It caught and started to smoke. Her father reached for the pan and took it off the element.

"Careful," he said. "You'll have us all going up in smoke. Now, what about you, lass? Now you've done your exams it may be time to look for a job. What about talking to Reg, down at the Four Square? That's good, clean work."

Sandra broke four eggs into a bowl. The yellow yolks stared up at her. She stabbed the slimy viscosity, again and again and the incipient life broke and spread.

"Dad, before Amy … "

She stared at the yellow mess of eggs in the bowl. It was too late to pretend this wasn't happening.

"Dad, remember, I told you. I told you and Mum. I'm pregnant."

"Here, look, lets pop those eggs in the pan. You get some plates out."

"Dad, did you hear me?"

Sandra felt her father, like a brick wall beside her. He stirred the eggs in the pan, divided the rubbery mess into two parts on the blank, white plates. He carefully picked up the two plates and, with eyes fixed on keeping them steady, placed one each side of the kitchen table.

"Dad? I'm having a baby."

"Yes," he said. "There's that too. Come and have something to eat, lass, come on, you need to keep your strength up."

Sandra sat opposite him and watched him eat the egg. He gestured to her to do the same. She moved her hand automatically from plate to mouth. The noise of the fork scraping on the plate tore at her.

"How old are you, Sandra?"

"I'm fifteen. I'll be sixteen in February."

"Good. You can get married then. In February, when you're sixteen."

A picture of Rewi's flat nose, his brown eyes, his soft, large mouth, his Māoriness hovered. *You've got to be taught … A bit of the tarbrush.*

Sandra held her breath.

"He will marry you, won't he? The father? He will if I have anything to do with it anyway. Who is he, Sandra."

"His name's Rewi. Rewi Stanton."

"Rewi. Rewi. What sort of name is that?"

"He's Māori, Dad."

Her father stood up. His face twisted, his hand came up and he leaned forward with a promise of force that had all the power of anguish in it. Sandra stared, transfixed as it froze in the matrix of tense muscles and pain. The matrix shifted. The kitchen filled with the sound of his long, slow sigh. Despair, a soft, slow slipping away, like breath from a collapsing lilo, it seeped out to sit heavy in the space between them. He slumped back on the chair.

"This isn't what we came for. Not for you to get off with some native. Not for your sister to, to … Not for your mother to go doolally. This isn't what we did it for, lass. It just isn't."

They sat, the two of them, staring at empty white plates.

There was a knock on the front door. It broke the trance.

"I'll get it," Sandra said.

It was Mrs Simpson. She followed Sandra back into the kitchen. She said it was good that Ian and Pat were both going back to work. She said it was good that exams were over. She hesitated over what to say next.

"I've told him, Mrs Simpson," Sandra said. "He knows. He knows it's Rewi's baby."

"Well, then," Mrs Simpson said. "What do you want to do, Ian?"

Her father looked blankly at her.

"What do you want to do about the baby?"

"I don't know. I suppose she needs to get to a doctor. I don't know if Betty can take her."

"I told Sandra I'd go with her. While I'm at it, I'll take Betty."

Rewi. It's Rewi's baby. The words echoed inside Sandra. Rewi's baby, not just an alien taking over her body, but Rewi's baby. They were soft words, words that remembered the soft pine needles and his soft, black moustache.

"That boy, what's his name? He'll marry her. She's almost sixteen. He can marry her."

"I know the family, Ian. They're Catholic, some of the family come to our church."

"Oh, bloody norah. They're bloody left footers as well."

"Well, yes. They're Catholic like we are, our family."

There was an awkward silence. Her father sighed.

"All right then," he said. "She's pregnant to a Hori left footer. What the hell did you get yourself into here, girl?"

"Dad, Dad," Sandra pleaded. "He's really clever and he's kind and he's, well, he's, I love him."

He pushed his chair back so hard it rocked and crashed back on to the floor.

"What's that got to do with it? Just what did you think you were doing, you stupid girl!"

"Now, now, Ian," Mrs Simpson said. "You're not helping. I suggest we get a meeting together with the family. We can get Father Searle to help and meet with the Stanton family. They're good people, Ian."

"Make good bloody in-laws will they?" he said.

"Will you come, Dad," pleaded Sandra. "Please."

It was back again. The slow death of despair. Sandra felt it and she felt it pull her father back into his chair. He nodded.

Sandra was counting the cracks in the floorboards as Rewi and his family came into the hall. From the edge of her vision to the beginning of the pews facing her, there were twenty-nine cracks separating the rimu boards. With her eyes down at floor level, she could see shoes walking in. Three pairs of black men's shoes, newly polished; two pairs of women's shoes, with stockinged legs. Her heart raced as she recognised Rewi's worn school shoes, with the backs trodden down.

She risked flicking her gaze up, underneath her lowered eyebrows. With the first flick she saw Rewi, sitting with three older men. With the second flick she worked out that one of the men seemed to be his father, he looked about the same age as her father. The other two were older, much older. One of them had a walking stick. She assumed they were his grandfathers. *Pregnant. Not married.* The words floated in the air between them.

Sandra willed Rewi to look at her, but his head was down, his eyes on his hands folded in front of him. Next to the men were two women. One looked so like Rewi that she knew it must be his mother. She stared past the neon of those words, flashing in the space. *Pregnant. Not married.* They flashed bright red, and Sandra felt her face flaming to match. She rubbed her hot cheek. *Not married yet.*

They all sat in the Catholic church, with the pictures of Jesus and his Mother hidden behind a heavy curtain.

Her father was fidgeting next to her. Sandra inched away,

towards the solid black-clad Mrs Simpson on her other side. Father Searle stood up and cleared his throat.

"Let us pray. In the name of the Father, and of the Son and of the Holy Ghost."

As he said Amen, there was a concert of hands, up, down, across they went. Sandra lifted her hand and let it drop again. Her father crossed his arms tighter.

"As we meet here today, may Blessed Mary, ever virgin, pray for us and all sinners."

Sandra pulled her shoulders up to her ears. She could feel the disapproval of Mary behind the curtain, ever virgin.

"As we meet, we pray especially for the souls of the recently departed, our beloved children Colin and Amy. May they rest in peace."

Her father started up from his seat, Mrs Simpson reached across and put a calming hand on his arm. Sandra's throat hurt.

"We're most grateful, Lord, that the people have gathered here, in your holy church, to discuss important issues that sit heavy on their hearts and minds. May the grace of our Lady help us today to plan for the future."

Sandra was sinking, in the Amens that finished the prayer, in the tears that had flooded her. The cracks in the floor blurred as if her heavy, un-virgin body could sink, oh how she wished it could sink, and disappear.

The flurry of whispering beside her pulled her back. Her father was spluttering and hissing, his body tensed to leave. Mrs Simpson frowned at him and nodded towards Sandra. Through her tears, Sandra watched his jaw tighten, and the soft stealing of despair into his eyes. He folded his arms again.

One of the old men was standing, leaning on his walking stick. He was nodding towards Sandra. She blinked hard and she was at the back of the Simpson's chook house again with this old man, who was crooning at the bone that he tenderly lifted and cradled. Then she was watching him help her mother away from the steaming mud, back into the manuka and safety. With his nodding he was saying —'Yes, I remember too.'

He was telling a story. A story about the mountain, about Putauaki, also called Mt Edgecumbe. How Putauaki took Tarawera, the mountain who split herself asunder, to wife and she bore a child, a son, Whatuira. But Putauaki could not settle with her and he looked towards Whakaari, a steaming island out at sea. His love for her grew so big that he travelled, at night, as mountains do, to join her. He did not know his son had followed him. When the sun rose, they were frozen on the plain. Now Tarawera forever mourns for her lost husband and her lost son, her tears making the Tarawera River and the Falls. Putauaki stands sentinel on the plain, with no wife, with his little son at his side.

"They are here," he said. "Looking over us, the father Putauaki and the son. Tarawera may cry for her son and her husband but, they must stay here, with us."

He sat down, leaning on his walking stick. There was silence. Her father pulled himself slowly to his feet. His words were strangled by his taut body.

"We are here. Because. Your son. Your grandson. Has got my daughter up the duff. Pregnant. You understand? She's having a baby. That's what we're here to talk about. Not some bloody rambling on about a mountain."

As if his tight body was being pulled involuntarily, he walked forward, heading for Rewi. There was a shifting amongst the family around Rewi's bowed head, an imperceptible barrier was raised. It stopped her father, half way across the twenty-nine rimu floor boards that separated the two families.

"Marriage." He spat it out. "That's what we need to be talking. Marriage. My daughter and this boy."

Father Searle moved in behind her father, quietly put a hand on his shoulder and walked him back to sit next to Mrs Simpson. Her father folded his arms again. He sat clenching and unclenching his fists.

The other elderly man stood up, stepping in front of Rewi. Sandra shrank from his deeply frowning eyebrows and flashing eyes. This must be grandfather Stanton that Rewi had lived with, in Taupo.

"I sit here," he said. "With my son, and his wife and her mother, and with our mokopuna, our grandson. And I hear your words with sorrow. I hear them with sorrow because, as you heard Mr Watene say, the child of this union must stay here, with its people and my grandson must go to his other love. He's going to go on with school next year. He carries the mana of his people with him. He must go on. That is final."

He stood hard and straight, immobile as the mountain. Sandra caught her breath. *Pregnant, pregnant and not married. Not married now, not married ever.* Her father leaned back in his seat. He sneered.

"Are you telling me that this boy of yours is just going to bugger off? He's just going to leave our Sandra here, with a bun in the oven, to deal with his little bastard by herself?"

"Now, now, Mr McLeod," Father Searle said. "I'm sure that's not what Mr Stanton meant."

"Well what does he bloody mean?"

The first old man to speak stood again, slowly. His weight shifted as he leaned on his walking stick.

"My friend," he said. "My moko loves your daughter, Sandra. He loves her. He told us so. They are both very young. He must carry on with his education. Sandra, your daughter, she is now our daughter too. She carries our mokopuna. We will help take care of her, Mr McLeod, as much as your whānau needs us to."

Sandra caught a sob, it lodged in her throat. *Rewi loves me.* These words danced faster, they danced her heart under her ribs and settled, quivering. It was, what was it? Like the soft tickle of a black moustache, like the quiver of the earth before it settles again on its hot core. Their baby, quickened by those words: *Rewi loves me.*

"Sandra," the old man continued, "you are welcome to our whānau. Your baby has a home with us."

"And now?" her father said. "What about now?"

"We leave," said Mr Stanton. "Rewi comes with me, back to Taupo."

Of one accord, the other members of Rewi's whānau stood up. Rewi was carried with them, eyes still downcast, carried out of the church hall. Sandra wanted to run after him and shake him and shout in his face. *Is it true, is it true …*

"Well then," Father Searle said. "Shall we close with a prayer?"

"Not bloody likely," retorted her father.

This time Mrs Simpson's hand on his arm was not enough and he stormed out of the church hall. As the door slammed, the heavy curtain over the picture of Mary with her son, both giving their hearts away, bulged and surged.

"Come on love," Mrs Simpson said. "Let's take you home."

Chapter Twenty-One

Kawerau February 1975

Bea pulls the gate closed on the chicken coop. The hens are squabbling over last night's potato peelings. Sandra pauses with the wet sheet half over the washing line, straightening it, trying to find the edge. These are the sheets from her mother's bed, the ones she died in. They're clean now and smell of washing powder. Her mother's been washed away to a coffin in a funeral home in the next town. Tidied away, neatly, for now. Sandra pushes a peg down on one corner of the sheet.

"Have you got something suitable to wear, Sandra?"

"Do you mean for the funeral? Well, I've got that red trouser suit. You know, the one I had on when I arrived and a dress, I've got a dress."

"What colour is it, love?" asks Bea.

The second peg jumps out of her hand. It was the 'love' that did it. She can't see where it's gone. The sheet and the washing line are blurry and her throat aches. She holds on to the wire for support. There's a hand on the middle of her back.

"Come on, Sandra," Bea says. "Leave the washing. We'll do that later. Come on, love, come inside. I'll put the kettle on."

It's gone again; the crack has closed up again. That second 'love', no it will not get in. She straightens up and reaches for another peg.

"I'm all right, I'll finish this."

By the time she gets back into the kitchen, the kettle's boiling.

She pulls her cigarettes out of her pocket. The packet's empty.

"Oh, I'm out of ciggies."

"Do you want to pop round to the dairy?" Bea says. "I'll get you to get some more bread anyway, for lunch."

The streets are quiet. There's no-one at the playground, on the broken swings, or the broken roundabout that leans crookedly on its concrete base. She hurries past. *How many days have I been here? It must be several hundred, except I arrived on Saturday and it's only Monday.*

Monday. On a Monday she used to walk this way, to go to school. At the corner here, on a hot day, she would take off her roman sandals and put them in her bag. Her mother never approved of bare feet; Sandra never approved of roman sandals. The house she's passing didn't used to have grass, the front yard always had kumara growing. There's a glimpse of a small body, crouching on the pavement, looking for the big green caterpillars that lived in the heart shaped leaves and the hot breeze coming from the mountain lifting her white blonde hair. Then she's gone, flown from the greedy caterpillars, carried on the wind. Sandra walks faster, trying to pay attention, stepping over the cracks so that she doesn't let these memories in.

At the end of the street with the dairy on the corner, trees have been planted along the grass verge. They're straggly, with few leaves. One of them has been snapped off at the base, the remaining thin trunk a sharp stake. A bike leans drunkenly in the bike rack outside the dairy. It's rusty. She wonders how long it's been there and who it used to belong to. She walks into the dairy with her heart pounding. Maybe someone will recognise her and then what will she say? The bread is bought, the cigarettes are bought, from a stranger who asks if she's visiting. She says she is, and that's all. She lights a cigarette as soon as she's out the door. She walks very fast, to beat those glimpses that sneak in from the past, the ones she's run from for so many years. She turns the corner back into that little dead-end street with its broken playground and its ghosts.

There's someone on the roundabout, a young woman in a school uniform. She's sitting on the high part of the metal drum, facing the road, waiting. It may be the way she's sitting, with her feet pulled up underneath her, hugging her knees, or it may be the way she holds her head on the side, while she rocks back and forth. Sandra thinks she might know this girl, this waiting girl. Then it's gone and she's a stranger on the playground again.

She wipes her feet on the doormat. The door is opened before she can knock. She wants to stay just where she is. On the doorstep. She doesn't want to step into this past. On the sofa is an elderly man, his white hair carefully combed over his balding head, his hat on his knee and next to him is a walking stick. He's nodding. For a long moment she stands at the doorway, not going in, not leaving, she stands at the doorway and she knows if she steps in, there will be no turning back.

He's struggling to stand up, holding on to the arm of the sofa, reaching for his walking stick. There's no decision left to make. He's standing up now, leaning on his stick and he reaches out one hand, one unsteady hand. She can't help it, she stumbles in, grasps the brown, gnarled fingers and the two of them lean on the walking stick. His old man eyes are watering as his mouth struggles with the words.

"My daughter," he says. "You've been gone too long."

Someone else is crying, someone else is bowing down to it, the grief, the pain. She can see that person. Someone standing on a swirling carpet, holding an old man's hand, leaning with him on his stick. Someone. She watches her from a corner of her mind, where she sits with her feet pulled up underneath her, hugging her knees, rocking back and forth and she wonders who that someone is and what happened to her that she's so mortally wounded. She must be helped, brought back, before she's lost.

"Sandra."

It's Bea's voice that points the way home. Sandra steps back, just one step. The carpet stops swirling. Bea helps Rewi's grandfather sit down. Sandra knows that it's started when she sees the girl standing at the door; the one who was sitting on the roundabout, the one who's now staring at her with eyes that are now brown, eyes that were once neither blue nor brown, eyes that had invited the possibility of her. She had not been able to say yes. Her eyes are drawn to the widow's peak, that matches her own, where the hair makes a point in the forehead, forever denoting mourning. The girl stares, not smiling, for a long time, for an eternity. Between her brown eyes, so like her grandfather's and her father's, and the blue eyes of the Virgin Mary, so like Amy's eyes; she's transfixed. The accusation in those eyes exposes her, pares her to the bone. Her mouth is dry as she opens her lips and only a tiny puff of breath escapes, soundless. There are no words to use.

"You must be Lady Macbeth," says the girl with the widow's peak, the one that matches Sandra's brow and that of her mother before her. "That's what Dad said he used to call you—Lady Macbeth."

Now the full lips and the flat nose say that this is Rewi's daughter. Sandra swallows and the ache in her throat brings her home to herself.

"I'm sorry about your mum, my nan. I'm sorry she passed away."

For the first time, Sandra wishes she was sorry too. One hand, under its own volition, has drifted up from her side and is reaching out towards this stranger. It's trembling. It sits, that hand, in the air between them, a bridge, maybe. The girl's movement is subtle; she leans back and looks over Sandra's shoulder, past her, as if she's not there.

"Koro, we need to go," the girl says.

Sandra catches the uneven movement of Rewi's grandfather as he moves over the swirling carpet to his great grand-daughter. He stops and there are tears in the furrows of his old face and one drop of mucus sitting on the end of his nose. He places his free hand on Sandra's shoulder and nods. Her hand, the one that reached out for the girl, lands on his elbow. In his eyes—what is it, it's sorrow that brings that lump from her throat up to sit in her mouth and hold them both silent.

He turns and his great-granddaughter helps him down the steps, gently moving his elbow away. Sandra's hand touches hers briefly, very briefly, and the girl pulls her hand back, fast. Sandra wants to reach out again and, at the same time, wants to pull back. Petrified by indecision, her arm stretches out in supplication as she watches them walk down the path and away. He's uneven, his stick pulling him along the path, leaning on her, the girl who knows the name. Rocking as she walks, she holds the world for him, leaving Sandra on the doorstep. It's as if there's a space there for her, cut out of time, where she should have been. It's too foreign, that space, too far away and it's been empty for too long. She aches for it.

"They're going to come to the funeral," Bea says. "Mr Watene and Hana, they're going to come to Betty's funeral."

Hana. Hana. What about Rewi, will Rewi come? But she can't ask. She can't get words past that sob in her throat, that's rising, pushing upward, threatening to erupt. She runs across the road to where that girl, that Hana with the widow's peak had sat, on the broken roundabout. It leans further as she cannons into it, holding on to the metal partitions to steady herself. She pulls her legs up underneath and wraps her arms around herself. This was where that girl's father had sat that night, that last time he'd called her Lady Macbeth, with the Sandra that was then and the tiny beginnings of his baby, this Hana. Sandra rocks back and forth, back and forth.

There were the months of two heartbeats. The baby's growing stronger as she pulled her life from her mother. Sandra's growing heavier as her own mother drifted further into some other reality. There were the months of waiting. For life and an end to the almost-death. A featureless time, a stasis that did not break until the morning when her body clenched and the floor was soaked and she knew it had begun. Hours, measured at first by regular periods of pain, then passing into one continuous, impossible attempt by her body to turn itself inside out.

When the baby was born, it was into the hands that took her away. She only had a single meeting with those blue eyes that invited so much. That she didn't deserve. Then Sandra waited again. Alone.

He came at the end of the week.

"Well lass, I've come to take you home."

Home. Home. The word echoed off the bare walls, magnified as it bounced from the ceiling, escaped through the open window, to melt in the drizzling rain.

Home. It echoed in her empty belly and sank.

"I'm not coming."

She hunched her shoulders as he pushed the door open, pulled the rest of his body into the room and leaned on the rail at the end of the bed. The chart on the rail rattled; her chart, with the story of this last week in numbers and graphs. One raindrop trembled on the end of his nose.

"What do you mean, you're not coming?"

"I'm not coming back. Ever."

She followed his eyes—to the floral curtains, the sink in the corner, the white hospital bed. This was the first time he'd come to see her. He put a bag next to the chair at the side of the bed, took his jacket off and draped it over the chair back. They both looked at her knees, mounds under the cover. She could smell brylcream and wet wool. From the edge of her eye she saw his fists clench. His voice was tight.

"Well, you can't stay here, lass."

Under the white cover, hidden by her knees, she pressed one hand on her belly, warming it. She shifted slightly to get the weight off her tail bone. It still hurt.

"Come on now, it's been a hard week, I know. But it's over now. It's all over lass, you can come home now."

"What for?"

"What for? What do you mean what for? Don't be stupid, girl. Your mother."

He moved back behind the bed-rail. She let out her breath that had trapped itself. He leaned over the rail with his hands white-knuckled.

"Look, I've brought you some clothes. I'll leave them here. You get yourself changed and I'll go and sign you out. Then, we'll go home."

His hand came off the rail and rose, as if involuntarily pulled, and the forefinger pointed at her. It wavered and fell. The door closed with a kerthump behind him.

She sat on the edge of the bed and opened the zip. It was her old school bag. Inside were clothes, ones she hadn't seen for some time. He must have looked carefully to find things she could wear. There was a skirt and a shirt, but no underwear, he hadn't thought to find her some underwear. She pulled a jersey over her head, thrust her feet into shoes—her old school shoes. At least there were socks.

There was a noise in the corridor, wheels on polished floors and a moan from the person being moved. She waited but he wasn't coming back. Not yet. She turned her back on the door and groped in the pockets of his jacket. A dirty handkerchief, a lighter, and his wallet. She took all the money, a tattered envelope with black and white photos in it and his silver lighter with the initials I M.

When she opened the door, the corridor was empty. The black and white tiles marched with shiny precision, one way to the main entrance where he was signing her out, the other way to the laundry with its back door that would take her to the path alongside the river. No-one saw her leave.

She walked as fast as she could, trying to feel herself at home in this body. Without the weight she felt insubstantial, as if she would lift off from the earth, as if she was dissolving into the damp manuka and the spray that reached out for her as the river pulled itself down to the sea. It drifted her along the edge and silently invited her in but she didn't go. It was the ache in her breasts that pulled her back. One hand came up, involuntarily, to hold and support her aching.

If he'd come looking for her, he could have found her easily enough. He could have found her at the bus station where she sat for a time, resting, watching the rain stop and the cloud lift from the mountain, watching the cloud reach arms around the girth of the mountain to touch the small mound tucked into its side—the baby mountain.

But he didn't.

There was a bus. A long day in a bus and an old lady who asked her where she was going. She didn't reply. As the silver lighter warmed in her hand, she looked out of the fogged window and listened to the tyres on the wet road.

"I'm not coming back, ever."

Sandra McLeod, the real estate agent (successful) from Auckland, rocks on the broken roundabout with her ghosts. The swings move. The broken swings, one hanging drunkenly with the chain snapped, one slung up over the frame—suddenly they're swinging. In, out, they go, in, out. A halo of white curly hair is flying and she's laughing. Richard's voice echoes: *Amy, will you marry me, Amy?* and the pig dogs are barking, barking, barking and it turns into her name.

"Sandra, Sandra!"

It's Robert's face in her face and his hands shaking her shoulders and the fear in his voice that pulls her back.

"Sandra!" he calls again.

She shudders, a deep earthquake of a shudder and the metal beneath her is cutting into the top of her legs and the swings are still.

"Sandra? Come back!"

She shakes her head. All of her is trembling. She's being crushed by the weight of it: the weight of the air that breathes her, heavy with sulphur and steam hissing from the violence of the steam bores: the weight of the mountain that leans on her, insisting it will crush her. She shakes her head, hard.

He holds her chin, forces her eyes up to look into that solemn face and those brown eyes. He makes her focus on him, on now.

"Come inside," he says.

He pulls her up from the roundabout, holding her hand to keep her here in this present, as he walks her back across the patchy grass to Bea's house. Most of her is walking with him and part of her is not. Part of her is still on the roundabout, on a night when the new moon was held in the arms of the old and Amy's white cardigan showed like a beacon in the dark.

Lady Macbeth, Lady Macbeth. It's Robert's voice that stops the whispers.

"Bea wants you to help sort out clothes for Betty," he says. "You'll need to go through her wardrobe and get something nice for her to wear."

Sandra almost jolts into laughing. *Who cares what my mother wears, she's dead, no-one will see her.*

The absurdity of it swings her back from the crushing suffocation of the past to her own feet walking up the pathway and climbing the steps into the house. She's light-headed with relief, this she can do, choose a dress, even if it does seem ludicrous.

"The funeral director rang, Sandra," Bea says. "We need to take some clothes in to the funeral home."

She nods, trying not to smile, almost drunk on her choked laughter. She follows Bea into the bedroom that was once Maria's, that was once her mother's. The bed and the chair are empty. She opens the wardrobe. She can do this. There are few clothes, little to choose from and she pulls out a dress of pale blue. Somewhere she remembers this was her mother's favourite colour.

"That will do nicely, dear," Bea says, laying it down on the candlewick bedspread. "Now, what about some shoes?"

Sandra bites her tongue. Shoes. *What shoes do dead people wear?*

What's the point? Is my mother going to need shoes to walk to heaven in?

Anyway, there are only slippers in the wardrobe as far as she can see. She pulls out a box to peer into the back shadows. Still no shoes. She opens the box, carefully pulling the cardboard aside. There's a dress and she pulls it out; Amy's dress, her best one with the fake fur around its neck and her school dress and the white cardigan with the stain just above the elbow.

Under the clothes there is a built up shoe, size two. She reaches for it. It's surprisingly light. Sandra remembers the weight it used to be. She holds it carefully. It's so small, so very small. Her little sister, what a tiny body she was, clinging to this world. A vortex of memories is pulling at her; she's patting that little body dry, piggy- backing her when she's tired, holding her when there's nothing else that is stable to hold on to. Sandra's lost in the memories, the quagmire has pulled her in. She holds the shoe, carefully carrying it out of this room where her mother died, back along the hallway to the lounge.

Robert looks first at the shoe, then at her face.

"We're going," he says. "It's time."

Your feet follow him, out of the house to his car.

"Get in," he says.

You do as he tells you. You can hear his voice, whispering underneath the sound of the car.

"You know where we're going, don't you?" he asks.

You nod.

"I have to go there often. It stalks me, that place. I go for real, like now, and I go there just as I'm going to sleep, or maybe sitting thinking of nothing very much. It's as if there's something I need to understand, some piece I have to find that I missed the first time."

You nurse the shoe. It's scraped and torn on one side, telling a story about a journey, one that Amy never made. You clench your jaw.

You can do this, you have to.

Robert drives silently, past the end of the tar-seal and on to the sandy pumice road. While your body is jerked by the potholes and the sand humps, you're still. It's silent in the eye of the storm.

He parks the car and locks it. You wonder what for.

"This is where we left our bikes," he says.

The path is not very well defined but he seems to know it. The overhang of manuka gently pulls you in. It's holding its breath, this bush, as if it's been waiting for you. As you move through its quiet, your noise disturbs a fantail. It scolds you for your intrusion. Now there is another voice pulling you in, it's the sound of water.

As you walk, the sound amplifies in you, from a soft falling to a loud insistence and the river is there in front of you and the water it carries dances and leaps as it settles from its journey back into its riverbed. Now the noise is deafening you and you're damp from the spray of it and it's falling, a small fall of water at first, then a vast pluming out from the tumbled rocks halfway down, where the earth has another opening, another doorway. Another doorway. Then the water is becoming air, then water again as it throws itself down, gathers itself down the steep escarpment. This is the way out, for the water, and all it carries.

This is where Amy's shoe was found, here in the shallows with one side of the leather scraped and torn.

"Follow me," shouts Robert and he pulls you away from the entrancement and violence of it. The path goes upward. The manuka reaches out with handholds, and your breath sounds loud in your own ears. You climb up to where the water begins its falling but you don't go there, to the steep cliff edge. Instead you follow Robert along a small stream, so small that you jump over it, twice.

"Some of the water goes down here," he's pointing to a vortex, a hole where some of the water disappears, to leave the small stream you've jumped over. The roar of the falls is muted here, it sings to you, enticing you.

Come in, it says, *come in. This is the real world.*

"Come on!" he says.

And you follow him instead, past an uprooted manuka, with its fingers that once clung to the earth, now curling in on themselves, clinging to the insubstantial pumice and drying clay; dying.

Around a rocky escarpment you go, to a churning pool and another fall of water. This one's not so high, but there's so much violence in the water that underneath, it's a churning mass of white. You know that this is where some more of the water goes and you know this was the beginning of the journey for Amy's shoe.

"We came here to do a magic spell," he says. "To get rid of Amy's ghost. We brought the little Mary statue with us. I'll show you."

He pulls you to the edge of the white water, around an old tree, one that digs its roots into the slippery rocks, clinging on to the solid land. You lick your lips, they're wet. A fine mist is settling on you. He's pointing to a flat rock at the very edge of the falls. Slick, wet and weedy, it stops just short of where most of the water disappears. This is where they disappeared, Amy and Colin and Mary, the Holy Mother.

Your little sister. The one who was so lightly held on this earth. The one you loved, not just as a sister does, but as a mother. The one you failed. The one you didn't protect enough. The one that was drowned, engulfed by this violent water and never, never released.

It rises in you, a long wail of pain, of wounding, pushing itself up through your belly. It shakes you and, gasping, you wrestle another breath that takes it deeper, to the very roots of you. It's the pain that has sat festering in your being, nesting in you so that you could never hold your own baby, nor grieve at the death of your own mother. This ancient wail of loss comes from your feet, from the unknowable depths below your feet and is swallowed by the noise of the falls. You're falling into a deep hole, like this one where Amy disappeared, you can feel your body falling with her. The violent churning of it. Undoing you. The wet gritty ground is under your cheek and you're sobbing into this earth, pulling the wet air deep into yourself. The earth absorbs your sobbing but holds your body out.

Not you. I will not take you.

There's a hissing under the insistent roar of water, a hissing you can almost hear. You strain to listen. Maybe she'll tell you, Amy's old woman, maybe she'll tell you what happened here. The roar of the water and the hissing persist, fill your head until you feel yourself dissolving, becoming particles of shining wet obsidian but, it will not let you understand. Your gaze is wrenched away from the violent water to the small remains of river that catch the sun and dance around an islet. There's a small island, just out of reach of the violent water and three manuka have managed to lodge themselves there. Under the manuka is a rock with a mossy surface. It stares into the fall of water, into the violence of its churning.

These waters are the tears of Tarawera. That mountain, she will always cry for her child, the one that was taken from her. She split herself apart with the grief of it, that mother. It is the way of the mother, to do that and to eternally lament for her child. It is greedy, that grief, it will consume everything. It was the way of your mother and of your Mary and of you and it will always be the way. That is how it is.

In the deep sentience between your skin and the skin of this place, you know this is true and you know you don't want it to be true.

What about Amy? Why take her?

But the guardian will not tell. There's a doorway here at these falls, this you know, and it goes to the depths of the earth, the shattered earth, the earth that destroys and that holds. Somewhere in there are her bones and Colin's bones, in wet caves in the place that you will never know.

You pull yourself away from the earth, the gritty obsidian ridden earth and under your belly is Amy's shoe. You hold it where the leather's been ripped, there at the heel, where support was most needed. A hand appears in front of you and you take it. Robert helps you stand. He takes the shoe from you and walks, carefully, each foot tested, on to the flat rock.

He pulls his arm back and throws the shoe into the water.

As he stands there on the rock, with the water suspending itself around him, the sun comes through the three manuka on the small island. For a moment you can't see him. Between you and him is a rainbow, for a brief moment it shimmers, dissolving him, absolving him. Then it's gone.

He makes his way back across the slippery rocks, over the roots of the old tree, to stand beside you. His hand finds yours.

"Come home Sandra," he says.

Chapter Twenty-Two

She wakes up to the light coming in through the window. She pulls her pillow up and the bed head creaks. Out of the window are the broken swings and the stationary roundabout. Ribbons hang limp in the morning damp. Strips of corduroy and cotton, torn and tied; Amy's clothes, tied there last night, with Robert.

Today is the day of her mother's funeral. There are sandwiches and cakes to be picked up from the caterer. She'll help this almost family of hers; she'll help these people who loved her mother in her absence. She swings her legs over the side of the bed and puts on the dressing gown that Bea has lent her. She walks quietly down the hallway to the empty kitchen. She knows where it all is. She plugs in the jug and spoons the tea in; one spoon for Pat, one spoon for Bea and one for the pot. She tips the boiling water in, puts the lid on and tucks the orange woolly tea cosy around the pot. She turns it three times. It's a magic spell she learned once. The milk goes in first, then the sugar. She pours the tea, long brown streams of hot tea and she carries the cups, with her tongue protruding just a little, to keep the cups steady. Down the long hallway she goes, to Bea and Pat's room. The door is ajar and she pushes it open with her foot.

"I brought you a cup of tea," she says and places one cup carefully, so carefully, on the bedside table next to Pat and walks around, carefully, so very carefully, to Bea's side of the bed to place the other cup next to this almost mother of hers. It spills, just a little, into the saucer. The two bodies in the bed stir, under the pursed lips of the Virgin Mary watching the ceiling, her face blank. She tiptoes out of the room.

She decides to wear the red trouser suit.

From the lounge window she looks out at the playground. There is someone on the swing. It's that girl, the one they called Hana. She's pushing her body back and her legs out and the swing is arching high and the ribbons of Amy's memories are whipping exuberantly, up towards the freedom of the air and sun. As the chain pulls taut at its peak, the girl disappears, absorbed into the brightness. Now you see her, now you don't.

Sandra is there, without knowing how she decided, standing by the swing, watching. Watching the face with Rewi's nose and the smile that he always had when he saw her. Rewi's daughter. Watching the girl with the widow's peak. She's burning, with a fierceness that she does not recognise, to pull this girl off the swing and hold her so hard that she will never, never get away. This girl. Her daughter. She has no right. The swing slows while Sandra's blood is galloping, thundering in her ears. With one foot, Hana stops her motion and sits staring at the pumice sand. Sandra holds her hands tight under her armpits and waits.

"Can I ask you some questions, Lady MacBeth?"

Sandra nods.

"Do you still live in Australia?"

"I never did. I live in Auckland."

"Oh."

Hana is still staring at the ground. One of the shreds of Amy's best dress, the green corduroy, has come untied and is lying in the sand. Sandra crouches to pick it up. Now she is facing her, this Hana, and their eyes cannot escape, the brown ones from the green ones, each searching. The brown ones narrow just a little as if in protection from the glare. It is Sandra who breaks this communion, her eyes snapping back to the corduroy strip in her hand. *No right. I have no right.*

"How old were you when I was born?"

"Sixteen."

"That's how old I am."

"I know."

She's sixteen again and she can hear those words. *You'll have to be brave, Sandra. Look, you unfold the towel. Your baby, she's beautiful but look carefully, there's just one little thing.*

She can feel the weight of that slippery creature that she's just laboured so hard to birth and the towel is soft and warmed and the soft, black hair is still wet. The fontanelle is pulsing, remembering her.

The blue-brown eyes that seem to know her are inviting all of her in. A hand reaches over to unfold the towel and she looks down at the small brown body to see the thin little leg, with a foot that looks like a beached tadpole, sitting bent over itself.

Hana slides off the swing. The right leg is stronger than the left and she leans hard on that side. Sandra's hand comes up to steady her but Hana has already got her balance and is walking away. A rolling walk, one shoulder higher than the other. It is so familiar. She stops and looks over her shoulder.

"One more question."

"Yes?"

"Why didn't you ever come back?"

Hana doesn't wait for an answer. She turns and walks across the scrubby grass, crosses the road and is gone. Sandra stares after her. *Would you listen if I tried to tell you?*

The funeral is at eleven. The boot of Robert's car is full of food. As they get in the car Sandra looks at each of them; at Robert, his hair cut neatly, looking as if he was born to wear a suit and tie, at Pat, his tie uneven and one wing of his collar sticking up, at Bea with her hair falling out of its bun, in a dark shapeless dress. Sandra looks at each of them and a small warmth sits between her and them, waiting for her to take it in. She blinks back tears. To stop her mascara running.

The undertaker is waiting at the door of the chapel. He shakes her hand and reaches into his jacket pocket.

"I didn't ask you, Sandra," he said, "but most people want to keep this."

In his hand is a thin gold band, almost worn through on one side. It's her mother's wedding ring. Sandra smiles at him and he takes both of her hands in his, smiles a smile that leaves his eyes sombre and slides them away to Robert. She thinks, *thank goodness I didn't have to take her ring off, or my mother may have become a ghost forever, like Emma Edgecumbe.*

She stands as the minister walks into the chapel and she unfolds herself carefully from the seat, her stack-heeled shoes sinking into the thick carpet. He's reached the coffin, with its lid secure. She looks down at that small gold ring she's holding and wonders if she'll ever wear it. Someone slips into the seat next to her. A pair of shoes, with one heel built up. Sandra drops the ring, her mother's ring, the one her father gave her mother to show he would love her forever. Her eyes go from the ring sitting on the carpet, back to Hana's shoes. This child, the one with the widow's peak, she is not precarious on this earth.

You walk on my feet, and on my mother's feet yet you have learned to stand strong on this land.

Next to her Sandra can see someone else's shoes. Men's shoes worn down on one side, with the backs trodden down. He's leaning down to pick up her mother's wedding ring.

Praise for A Place To Stand

This story brings alive a 1950s timber town in Aotearoa/New Zealand, the dark and the vivid explored through a young woman's dilemmas. It is an unpretentious picture of a unique place and the struggle to reconcile family, identity and culture which adds to our national understanding of ourselves.
— Catherine Delahunty (author)

Helen McNeil's story, set in Kawerau during the 1950s when the town is being constructed around the mill, is uniquely New Zealand.

The main character, Sandra McLeod, arrives as a child from England with her '£10 Pom' family, but their new life isn't what they'd hoped it might be. Via flashbacks recalled by Sandra when she returns to Kawerau to visit her ailing mother in 1975, Helen McNeil skillfully describes the gradual disintegration of the McLeod family in realistic, evocative and sometimes grueling detail. There is a sense, too, with the presence of the Māori and Catholic elements of the story, that Kawerau, perched as it is on a brittle volcanic crust, is a mystical place where both good and bad fortune can be magnified.

The revelation of Sandra's secrets is perfectly timed to keep the reader turning pages, and the conclusion is as satisfying as you could hope for. A compelling and really quite haunting read from a new and distinctive voice in New Zealand fiction. I thoroughly enjoyed it.
— Deborah Challinor (author)

OMG, finished your book this morning. Haven't read under the blanket with a torch for forty years …
— Christine from Kawerau

Acknowledgements

I would like to acknowledge the following people who helped make
this possible.

My family: David for emotional and financial support, Robin for
creative conversations and for design, Kirsty for
proofreading and crying when she read it, Cris for the video help.

My mentors: James George for his supportive mentoring, John
Cranna for helping me redraft, Jocelyn Watkins for self-publishing
help, my writing buddies for support and feedback. And way, way back,
Carol White for saving my intellect when I was at high school.

My communities: Earthsong residents for endless conversations
of my latest obsession, Maggie and Wanda for liking the book, Heart
Politics friends for listening to my raves, Jo Ayres for insight into
Catholicism pre Vatican II.

My professional assistants: Geoff Walker for assessing the manuscript,
Catherine Delahunty and Deborah Challinor for reviewing it, PublishMe
for a professional product, Lighthouse PR Ltd for help with publicity.

Many, many thanks.

Disclaimer

Whilst I have drawn on my memories of life in Kawerau for
this book, none of the characters are true depictions of people
I knew. Rather, they are a mix of essences and themes. Please
forgive me if you recognize yourself.

www.ingramcontent.com/pod-product-compliance
Lightning Source LLC
Chambersburg PA
CBHW032011050726
47590CB00006B/2135